A
Stitch
in
Time

Rosemary J. Kind

Printed in the United Kingdom

The author can be found at: ros@rjkind.com

Cover image: 'A Framework Knitter at Work' by Mary Annie Sloane, watercolour, 1891, from the Leicester Museums and Galleries Collection.
© Mary Annie Sloane Estate.

ISBN 978-1-909894-48-8

Published by
Alfie Dog Fiction
Rose Bank,
Norton Lindsey,
CV35 8JQ

DEDICATION

This will be the longest book dedication I have ever written, as this book is inspired by a number of people, without whom I would not be here.

Great-Grandma Betsy (maternal side) - Betsy Brown (nee Walker) born 1866 with only one leg. She went on to live a full life, marrying and having eight children who lived.

Great-Grandpa Robert (paternal side) - Robert Kind - born 1863 and became a boot maker. He was educated through the Sunday school movement and went on to teach in Sunday school and be involved in establishing adult education in South Wigston. His own family were stocking framework knitters. Despite his humble origins, both his sons went on to university, after WW1.

However, before the war, my grandfather, Orson Kind, became a pupil teacher.

Mum - Brenda Kind, granddaughter of Betsy Brown and the first of her immediate family to go to college. She went on to become a teacher.

Dad - Alan Kind, grandson of Robert Kind, his interest in framework knitting and involvement with the Framework Knitting Museum in Wigston inspired this book, as did those of my ancestors who worked in framework knitting.

Finally, my dear writing buddy, Sheila Crosby, who lost her leg to cancer on her 60th birthday and whose determination and attitude is a constant inspiration to me.

AUTHOR'S NOTE

I have of necessity taken some licence with historical accuracy, as insufficient information is available on some areas. I do not know that the Methodist chapel had an organ at the date I have ascribed, however as the Independent chapel had one installed in 1861 it is not beyond the realms of possibility.

NOTE:
The characters are all fictitious and any resemblance they may have to persons alive, or dead is entirely coincidental. This book is not intended to suggest that the events portrayed happened in reality. It is purely a work of fiction, rooted in elements of real history.

I have taken the liberty to include the lawyer Hiram Owston as himself. His is such a wonderful name and he was indeed an up-and-coming lawyer at the time, who went on to live in Wigston. Beyond his name and his profession none of what is attributed to him is taken from real life.

A glossary of language is included at the back of the book to assist with the meaning of colloquial speech.

"We talk of all our principles, of believing in justice, equality and fairness, but principles are really rather pointless if you only apply them to other people." Samuel Hurst

PART 1

CHAPTER 1

1845, Wigston Magna, Leicestershire, England

The strand of wool Clara was winding slipped, no longer neatly wound. She huffed in frustration and unwound the yarn to the point where the wool was still tight. She could feel her heartbeat through her dress and apron. How could she concentrate today, when her mother was upstairs crying out in the pain of childbirth?

Clara was sitting on the low wooden stool in the corner of the workshop, with her tongue pushed between her lips as she concentrated on the old, repurposed spinning wheel. It wasn't easy to use the treadle to turn the wheel rhythmically. Her job was to wind the skein of wool onto the bobbin as evenly as her eight-year-old hands allowed. Despite her youth and the softness of the yarn, Clara's hands were dry and calloused from the long hours she worked. Her family were stocking framework knitters, and she had to keep them supplied with full bobbins of wool, in order for them to work the knitting frames and meet their week's quota of stockings.

"The baby's nearly here," Clara's elder sister, Hannah shouted rushing past to the kitchen.

Dad stopped working his knitting frame for a moment. Clara could see his hands shaking, but then he sat a little straighter and continued working on the stocking.

Clara stared out of the long, mullioned window to the

high, wispy clouds beyond. The wheel sat idle and the hank of wool lay slack across her lap. In her nightly prayers, she'd already asked God for a brother, but it couldn't hurt to cross her fingers and make a wish. God wouldn't mind that too much, would he? Last week at Sunday school, one of the girls had said brothers weren't nice; they left beetles in your apron pockets. Despite that, Clara still wanted the baby to be a boy. Mind you, she shivered at the thought of beetles. But she'd given it some thought. By the time a brother was old enough to play tricks on her, she'd be almost as old as Hannah was now, and by then she doubted that she'd care quite as much about beetles.

A brother would definitely be best; she already had two sisters. Weren't they enough? There might once have been an older brother, born between herself and Hannah, but she only heard adults talking about him in hushed tones. Mam said he'd gone to be with Jesus, but although every Sunday Clara looked around the chapel, she couldn't see anyone who could be her brother. She'd built up a picture in her mind of how wonderful a brother might be and wished he were there.

Dad let out a long slow breath and looked over to his daughter. His voice was as gentle as ever, but with a firmness that brooked no argument. "You must carry on winding, love, or none of us'll eat next week."

Clara picked up the wool. She liked winding bright coloured wools best; they helped to cheer up the dullest day. Today she was winding plain black, but it didn't matter so much with the May sunshine lighting up the gentle blue sky outside. She turned the wheel slowly with the treadle, playing out the wool from the skein and taking it up onto the bobbin, moving steadily up and down in neat rows. White was the worst to wind. She worried it would go on the floor and gather dirt, or that her hands mightn't be clean enough. Black wool was less exciting, but less worrying too.

The knitting frame was much higher from the ground than the spinning wheel stool and her legs would need to be longer before she could reach those treadles. As soon as she grew tall enough, she would learn to make the stockings. By then, her younger sister Martha would need to take over winding. Martha was already learning, but, at five years old, she lacked the control and coordination to work quickly enough. Clara could still remember how hard she'd found winding at the start, but in time Martha would do as well as Clara did now.

She stopped again, wondering what was happening with Mam. Neither Grandma Herbert, nor Hannah, who'd gone back upstairs, had come to tell them anything more. She wondered how Dad could concentrate on what he was doing while they waited for news. At least they were plain stockings he was knitting rather than ones with a complicated pattern.

"Clara," Dad spoke more sharply. It was a tone she wasn't used to hearing. "Gerronwirrit, love. It's bad enough you can't work Hannah's frame while she's helping Mam. Until she's back, you and me must do the work of four of us or there'll be more than Thursday this week wirrout bread. Ya mam won't be working full hours for a while."

Clara fumbled with the wool in her haste to get back to winding. She didn't want to anger her father. She adored this mild-mannered man and hated the thought of displeasing him.

On a good week the bread lasted all seven days. On a

bad week… Clara preferred not to think of the hunger in her belly on a bad week. Thursday was the day before they were paid and the most likely for them to be without food. It was the same for the many families around them who worked knitting frames at home. They all struggled to find food enough for the whole week. Soon there'd be another mouth to feed, so further for the food to go.

To take her mind off Mam, Clara thought of other things as she focussed on the bobbin. Unlike some homes, like Sarah's next door, they didn't have a separate workshop behind the house. They had two single-width knitting frames, in what to some people might have been the parlour, and lived in the small room the other side of the hallway, and the kitchen beyond. Mam, Dad and Hannah worked the frames by turns, making sure they ran all hours when light shone bright enough to see by and as many hours as they could afford to pay for candles beyond that. The glass globes hanging in the window helped to focus the sunlight and lengthen the time before the lamps needed to be lit.

Even running fifteen or sixteen hours a day, they found it hard to make the number of stockings needed to earn a modest wage. Some houses had more frames and other family members or journeymen coming in to work, but Clara's family didn't have the space for that. Besides, Dad was worried about the cost of renting another frame when there were already some weeks when, as a result of the new factories, the work was short. Once Clara was trained, they'd find a way to fit a third frame into the small room, as long as Dad thought work would be regular enough to make it worthwhile. There'd be several years before the new baby could help winding wool and Martha wouldn't be able to wind enough to keep three frames running, so there'd be the extra cost of buying in ready wound wool to account for, as well as the frame.

Sunday was Clara's favourite day; except for the part where they had to sit still on the pews while the minister talked. Most of the time she didn't understand what he was saying, but she loved to hear the Bible stories, and it was all worthwhile for the opportunity to attend Sunday school and have at least some chance of learning. She wished more than anything that she could enrol at the school for weekdays; she wanted to hear about more than Bible stories and had so many questions, but attending school cost money, which was something they didn't have. Dad said they didn't have so much as a farthing spare and there certainly wasn't anything to pay for schooling. Nor did she suppose anyone else would want to pay her school fees and if they did, it still left her work to be done at home. She sighed. Mostly, everyone told her to stop asking questions, except Mr Cooper, her Sunday school teacher. He said she could always ask him questions, but she should wait until invited, rather than when they occurred to her. She didn't find waiting easy, especially as she thought of so many things to ask. Grandma Herbert said no good could come of asking questions, so Clara asked them when Grandma wasn't around.

A scream resonated through the house and Clara jumped from the stool, dropping the skein of wool on the floor.

"Hannah?" Clara was confused. "Whatever's wrong?" She was expecting to hear her mother's screams. She remembered those all too well from when Martha was born, but why was her sister Hannah screaming? She wasn't the one having the baby. The colour had drained from Dad's face, and he had stopped working. He was

7

looking wild-eyed toward the stairs. A baby's cry followed, but her father remained frozen in the moment as Hannah came clattering down the spiral oak stairs and ran out through the kitchen and into the back yard. She was followed at a more sedate pace by Grandma Herbert, their mother's mam.

"Don't fret. Hettie's fine and you've gorra baby boy, John James." Her smile seemed forced as she looked to Clara and added, "I think it warra bit of a shock for Hannah. I'll call when we're ready for you to see them, John." Grandma didn't wait for Dad to reply but went to the kitchen, where Clara heard a pan clang onto the range.

Dad seemed to pull himself back into the moment and Clara wondered what he'd been thinking. From the look that had been on Hannah's face, Clara wondered if Grandma's explanation was true, but doubted anyone would tell her, even if she asked. As she picked up the wool from the floor and brushed the dust away, Clara couldn't help but feel the corner of her mouth twitching. Her prayers and wish had been granted. She had a brother. She wanted to rush to their mother and see for herself that they were both all right. Above all else, she wanted to see her new brother. Her smile broadened as she felt a thrill of excitement. She sat back down on the stool. Until Dad said she could go, she wouldn't be allowed to leave the workshop. Besides, Dad wouldn't go up until Grandma said they were ready for him. She watched him closely as he returned to knitting the stocking and wondered why his hands were still trembling as he worked. Had he too heard something in Grandma's voice that left him concerned?

They didn't stop to eat until the light was fading. It took fewer candles for eating than to work by. Hannah had returned about half an hour earlier, in time to prepare the meal, but she said not a single word when she came in.

As Dad finished saying grace, Grandma came through from the stairs. "Hettie's sleeping. I'll fetch Martha home from our Jack's an' eat wir' 'er here before going home again. These old legs'll be worn out by the time I'm done." Grandma took up her coat and went out of the back door, where a jitty ran along behind the houses.

Clara let out a small sigh of relief. She'd thought Grandma might stay the night with them, but the times when she did, she took as much space in the bed as the three girls put together.

Clara looked at her older sister as best she could in the dim light, but could tell nothing from her expression, Hannah's eyes were cast downward to her plate as she moved her food around, without eating.

"When can I see Mam?" Clara asked, looking to Hannah for an answer rather than Dad. Hannah continued to stare at her plate as though she hadn't heard.

"I'm going up after we've eaten, but tomorrow'll be time enough for you and Martha," Dad said. "It's been a hard day and Mam needs to rest."

It wasn't fair, but she could do nothing. Dad had spoken and, as a child, it wasn't her place to argue.

In the end Dad relented and, although both Mam and her brother were sleeping, Clara was allowed to look in on them from a little distance. Her brother was cocooned in blankets with no more than his head and an arm visible. She wanted to reach out and touch him but knew that must wait until the following day.

In bed that night, Clara could tell by the sound of her older sister's breathing that she wasn't asleep. She whispered, "Why d'you scream? Warrit ever so bad?"

Hannah said nothing.

Clara never got far with her sister if she kept asking the same thing, so she tried a different approach, hoping Hannah might answer and then start to say more.

"Where d'you go when you ran out? D'you go to see Mary to tell her the news?"

"Never you mind," Hannah snapped at her and turned her back in Clara's direction.

Clara frowned. If she'd gone to see her friend Mary, why wouldn't she say so? Hannah might not be the best of friends with her younger sister, but she wasn't usually quite so unwilling to talk. Clara knew better than to ask another question. Hannah's temper could be quick at the best of times.

Grandma arrived before they were up the following morning. "It ain't right." She ladled porridge into their bowls with such force that it slopped over the edges. "You should get 'im christened, soon as you can. That won't be all that's wrong wir'im, I'll be bound."

Clara was used to Grandma being outspoken, but this time, try as she might, she didn't understand what the adults were talking about. Her new brother, John James or JJ as Clara had decided to call him, looked perfectly healthy to her eyes. He certainly howled as she thought a baby should, and Grandma said he was feeding well. All Clara could do was listen to the riddles of conversation and try to work out what they meant.

Saying he needed to be christened quickly made it sound as though Grandma thought JJ was dying and that surely couldn't be right. Hannah was still ignoring her questions, and the adults seemed subdued. Dad hadn't even had stern words with Hannah for running out when she should have been working the previous day.

The porridge had little flavour at the best of the times, but today as she worried about what they meant, it felt heavy in her mouth and hard to swallow.

Clara hated the workshop with everyone so quiet. Usually, Hannah sang as she worked, but not today. Why weren't they all celebrating that both Mam and JJ were safe? The hours stretched away ahead of them with the rhythmic sound of the knitting machines punctuating the silence.

She looked up when she heard JJ howling. Dad stiffened but carried on working and Grandma came out of the kitchen and went upstairs to Mam. Soon after, the house became peaceful again, except for the monotonous clacking of the frames which Hannah and Dad were working.

When Dad eventually said she could take a break from winding, Clara went up the narrow staircase and knocked quietly at the bedroom. Grandma opened the door and, without a smile, nodded that she could come in.

"She'll know sooner or later, Hettie. It may as well be now," Grandma said as Clara's mother held JJ to her breast.

Clara went across to the bed, where her mother was propped up against the headboard, JJ suckling contentedly. He was so small, although his head and hands already looked bigger than they had yesterday, when she'd seen them poking out from the confines of his blanket. Clara took in the tufts of hair on his head, his tiny pudgy hands which reached out without focussed direction. She felt wonder seeing the tiny, squashed nose and ears. Her gaze travelled from his rosy cheeks to his tiny toes and stopped. Clara frowned and followed the line of his body again. JJ was perfect - except for one thing. She stared down at the tiny nub where his right leg should have been.

"Why ain't he got two legs like the rest of us?" Clara asked. She watched her mother bite her lip and swallow hard.

It was Grandma who answered. "The good Lord has his reasons, I'll be bound. I don't suppose the boy'll be wir'us long and I'm sure it'll be a blessing for 'im if he ain't."

"He ain't 'the boy'. His name's John James." Clara knew she'd be in trouble for answering back, but she felt a wave of protective anger for her brother. She couldn't stop herself now she'd started. "Why would it be a blessing if we lost him? He's like a brother should be every other way."

"Well, my girl, he won't be able to work the machines and there's barely enough to feed those as can. He ain't gonna get far wi' one leg."

Clara took a step closer to her mother and reached a hand to touch the soft down on JJ's head. Then she touched his hand, and his tiny fingers closed tightly around one of hers. "I'll do the work of both of us, and I'll help take care of 'im."

"Will ya now?"

The doubt in Grandma's voice made Clara more determined. She looked at her mother, but her mother's face was grey with exhaustion and her eyes were closed. Instead, Clara spoke directly to JJ. "I'll be the best sister to you. I'll never let you down. Never." She leant down and kissed his cheek, before Grandma ushered her back out of the room.

Normally, Clara fell asleep immediately, but not that

night. She didn't try asking Hannah questions. What was the point when her sister wouldn't answer? Instead, she lay still, breathing as quietly as possible and listening for every noise coming from their parents' room. It was hard to hear what was happening over Martha's heavy slumbering on the pillow next to her. Clara moved her head around so that her ear was uppermost. When she eventually heard JJ cry, she smiled, and her eyelids finally closed. If he could cry, he was still alive. At least for now, Grandma must be wrong.

For the next few weeks, Clara's nights followed the same pattern, listening for JJ. In the mornings she felt anxious until she knew her brother was still safely with them. Her sleepless nights left her tired during the day and she was slower winding, making more mistakes and needing to correct them as she went. Thankfully, with Martha now helping, they wound enough between them to keep the frames running.

In the days following JJ's safe arrival, with all the girls and their father in the workshop, it should have been brighter and noisier. But the atmosphere was subdued and to Clara, the days felt long.

As the weeks passed, life began returning to normal and the atmosphere lifted enough for Hannah to resume singing as she worked. Dad once again talked about the possibility of renting a third frame, but from what Clara overheard, he couldn't see how the work they could produce would make it possible, at least until she could become proficient at stocking making and that took more strength than she had in her young arms. Hannah wasn't strong enough to produce the same amount of work as their father, or even their mother come to that. The competition from the factories meant the price of the finished stockings had fallen and their orders were sometimes low. On the busy weeks, none of the family could work longer hours than they already did. On the quiet weeks, the frame rent was due, regardless of whether they had enough orders to keep them running.

As for JJ, having one leg made little difference to his care in those early days and once Mam was working again, his crib was moved between the workshop and the kitchen as was needed. Clara liked it best when he was in the workshop, and she could look up from time to time to see him sleeping. She imagined being able to stop her work and sit close by his crib, singing him a lullaby, not that he'd have heard her much above the noise, with both knitting frames running full-time. Her voice was still small and thin compared to Hannah's. That was one of the things which had caused Dad to nickname her 'Mouse', because most of the time she was as quiet as one of the little creatures they so often shared their home with.

Eventually, even Grandma, when she visited, acknowledged that JJ was thriving and that the mysteries of God's ways could never be understood. Instead, her doom-laden words turned to what would happen when it was time for JJ to walk and he was too heavy to be carried. Clara could see that would be a problem.

CHAPTER 2

1846 (a year later)

Clara tried not to jiggle up and down in her excitement, as Mam secured the starched collar around the neck of her dress. On a normal Sunday Mam didn't go to these lengths to make her daughter look presentable, but this wasn't a normal Sunday. Today was the Sunday School Anniversary and everyone from the Wesleyan Chapel would be there, including those who only attended on high days and holidays. Even Grandma Herbert was going, and she normally went to an Anglican church with Uncle Jack's family, claiming she didn't hold with this 'non-conformist claptrap'.

Today, prizes would be given out to the children for regular attendance, and it was the first year when Clara hadn't missed a single week. Few children managed to be at chapel every week, and she couldn't stop smiling as she thought about it.

"Oh, please come along, Martha. I don't wanna be late." Clara was almost dancing from foot to foot as her younger sister hung back on the stairs.

When Martha came out of the shadows, Clara saw why her sister had been hiding.

"Martha Phipps, where did that stain come from? There ain't ote I can do about it now. There's no spare apron with washday tomorrow. Don't you go sitting on the front row."

Mam grimaced toward Dad, but Clara could see from the slight twitch of her lip and the twinkle in her eye that she wasn't really cross with Martha.

Clara doubted that Martha had any intention of sitting on the front row, unless she was made to do so. Breathing a sigh of relief as, at last, the rest of the family headed out of the door, Clara took hold of Martha's hand so her sister wouldn't dawdle.

"But I hate Sunday school," Martha whined, as Dad closed the cottage door behind him.

"It mightn't be too fond of you, looking like that, my girl." Mam shook her head as she looked at her youngest daughter. "I wa' no better when I wa' 'er age," Mam said to no one in particular, and sighed.

Martha made it clear at every opportunity that she didn't like attending Sunday school and would rather not have to sit still all that time. Unlike Clara, she was bored by having the stories explained to her and could never remember the words to the hymns. Much as she loved her younger sister, Clara found it hard to understand how she could show so little interest in learning. Martha was six and still knew few of her letters.

Clara waved to Sarah who lived in the neighbouring terraced cottage. Although she and Sarah were the same age and were as much friends as their precious free time allowed, Sarah's family attended All Saints church, along their road. The Anglican building was much older and looked grand compared to the chapel, although Clara sometimes thought the graveyard seemed quite scary after dark. While the church was much closer to where they lived, Clara didn't mind their walk to chapel, especially on a sunny spring day like today. Sometimes they went through the lanes and other times round by the road. She always looked into the grounds of the big manor house when they walked along Long Street and wondered what it must be like to live in a place like that. It might be lonely unless there were enough people to fill every room, as there were in the tiny home her own family shared. Although she'd heard of people having a bed to themselves, it was something she simply couldn't imagine. How could they possibly be warm enough? She thought it must be sad not to have someone else so close by.

Whilst Clara didn't envy the house itself, she would love to live somewhere surrounded by a garden. What stories could the great trees tell? How long they must have lived watching over the people who passed.

The new leaves were mostly out and looked so fresh, the green not yet darkened by the long summer days which lay ahead. The shape of the leaves on the great oak trees were her favourite and she never tired of looking to see if any squirrels were running among the branches or chasing round the trunks.

Their own home bordered the road, without so much as a thread of space between. On the rare occasions when both she and Sarah were free, they went to the fields near the canal, or better still to the river Sence, but it was quite a walk and Mam never liked her going there alone. The overwhelming gentleness of the riverbank, with tree branches reaching out to the waters, reminded her somehow of her own father's nature and she loved it the more for that. Its rages of flood were always short lived and passed back into tranquillity without much of a shadow.

JJ was wriggling in Dad's arms as he was carried. He'd reached the age of trying to crawl around the floor at every opportunity. In compensating for his missing leg, JJ's arms had become strong, making it all the harder when he didn't want to be held. Mam said other children of his age would be starting to walk, but she didn't expect JJ ever would. Clara thought that would be sad. She loved watching her brother's determination to raise himself to a standing position. He used his strength to pull himself up and, with someone holding his hands, he could almost balance on his one good leg. To her surprise, Grandma had helped and encouraged him too, but Clara supposed life would get harder now he wasn't so easy to carry.

It was a shame to think he'd never be able to climb trees or run around, not that they had much time for those games, but on the rare occasions when they did, being outdoors was a sheer joy. She would love to share those times with him. Perhaps she could think of other things they could do together. She would help him learn to read as soon as he was capable of concentrating, then at least he could enjoy stories the same way she did, until then she would tell him the parables she heard in Sunday school.

As they approached the chapel, Mr Preston, the Sunday School Superintendent, dressed in his three-piece suit, with pocket watch chain dangling from the waistcoat, was greeting everyone at the door and directing the children to their seats near the front. Normally, their classes were separate from the main service but today was different and Clara stood taller as she moved to her place on the front row of the main block of children's seats. Sitting here, she had only the smaller chairs for the young children between her and the minister who would lead the service. Hannah no longer sat with the children, at fifteen she thought herself far too grown up for things like that. Clara thought it sad that both her sisters had so little interest in learning.

Hannah couldn't so much as write her own name, which seemed especially grievous, as whether Clara wrote the letters forward or backward, they still read 'Hannah', which she thought was amazing.

The chapel was full for the anniversary; people squeezed in along every row of pews. Clara wanted to count how many people were there, but if she turned around to see, then she'd soon be in trouble. Instead, she looked ahead at the table where the prizes were laid. They were too far off for her to see exactly what was there, though she longed to find out.

As the organist began to play, Clara stood up with the rest of the congregation to sing the opening hymn. She didn't need to read the words; she knew so many of the hymns by heart. She sang as loudly as her mouse-like voice allowed. She loved singing almost as much as she loved learning and wished her voice was as strong as Hannah's.

The service continued and Clara listened to all that was being said, even the parts she didn't understand, but it was hard when she was so excited about what was to follow. She kept glancing over to the table at the front. Never before had she received any sort of prize, and she couldn't stop smiling with the anticipation. For the last week at home, she'd talked about little else. Mam said that however much of a hurry her mind was in, when Clara's name was called out, she must walk to the front at a sedate and respectful pace.

"Let us pray…"

Clara put her hands together and closed her eyes. At last, the sermon was over. She needed to sing one more hymn before the children, whose Sunday school attendance records were the most complete over the last year, would be called forward. There'd been a week when

Clara had hidden how unwell she was feeling, to make sure she wouldn't be kept at home. How different to Hannah who would feign illness at any opportunity in an attempt to stay away from chapel, although oddly that seemed to have changed recently, though she still complained about the services themselves.

When her name was called, Clara was on her feet so quickly she almost tripped herself up. Then she remembered her mother's words and took a deep breath, making herself slow down. She knew she had to shake the minister by the hand and say, 'Thank you, sir,' before moving back to her place, as the line of children continued behind her.

Sarah, next door, had received a small medal from her Sunday school. Clara hoped her own award would be something as nice.

Once out from the row of chairs, she made her way toward the front of the chapel. The minister was holding a small book. When she reached where he was standing, he held it out to her.

"For me?" She looked up at him, her mouth open. A medal would have been wonderful, but this was more than she could ever have dreamed of. "A book of my very own? Can I take it home?"

The Sunday school superintendent nodded and was indicating that she should move along.

"Thank you, sir," Clara stuttered and curtsied at the same time, once again tripping over her own feet and stumbling back toward the pews. She was grasping the Bible she'd been given as tightly as though she expected it to run away. Once she was seated again, she ran her finger over the embossed letters on the hard cover, feeling the words. Then surreptitiously she raised the book to her face and breathed in the smell. This book didn't smell of the countless hands that had touched it before her but held a sweet newness that Clara thought was heaven itself. With a book of her own, she could practice reading as often as she liked. No one at home would be able to help her with the difficult words, but if she committed them to memory, she could ask her Sunday school teacher the following week or carry it with her. She could take it everywhere she went, as long as she took care never to leave it anywhere. How she longed to read the stories she already knew and try to read others. Her favourite was the one about the loaves and the fishes, because everyone in the story had enough to eat and she thought that would be wonderful. She wasn't absolutely sure she'd be able to find it amongst all these pages, but she was sure if she asked Mr Cooper, who taught her class in Sunday school, then he would help her learn which page it was on. She wanted to open the book right now but knew that would get her into trouble. Her fingers danced from the book to her skirt and apron and back again. There wouldn't be long until the service was over, but suddenly the time felt endless.

When the last 'amen' had been said, and quiet contemplation completed, the congregation filed out. It was always such a slow process. People worked their way along the pews to the aisle and then joined a queue, as each one shook the preacher by the hand before they passed into the street.

Hannah was standing a little way off, talking to Mary Carter and Mary's older brother Frank. Mary and Hannah were the same age, Clara knew that, but she wasn't sure about Frank, a couple of years older maybe. Watching them, Clara thought how strange it was. Hannah kept twisting a strand of her long hair and was giggling, which wasn't like her at all, at least not at chapel. She was normally quite sullen while she was here.

Dad came to stand near Clara, once he'd finished talking to the minister.

"That's a bright girl you have there, John."

Mr Preston, the Sunday school superintendent had come over to speak to Clara's father. Clara felt her face flush. She didn't think Mr Preston had ever so much as noticed her, as he didn't teach the class she was in.

"You should send her to the British School. She'd certainly benefit from more learning."

Dad shook his head, and his shoulders dropped. "You know it ain't that easy, Mr Preston. I can neither spare 'er from working, nor pay for 'er to attend." He put a protective hand on Clara's shoulder.

She dropped her gaze, no longer feeling much like smiling. Whilst she knew that was the case, for a moment she'd felt a swell of excitement that maybe Mr Preston's words could make a difference. The chapel and the school were connected somehow, although she didn't understand how. And she thought the National School was connected to the Anglican church, but she knew less about that. If Mr Preston thought she should attend the British School, then surely there would be a place for her and she would like nothing more than to be able to spend all day, every day, studying and learning. She'd work as hard at learning as she did at home.

"There are benefactors who pay for some of the scholars' places. I could speak to the school board of governors if you think it would be helpful." Mr Preston rocked back and forward from heel to toe as he spoke.

Clara had no idea what benefactors meant and hoped that her father understood, but from the look of sadness on his face it seemed unlikely that this would change his decision and her heart sank. She loved Sunday school, but she wanted to learn much more than was held in the Bible. Although, she supposed it would take her a long time to read it all. She had questions too about the world around her and never had the opportunity to ask them. Downcast, she put her hand into her apron pocket and gripped the Bible. At least she now had a book of her own; that was more than she'd ever had before. Now she really could set about reading every page. Maybe then her many questions would be answered, but she doubted it, as it didn't seem to be that kind of book. It didn't tell her the names of the wildflowers or about the stars in the sky. She wanted to know where the river came from and where it went when it left them. Dad said he'd walked as far as Crow Mills and on one occasion seen it in flood, but he didn't know what lay beyond. Maybe there weren't books on things like that. She thought that one day she'd like to see it for herself.

Certainly no one she knew seemed to be able to answer the questions she so often asked. She would practise her reading at every moment she had enough light and wasn't working, although she didn't suppose she'd be allowed to have her book at the table when they were eating — maybe she would only have time on Sundays. She smiled. It was Sunday today and she would begin on the first page.

As the Phipps family walked home after service, Clara was quiet, listening to the conversations around her. Martha was clearly happy to be out of chapel. Hannah kept looking back over her shoulder as they walked away.

"He seems a nice young man," Mam said, causing Hannah to go very red.

"Mam." Hannah's embarrassment was obvious.

"You could do a lot worse. Couldn't she, John?" Mam

turned to Dad who was carrying JJ.

"Worse than what?" Dad asked.

Mam tutted. "You men notice so little. Frank Carter seems sweet on our Hannah."

"Does he now?" Dad's voice was distant as though not paying attention. A short silence followed before Dad said, "A lad like 'im's hardly likely to settle for someone as poor as us. Mind you, you hear things. By all accounts 'e's…" He went quiet for a while, and no one spoke. Then as though the previous conversation had not occurred, he said, "I ain't gonna be able to carry John James for ever. It's a fair walk to chapel and he does insist on wriggling."

"Like as not the good Lord'll take 'im 'ome long before 'e gets too 'eavy," Mam said, echoing Grandma and sounding resigned.

"Other than ya mam always looking for the worst possibility, we've no reason to think that now, Hettie. He's come this far. We need to find a way to 'elp 'im, though I've no more thought where to start than you 'ave." Dad looked sad rather than defiant as he spoke.

Clara frowned. She wasn't sure what it meant for Frank to be sweet on her sister, but she could probably guess. But how the Lord would take JJ on a Sunday when Dad was finding it so hard, she had no idea. Perhaps JJ wouldn't wriggle if someone else was carrying him. She wished there were a way she could help, but she certainly couldn't carry her brother. These days she found it difficult to pick him up. She thought about the Bible stories they heard in Sunday school. Jesus had made a blind man see and a crippled man had been able to walk again. Maybe Jesus could make JJ better. She wondered whether to suggest that to Mam and Dad.

JJ wanted to walk; Clara had no doubt of that. He

dragged himself around the floor, pushing himself along with his foot and pulling with his hands. But walking would be another matter when he couldn't balance on his leg for long without help.

Stopping listening to the adults, Clara set to thinking what might be needed for JJ to walk without help. She'd seen people with walking sticks, but that wouldn't be enough. Maybe two sticks. That wouldn't be easy. He was still too young to be as controlled and coordinated as that might need, quite apart from the fact he seemed to grow every time she turned her back for five minutes, but perhaps if he had some walking sticks it would be better than nothing. She was still thinking about where, near to home, she might find some wood and who could help her to make JJ sized walking sticks when they arrived home.

It was only when Mam said, "Why don't you read us a story from your Bible, Clara, dear?" that the sheer joy of the little book came back to her.

Clara took off her coat and sat on the stool in the corner of the kitchen. Opening the book at the beginning, she looked at some of the words 'generation', 'Abraham', 'begat' and, struggling, thought this might not be the best place to start. Each page had printed at the top which book of the Bible it was, so she turned pages a few at a time until she found where the Old Testament ended, and the New Testament began. While she knew some of the order of the books, she wasn't used to finding the one she wanted. She turned a few pages further. "At the same time came the dis…dis."

"Disciples," Mam said as she bustled around the kitchen. While Clara's mother couldn't read, they'd all heard the stories often enough in chapel for some of them to be familiar.

"…disciples unto Jesus, saying…" Clara's progression across the page was slow as she had to think what each word was before she said it aloud, but if she kept reading, she was sure it would get easier in time. She wished she had some way to write out the words she didn't know, so she could ask her teacher the following week, but they had neither ink nor paper in the house, or a slate and chalk. Her Bible was far too precious for her to mark it in any way. All she could do was try to memorise those words, but that was hard if you didn't already know how to say them to yourself.

She read on a few lines, then, marking her place with her finger, looked up and said, "I could read a story to JJ when he goes to bed each night."

"Why d'ya wanna do that?" Hannah asked, her voice as filled with contempt as confusion.

"'Cause I like reading and 'e might enjoy a story." Clara clenched the fist that wasn't marking her place.

Hannah laughed. "Reading's a waste o' time. That'll never find you a husband."

"And don't you be too keen looking for one either, Hannah Phipps. We've still got work 'ere we need you doing. There'll be time enough to go gadding about when you're older. Now pass me that trivet to put under this pan." Mam was holding a hot saucepan and was looking for somewhere to put it down.

Hannah pouted as she moved the trivet and placed it in reach of her mother. "I'm gonna find someone to marry who don't need me to work an' all."

"Are you now? Well, I don't s'pose 'e'll 'ave a lot o' time for the likes of us. You 'eard what your father said about that Carter boy. Bricklaying's a good trade, he'll do all right for 'imself, but money ain't everything. Besides, we might go to the same chapel, but that don't mean 'is parents'll want 'im marrying into our family." Mam mopped her brow with her apron and sighed.

Clara looked back down to where her finger was on the page of the Bible, her frayed cuff marking another line further down the page. She carried on reading quietly to herself, her mouth forming each word as she went. She said the words under her breath so as to avoid any more comments from Hannah.

But her older sister was preoccupied with Mam's words and flounced out of the kitchen calling back as she went, "Frank will want to marry me. You just see."

Clara frowned, wondering what her sister meant.

CHAPTER 3

Summer 1847 (the following year)

"Washing's finally done. I'll take over 'ere while you mind John James," Mam said.

She looked tired as she stood by the knitting frame where Hannah was working.

"Must I?" Hannah scowled in response.

Clara watched out of the corner of her eye. Not wanting to draw attention to herself, she continued to wind the wool onto the bobbin as she listened.

"You're better doing that wi' all your daydreaming, than you are knitting stockings. Come on, we need to get these finished."

Clara wished her own knitting was faster, but she was still learning and didn't get a great deal of time on the knitting frame. Although her legs were now long enough to reach the pedals, she needed to build the strength in her arms. The effort needed to move the bar which made the stitches, was hard work, even at the age of ten. She was getting stronger, but it would take time. After a short stint working the frame, her arms felt as though she were being branded with coals from the fire. The way Mam used the machine it was no wonder Dad said it was a hundred times faster than knitting by hand, but for Clara that was definitely not the case.

Hannah shuffled along to the end of the bench seat and

made room for Mam. "I'll wind; Clara can look after John."

"Can I?" Clara's heart lifted. She knew Hannah hated winding but disliked keeping an eye on JJ more. Clara carefully put her finger on the thread so that it wouldn't slip when Hannah took over and got up from her stool in the corner of the workshop. She didn't need asking twice if it meant she could spend time with her precious brother.

There'd be chores to do, but if she finished those, she could always find ways to pass the time. She loved keeping JJ out of trouble as he crawled with ever more determination around the kitchen or back-room floor. She'd read him the story of when Jesus was born, irrespective of the fact that it was summer. JJ seemed to like hearing about the donkey and the manger as much as she did. Maybe she'd save that for later. Light was streaming through the workshop windows, and the sun was high in the sky. She longed to feel the warmth on her face. Perhaps the chores could wait a short while.

"Come on, JJ." She picked up the two short branches she'd left propped against the wall of the workshop.

"Out?" JJ said, his face brightening.

"You're wasting ya time," Hannah said, as Clara went out with JJ crawling rapidly after her.

Clara ignored her sister. She was determined that eventually she would help JJ to walk. JJ found it easier outside where there were no fire irons or spinning wheels to land on. Horse dung in the road might not be nice, but it hurt less when he fell on that, rather than the coal scuttle. She couldn't carry him far now he was two years old, so they could go only the distance he could crawl. Mam was always cross about the state of his clothes and the smell, but Clara would worry about that later and besides, Dad said that was to be expected with a growing boy.

Finding sticks which might be suitable was one of the hardest parts. Every piece of wood she'd found so far was either the wrong height, or so dry that it snapped when JJ put his small amount of weight on it. The wood then became kindling, and Clara was left searching for replacements.

"Hold onto me, so I can measure the stick."

JJ pulled himself up. Clara had learnt to let him do it for himself. He could stand quite well on one leg and now understood what Clara was doing as she held the sticks against his sides and then broke them off at the right height. JJ giggled as Clara passed the first stick to him.

Breaking the second one didn't go quite so well and it was slightly shorter than she intended. Clara passed it to JJ all the same and then as he leaned on the sticks, she moved behind him and held him around the waist. She wished Dad didn't have to work all hours and could come out here to help.

"Move the sticks forward," she said, gently supporting him and trying to change the position of the stick in his left hand at the same time. "Now hop."

She'd shown JJ what she meant so many times by doing it herself and he understood the game, but yet again as he hopped forward, he stumbled and landed on the compacted dry mud of the road, making his landing hard. The mud would brush off more easily than dung, but he was crying rather than giggling today.

For the number of times that JJ tumbled, Clara wished there was grass nearby that he could practice on. None was close enough to their terraced cottage. JJ himself didn't want to crawl too far. She wished they had one of those wheeled chairs that rich families had to take out their young children, then she could take JJ further from the house. What kept her going was the promise she'd made when he was born and the fact that his own fierce determination mirrored hers. He was soon consoled when he fell and wanted to try again. It was part of the game, and he accepted the bruises and grazes that came with it. Clara loved him all the more for it. He was still too young to realise the problems he faced weren't normal. Once in a while he moved forward a pace or two before the sticks broke and he would smile so wide that his face was split in two. Those were the moments she cherished.

Today wasn't one of those days. Clara sat on the ground next to him and hugged him to her. "We'll do it. We'll keep trying 'til we do it." Then she looked at the hand he was holding out and saw the large splinter from the stick. He couldn't crawl back with one hand. "Wait 'ere. Don't go anywhere." She ran inside to find one of her mother's needles to remove the splinter.

When Clara came back outside, she stopped suddenly. A smartly dressed boy of about her own age was sitting next to JJ on the road, trying to comfort him.

She rushed over to her brother. "Who are you? What are you doing?"

"I'm sorry," the boy said. "He was crying, and I was passing so I came to help."

Clara nodded warily and held up the needle for the boy to see. "Splinter."

JJ's face lit up when he saw his sister returning and he obediently held out his hand for her. "Spinter," he repeated.

Clara couldn't help but smile. How could anyone not adore her little brother? He seemed oblivious to there being any concern over the newcomer and was proudly holding up his broken stick to show him, while Clara removed the splinter.

"What happened to his leg?" asked the boy.

Clara shook her head. "Nothing. 'E were born that way."

"I were," JJ added almost proudly, making both Clara and the other boy smile.

"Why are you in the road? What if a cart goes by?"

Clara frowned. "We ain't got nowhere else to go."

"Don't you have a garden?"

Clara laughed. People like her didn't have gardens. She shook her head. "Who are you?"

"I'm Samuel," said the boy. "I'm staying with my aunt."

Clara nodded. "Clara," she said cautiously "and this is my brother JJ."

"Pleased to meet you."

The politeness of the boy made Clara laugh.

The boy looked around them at the road. "Where do you get the sticks?"

Clara shrugged. "In the lanes, when I can find any."

The boy nodded. Then to Clara's surprise he gently supported JJ to stand and helped him with the sticks that Clara had found. They worked together without saying much for the next few minutes, until the other stick broke and it became impossible for JJ to carry on.

"We'd best go. I have work to do," Clara said.

"Work?" The boy sounded surprised.

Clara nodded and turned to go toward the house.

"Goodbye then," Samuel called. "It was nice meeting you."

Clara frowned and turned back. She smiled. "Yes," she said. "And you. Bye."

Later that day, when Clara was sweeping the hall, she

opened the front door to sweep the dust out into the street. On the doorstep were a neat pile of six sticks of about the same length she had been using with JJ. Clara smiled and looked out into the road to see if Samuel was still there, but she could see no one.

The following week in her Sunday school class, they read from John's gospel, chapter 5. As the passage came to an end, the only words which Clara could focus on were when Jesus said to the man 'Take up your bed and walk.' The man hadn't been able to walk for thirty-eight years and yet suddenly he did so. If Jesus had helped that man walk, then surely, he could help JJ. Maybe the man had two legs rather than one, but Clara was convinced that somehow Jesus must be able to help her brother.

At the end of the class as the children trooped out, Clara approached her teacher. "Excuse me, sir." He didn't look up from what he was doing so she gently tugged at his coat sleeve.

"Mr Cooper, sir." She felt herself flush. Maybe Mr Cooper wouldn't know what to do, but he was always willing to help her with her reading, so perhaps he wouldn't mind her asking.

"Miss Phipps." He looked up and smiled, his bushy eyebrows twitching, seemingly into a smile of their own. "What are you struggling with this week?"

He had a twinkle in his eye, and it gave Clara confidence to be bold. "In the story you read today, Jesus made the man walk. Could he help my brother JJ walk too?"

Mr Cooper looked at her with a benign smile. "Ah." He hesitated. "I've seen you in the street trying to help him. Is it not going well?"

Clara shook her head and explained about the sticks breaking and the splinters and JJ falling over. Sadly, the extra sticks that Samuel had left for them were already broken. "When you read that passage to us, I thought maybe Jesus could help instead."

Mr Cooper nodded but looked far away. "Sometimes the Lord works in different ways. Let me have a think about that." He patted her shoulder.

"Thank you," she said shifting her weight from one foot to the other and wondering if she should go now. Mr Cooper turned back to what he'd been writing, and Clara went to find the rest of her family.

She didn't know what it meant when an adult said they would think about something. If it were Mam, then it would probably be a way to stop Clara from asking again, but something in Mr Cooper's manner suggested he might be different, and she hoped that would be the case. In the meantime, she would try to find some more small branches for JJ to practise with.

It was two weeks later at the end of her Sunday school class when Mr Cooper called her back as she was about to leave. "I'll walk out with you and talk to your father."

"Yes, sir." Clara's stomach tightened as she wondered what he intended to say. She thought back over the morning. She hadn't spoken out of turn. She'd remembered to raise her hand to ask a question and when she was asked to read a short passage she'd done so willingly, although she'd struggled with some of the longer words. She said nothing as they walked through the schoolroom to find her waiting parents.

JJ was sitting on the floor next to their feet. It was hard to hold him firmly on a hip as other parents did with young children. With only one leg to wrap around you it was difficult for him to balance, and it soon became tiring, even for Dad.

"Mr Phipps, Mrs Phipps." Mr Cooper bowed his head slightly in greeting her parents.

Clara stood close by, twisting the sleeve of her dress as she waited to find what he was about to say. It was then she noticed that in the hand behind his back he was carrying some pieces of wood.

Mr Cooper seemed nervous. "I hope you don't mind, but Miss Phipps spoke to me about young John here when we read the lesson two weeks ago. She was telling me all the things you've done to help your son learn to walk."

"It's a bad business and no mistake," Clara's father said, shaking his head. "I dunno there's ote we can do, but that dun't look good for the child."

"Might I be so bold…" Mr Cooper brought what he was holding into full sight, "… as to offer these to Master Phipps?"

In his hands were pieces of wood, carefully finished, longer and more solid than the sticks which Clara had been trying to use for walking sticks. They ended with blocks of wood, smoothed and shaped into a gentle curve, without splinter or roughness. She frowned. They were far too long for JJ to use as walking sticks and would be hard for him to grip. She was surprised that Dad's face darkened.

"But we couldn't pay you for 'em, we…" He trailed off and seemed to be finding words difficult.

"Good Heavens, sir, no." Mr Cooper seemed embarrassed. "I don't want payment. Please take them as a gift. I had a word with Mr Bailey and asked if he had any wood to spare and then put them together myself. I dabble in a little woodworking as a hobby, and I thought I could make myself useful in doing so. They may be too long, but I didn't have the right measurements. I could either cut a small piece off the end or you could maybe wait for him to grow a little."

Clara could contain herself no longer and, scared that her father would not accept the gift, spoke up. "Excuse me, sir, but what are they?"

Mr Cooper brightened at her question and the opportunity for her father to refuse seemed to have passed. "Here, let me show you."

Mr Cooper put the ends of the sticks on the ground. "They're crutches. Master Phipps can put them under his arms here." He put one under his own arm and indicated the curved tops.

Clara clapped her hands together, then bent down to JJ's level. She held out her hands for him to grasp and pull himself up. "Look, JJ." She wasn't sure how to explain to him. He'd picked the idea of walking sticks up quickly, but that was by copying her. These crutches were too small for her to show him.

As she held JJ's hands, Mr Cooper slotted one of the crutches under JJ's arm, but it was too long for him to use to stand, if he stood with them wedged under his armpits his leg would be off the ground.

Clara felt an overwhelming sense of disappointment. "Sorry," she whispered to her brother, lowering him gently down again.

"Sticks?" JJ said, hopefully, looking up at her.

Clara shook her head. "We don't have any of those either."

"Not to worry," Mr Cooper said, straightening up. "I need to take about an inch and three-quarters off the bottom and if I do it quickly, he won't have grown in the meantime. I'll bring them round tomorrow evening."

Clara looked up at her father, holding her breath.

"If it's really no trouble…"

She thought she saw a tear in her father's eye as he spoke.

"It's very kind of you and if he can use 'em, even for a while, it'll make a big difference."

"No trouble at all." Mr Cooper seemed flustered by the gratitude. "I rather enjoyed making them. If I can get hold of the wood, I might be able to make some more when he grows out of these. To be honest, Mr Bailey did help and lent me some of the tools."

"I ain't met Mr Bailey myself, but if you'd thank him for me, I'd be grateful." Dad was looking at his hands, clearly struggling with the generosity of spirit from someone who he hardly knew.

"I most certainly will. I'm sure he'd like to meet young Master Phipps one day. I explained to him why I needed the wood, and he was most interested. Most interested indeed." Mr Cooper then nodded to Mrs Phipps before retreating from their little group.

Mr Cooper was as good as his word and the following evening called at their house with the newly shortened crutches.

"Well, I never did know such kindness," Mam said, shaking her head as though not quite believing they were real.

Clara thought it strange how much her mother's mood seemed to have lifted. She'd thought her mother cared little for JJ's progress and now to Clara's delight, Mam was the one holding JJ straight while Clara gently put the crutches under his arms.

JJ giggled in enjoyment of all the fuss and excitement.

"Let go of him, Mam," Clara said. "You can stand on your own, now," she said to JJ as he remained motionless in the middle of the kitchen, a look of concentration on his face.

Clara saw Mam dab the corner of her eye with her apron.

Thinking how she would need to move the crutches if she were learning to walk with them, Clara stood close by JJ trying to work it out. As she was still thinking, Dad came in and looked at them all.

He smiled and spoke to his son. "Now, John, move them sticks forward a little and then hop toward me."

JJ landed in a pile of crutches and flailing limbs, giggling on the kitchen floor. Dad lifted him gently to his feet and, with his usual determination, JJ hopped again… and again, though, as so often happened, he made little progress.

Within half an hour, JJ was exhausted but at least he had understood what needed to be done. He would have continued all night, had Mam not insisted it was time he was in bed.

Every day, JJ practised with his crutches. Within a couple of days, although his armpits were clearly sore, and he showed Clara where his shoulders ached, he could complete a circuit of the small kitchen table. Outside was harder, due to ruts in the road and the slippery patches of mud and waste, but Clara helped him all she was able. By the following Sunday, JJ made slow progress covering some of the distance to chapel on his crutches, until he was too tired to go further.

Clara wished they could show JJ's progress to Samuel,

the boy who had helped them a few weeks earlier. She smiled at the recollection.

"Come on, John, let me carry you now, or we'll never get there." Dad reached his hands down and lifted JJ, passing the crutches to Clara to carry.

When Mr Cooper saw Clara with the crutches in her hands, his face fell. "Do they need more adjustment?" He asked reaching out to take them.

Clara drew back. "Oh, no, sir." She shook her head vehemently then broke into a broad smile. "JJ, that is John James is doing well, but he was tired from using them so much. After a while, it hurts his hands and arms to hold them so, but it's getting easier." She indicated where JJ had to grip the pole of the crutches. She passed the crutches back to JJ who delightedly swung himself forward the last few steps into the chapel.

"Look," JJ called back to them, as though he thought they weren't all watching him.

Mr Cooper broke into a broad grin. "I see the problem, I could perhaps…" He picked up one of the crutches from where JJ was now sitting on the floor, smiling proudly after showing off his new skill.

Mr Cooper nodded before handing the crutch back to Clara but said no more.

JJ and Clara were as determined as each other. Whenever Clara was free from working, she sat with her brother reading to him or took him outside to practise with his crutches. She used a herbal preparation that Grandma gave them to soothe the hard patches of skin that developed on his hands and rubbed his shoulders when they hurt from too much use. When she was tired, but he was still in want of help, she thought about how much she loved him and remembered her promise and pushed herself to continue.

Within weeks, JJ could move around almost as well as any child of his age. He tired easily, but rarely cried and, despite finding the stick of the crutch hard to grasp at times, he never gave up.

"You mind what you're doing wi' those things." Grandma picked up a pan that had clattered to the floor as JJ made another circuit of the kitchen.

"He'd knock things off wi' or wirrout the sticks," Mam replied, smiling. "He's a growing boy. I should think our Jack wa' as bad when he wa' that age, although he weren't much younger than me, so it's hard to remember."

"That's as maybe, but if young John hits my ankle wi' those crutches one more time…" Grandma shook her head and turned back to the stove.

Clara noticed that her grandmother broke into a smile as she worked.

"You wa' at least as clumsy as Jack ever wa'." Grandma looked across at Mam and shook her head. She picked up the corners of her skirt and effected a posh voice. "I think delicacy passed our family by." She raised an eyebrow as she looked at them all. Then shook her head once more and went back to peeling vegetables.

Although JJ was doing well, he was still clumsy in his movement. For an ordinary young child that meant bruises and scratched knees for themselves when they tumbled over, but with JJ it could mean those around him sustained injury as well. Clara didn't complain about the times he put his crutch down on her toe without realising or hit her shin as he and the crutches went falling in all directions.

"He's doing ever so well, sir," Clara said to Mr Cooper at Sunday school.

"And how are his hands doing?"

Clara frowned. "Sore, sir, but Mam says they're toughening up the more he uses 'em."

Mr Cooper nodded. "Are the crutches still the right size?"

This time Clara laughed. "They were last week, sir, but he seems to have grown again. He's getting quite big."

Leaning forward and whispering as though conspiratorially, Mr Cooper said, "I've made him a bigger pair of crutches with special handles so that it's easier for his hands. I'll bring them round for him this week."

Clara didn't know what to say and stared at him open mouthed.

"Don't say anything yet. I'd like it to be a surprise."

She nodded earnestly. "Thank you," she said finally remembering her manners and went away grinning broadly.

CHAPTER 4

1847

Clara went into the kitchen to prepare supper. Grandma had been ironing and was standing with the iron in hand, talking to Dad, her eyes screwed into a tight frown.

"You shouldn't be encouraging 'im." Grandma slapped the iron down on the stove. "What's he gonna do? No good can come of it. You can't support yourselves. You should be sending 'im to an orphanage now, if anywhere'd take him. I know it's hard on the lad, but if it's not the orphanage now, it'll be the workhouse for all of you before you're done."

Clara gasped. She thought Grandma loved JJ as she did, although it had taken the old woman a while to show any affection toward him. What had made her say something so dreadful?

"That's enough." Dad looked furious. "He's as much part of this family as you an' me."

Clara had never heard her father speak to Grandma like that, certainly not in front of her.

"So much so that our Hettie went wirrout bread yesterday so 'e could eat. It would've been better if 'e 'adn't lived. "'E's never gonna get along wirrout 'elp. What d'you think's gonna happen? It's wearing our Hettie down and no mistake."

Grandma clearly had no intention of being stopped

from speaking her mind and Clara hated to hear what her grandmother was saying.

"I said, that's enough. Don't you think you'd better leave the ironing and go back to Jack's for today?" Dad said.

His fists were balled, and Clara could see the whites of his knuckles. She stood still where she was in the doorway. If nothing else she would stop JJ coming in and hearing what was being said.

"And what's 'e gonna do when 'e's older, that's what I wanna know?" Grandma had avoided answering Dad's question. "He'll be no use wirra knitting frame when there's two pedals to work, so where does that leave 'im?"

"There's other work." Dad threw his hands up as he said it.

Clara held her breath, waiting to find what her father would say next. Instead, his shoulders dropped, and he looked defeated. He left the kitchen and went past her in the direction of the workshop.

Grandma snorted as he left. "I ain't seen many jobs 'round 'ere for them of us wi' two legs. You wouldn't spend all hours keeping this lot goin' if there wa'. He can't go into the factories. He'd be a danger to everyone."

As soon as Grandma picked up the iron again, Clara left the kitchen. Preparing the vegetables would have to wait. She couldn't be that close to Grandma without saying what she thought. She loved JJ and would do anything for him and Grandma should feel the same.

As she went through the hall, the door to the workshop was ajar and she peeped through the gap to see what Dad was doing. Surely, he wasn't working again, however bad things were. They'd already had a long day, and he wouldn't want to relight the lamps. Besides, he said the order was finished.

Dad was sitting with his head in his hands and his shoulders slumped. Clara wondered if she should go to him or tell their mother what had happened. But Grandma was her mother's mam, and complaining about Grandma wasn't likely to go well. Clara decided it was best to say nothing, but leaving Dad looking so sad was hard. She took a deep breath and returned quietly to her chores. It was true, Mam hadn't taken a share of the bread yesterday, but she'd said she wasn't hungry, and Clara had believed her. Now that she thought about it, there had often been times when Mam said she didn't need anything when food was short.

The supper table was a sombre affair. Except to ask for something to be passed to them, no one spoke. The children weren't expected to say anything unless spoken to first, but normally the adults would have some conversation. Now Hannah was older she was allowed to speak more freely at the table, but she remained quiet today. Clara couldn't wait for the meagre meal to be over.

It was unusual for anyone in the house to argue, and Clara presumed there would be apologies made, and all would soon be forgotten, although she didn't feel she could easily forgive the things Grandma had said.

The following day as they worked, they did so with little being said and Dad looked tired and worn, as though he hadn't slept. In the afternoon, when Mam came to spend time on the knitting frame, Hannah was given the choice of winding wool or taking over the housework and looking after JJ, a job that Grandma had been doing recently when she was there.

"Where's Grandma?" Hannah asked.

Clara was surprised at her asking so brazenly, but then

Hannah hadn't witnessed the argument.

"She ain't 'ere." Mam sighed heavily. "She said Uncle Jack needed 'er today and she'd rather be where she was appreciated." She gave Dad a sideways glance as she said it.

Hannah gave out a loud breath. "I s'pose I'll do some winding then." She came over to where Clara was sitting and although nobody had said in so many words, Clara took that as her cue to spend the afternoon with her brother and doing the household chores. She was more than happy to leave the atmosphere of the workshop behind even if it was to exchange it for mopping the floors.

Once Clara had finished with the mop and before she prepared dinner, she took JJ outside for some crisp autumn air. JJ began by seeing how far he could go on his crutches while Clara sat reading her Bible. She looked up at intervals to make sure he hadn't gone out of sight. When he tired, JJ came and sat beside her and rested his head on her lap. Clara smiled. In moments such as these she felt truly happy.

"One day, when we're older, I'll find a way to look after both of us," she said, as JJ fell asleep. "Maybe I could work in a factory, and it'll be all right if you can't work." She had no idea what she would be paid or if it would be enough, but somehow she would take care of him. She stroked JJ's hair as he slept. To her, he was perfect. None of this was his fault. Every night she prayed that Jesus would find a way to help JJ. She was sure that if she prayed hard enough somehow everything would be all right.

It was strange seeing less of Grandma over the following weeks. Clara was struggling to work out how she felt about her grandmother after what she'd said. Of course, she loved her, but she couldn't forgive what Grandma had said, whatever the Bible told her about forgiveness. When Grandma was at the house, things remained strained, and Clara wondered what else had been discussed between the adults that she hadn't heard. Without Grandma helping there was much more work to do, washing, ironing and preparing meals and as Hannah preferred to wind wool and Mam was so much better on the knitting frame, much of that fell to Clara. The work could be as hard, harder on wash day as she struggled with the weight of the wet laundry, and cranking it through the mangle, but she was happy with JJ moving around the kitchen while she worked. She did get cross with him when his crutches stamped muddy marks onto a freshly laundered sheet, waiting to be ironed, but he was only like she and Martha had been when they were younger. No child was careful all of the time, but it made more work.

Clara was too small to do some chores alone and others she didn't yet know how to do, but for those things they would swap around, and she would go into the workshop for an hour or two, while Mam came to the kitchen. Hannah never seemed keen to take on the domestic chores, although she didn't seem much happier to be in the workshop, but when she was there, Martha sat winding close to Hannah, and they talked to each other or sang as they worked.

The days passed quickly, and JJ grew stronger. Without Grandma there, no one talked about what would happen when he was older, but Clara felt confident that God would have a plan. After all, wasn't that what the minister said so often in the services at chapel? Besides, as far as she could see, JJ could do many of the same things as other children his age. He was a strong and happy boy and rarely demanded attention when she couldn't give it. Nor did he complain about the difficulties he faced, apart from the occasional tantrum in frustration when he'd tried something a hundred times and still couldn't do it. When the tantrum was over, he'd try for the hundred and first time.

It was Monday morning and despite the dampness of the air, Clara was hanging out washing in their tiny back yard. She frowned. In the corner of the yard hunched over the dirt, Hannah was being sick.

Between her retches, Hannah snapped at Clara, "What you staring at?"

"I was just…" Clara didn't know what to say. She wasn't used to Hannah being quite so rude to her. If Hannah was ill, she should tell their mother. She turned to go back into the house. "I'll fetch…"

"Don't you dare. If you say a word, I swear I'll…" Hannah didn't finish the sentence as she retched once again.

Clara hesitated. She had no idea what to do. "I won't. Not if you don't want me to, but if you're ill…" Clara wrung her hands miserably. "… I'll fetch you some water."

"I'm fine. Leave me be." Hannah wiped her mouth on her sleeve and straightened up. She took a few deep breaths, kicked some dirt over where she'd been sick and walked past Clara back into the house.

When they were in bed that night, Clara whispered to Hannah, "Are ya better now?"

"Shut up, Clara," her sister hissed. "I told ya not to say ote."

"What ain't she to say ote about?" Martha asked much louder than a whisper.

Clara froze. She thought Martha was asleep and wouldn't hear what Clara said to Hannah. Now her older sister really would be cross with her. As gently as she could, Clara said, "There ain't 'ote to worry about. Go to sleep, Martha." She said nothing more, even when Hannah prodded her quite hard in the back.

Martha at seven years old was regarded by everyone as a child, despite spending her days winding in the workshop. Clara was only three years older than her sister, but she still felt it her responsibility to look after Martha, despite them having so little in common. Neither of her sisters wanted to learn to read and write and preferred spending time talking rather than being quiet.

Clara slipped out of bed and went to prepare breakfast early the following morning, before Hannah was awake. She hoped her older sister would have forgiven her for the night before and that maybe Martha wasn't awake enough at the time to remember. Clara was taking the dishes out of the cupboard as Martha came bouncing into the kitchen.

"Hannah's gorra secret. Hannah's gorra secret."

Their parents were already in the workshop and would come for breakfast when Clara had finished preparations.

"Shurrup," Hannah hissed at their youngest sister and glared at Clara. "Now look what you've done."

Clara couldn't help thinking her older sister looked pale. "Why does it 'ave to be a secret that you're sick? Everyone gets sick sometimes. Maybe it wa' summat you ate. Mam says when my belly hurts that I've maybe eaten too many berries from along the lane. 'Ave you bin eating berries?"

"An' where would I find berries that I could eat, so late in the year? Just shurrup." This time the look Hannah shot to Clara was pure venom and Clara recoiled.

That was the moment Mam came through the door. "What's going on wi' you girls? It's too early to be fighting already."

"Hannah's gorra secret," Martha chanted once again.

"Has she now? I'm sure she'll tell me when she's good and ready."

Clara breathed a sigh of relief at Mam's response and thought her words would probably be the end of the matter. And so, they might have been had Hannah not rushed from the room toward the yard with her hand over her mouth as soon as Clara placed a bowl of porridge in front of her.

Mam was about to sit down, but instead she made an apology and followed Hannah out through the back door.

Clara finished serving the food in time for Dad joining them at the table. Mam had still not returned, and Dad seemed to sense the atmosphere. Whilst they would normally wait and eat together, he said, "I think you girls best gerron and eat wi' me now. There's work to do."

Clara had completely lost her appetite worrying what might be wrong with Hannah. Instead of sitting to her own bowl, she helped JJ eating his. It wasn't easy for him to balance on a chair with his stump giving him an uneven position to sit. Clara bent down to his level on the floor where, supported by the wall and a cushion he was less likely to overbalance.

When Mam came back indoors her face was as grey as Hannah's. "John," she said to Dad, sounding strained. "I need to talk wi' you after breakfast. The stockings'll have to knit 'emselves. Clara, you can take young John and Martha into the workroom and make a start."

Clara looked up. There must be something seriously wrong with Hannah if the frames were to lie idle for any time at all. Perhaps if she could work hard on the knitting it might help to make amends with her sister. JJ would be happy enough with some wool ends to play with and Martha could wind as normal.

As soon as Martha's bowl was empty, Clara took the pots over to the sink. She didn't stay behind to wash them as she usually would but helped JJ to stand and then ushered Martha ahead of her to the workroom. Martha still seemed unaware of the growing storm that her words had caused, and Clara thought it might be best for her to stay that way.

Clara needed to use all her concentration when working the knitting frame and she was much slower than either of her parents or Hannah. The machine was already threaded up, so that was one less thing to worry about and thankfully they were working on plain unpatterned stockings. Rhythmically operating the treadles to take the yarn across the row, while moving the bar that engaged and disengaged the needles, by pulling it toward and away from her from both sides with her hands, was difficult enough. It was hard work, but at least her arms ached a little less now than when she'd first learnt to use the machine. She still made errors and needed to go back a little way to correct them. She worked steadily and only looked up when she heard raised voices from the kitchen.

It was rare that anyone in the house shouted. Clara stopped what she was doing, fearing she would make mistakes, quite apart from wanting to hear what was being said, which was impossible over the noise of the knitting. She wished now that she hadn't closed the door as they came into the workshop as the voices from the kitchen were muffled. She stared out of the window, wondering what was happening.

After a moment or two, the voices stopped and Clara was about to continue knitting, when to her surprise she saw Dad marching out into the street still putting on his hat and coat, with Hannah, red in the face trying to keep up with his strides. She was watching them go when the door opened and Mam came into the workshop, looking as red-faced as Hannah.

"Gerronwi' your work, Clara, there's note to see." Mam's hands were shaking as she sat at the second frame knitting the next stocking.

Clara didn't dare say a word.

"What's wrong wi' Hannah?" Martha asked.

Clara held her breath, unsure how Mam would react to the question.

"Never you mind."

Mam wiped her eyes and Clara frowned.

A couple of hours passed before Dad returned, without Hannah. He came into the workroom, saying nothing. Clara slipped from her seat at the knitting machine to allow him to take over. She was glad to leave rather than continuing to sit there in silence. She took JJ through to the kitchen and was surprised to find the breakfast pots without so much as water in them, still waiting to be washed. Whatever was discussed must have been serious for Mam to leave the kitchen in a mess. Clara began clearing up and her thoughts moved away from Hannah.

Clara set the same number of places at the table as usual, though her older sister had not yet returned.

"Where's Hannah?" Martha asked when they stopped work for lunch.

"She'll be back when she's good and ready," Mam replied and glanced at Dad who raised an eyebrow.

"Is she very ill?" Martha seemed oblivious to their

parents wanting to close down the conversation.

This time Dad looked beseechingly at Mam.

"Not sick exactly." Mam seemed hesitant to reply.

Clara gasped and covered her mouth with her hand. If Hannah wasn't ill, but was being sick, surely that didn't mean…? She couldn't be. She wasn't married. But Clara remembered how Mam felt before JJ was born. Dare she ask? She thought not, certainly not in front of Martha, but from the look on Mam's face at her reaction she presumed her guess must be right. She didn't suppose even Hannah would tell her if she asked directly.

To Clara's surprise, when Hannah returned in the middle of the afternoon she was smiling. The sight of her seemed to lift Mam's spirits.

"Will ya take me to see the minister later, Dad?" Hannah asked, almost shyly.

Their father nodded.

"The sooner all this is sorted the better," Mam said.

"We'll say no more about it 'til arrangements are made. In the meantime, you're gonna have to put in some work, as once you ain't here it'll be the harder for the rest of us." Dad went back to his stocking frame.

"You take over 'ere," Mam said, stepping aside for Hannah.

"But…"

"We'll have no buts. If we're all gonna eat, then you'll take over. We've lost time sorting out this mess, you need to do ya bit." Dad spoke sternly and Hannah said no more.

CHAPTER 5

1848

"There'll be as little fuss made on Saturday as possible, my girl." Grandma had, despite their differences, offered to help alter a dress of Mam's for Hannah to wear at the chapel ceremony.

"But it's my wedding day and I plan to enjoy it." Hannah was struggling to stand still as her grandmother finished pinning the hem of the dress to the right length. Grandma had already let out the side seams as far as possible, but the dress was still a little tight around Hannah's expanding waist and attempts to conceal her condition were proving futile.

"That's as maybe, but you're still sixteen and everyone knows why it's all happening so quick. Look at you."

Hannah pouted and Clara turned back to the washing she was doing before her sister accused her of staring.

Although Hannah marrying would mean fewer of them to do the work, Clara was secretly looking forward to Hannah moving to live with Frank's family. She'd miss Hannah singing while they were in the workshop, but she wouldn't miss her moods and it would be good to have more space in the bed for JJ, Martha and herself. She wondered if Frank's family really wouldn't expect Hannah to work and what she'd do with her time otherwise. Clara hoped they'd find Hannah easier to live with than she did.

From what the adults said, it would most likely be a long time before Hannah and Frank were able to have a home of their own. Although Frank was older than Hannah, he was still apprenticed to his father and would be for another couple of years.

Clara sighed. Somehow, she planned to earn enough to support herself and JJ and that would be hard to do framework knitting. She couldn't see a husband taking on her brother as well as herself. The new factories were probably the answer, but she didn't know much about them, except that women were paid less than men and they didn't employ married women, but that was the same for almost every job, which meant she doubted she'd ever marry. She carried on scrubbing the clothes and wondering what her life might be like if she could go to school. She'd heard people say that a girl might do different jobs if she had an education. After a while, Clara looked around the kitchen remembering she wasn't on her own.

Hannah had taken off the dress so that Grandma could get on with the sewing. Despite the cold of the January day, she was sitting in her petticoat at the kitchen table looking far away.

"Hannah Phipps, that's quite enough daydreaming. While you're still under this roof there's work to be done. Get yourself dressed and back 'ere into the workroom to take over from me." Mam had come into the kitchen to fetch a drink.

Both their parents had looked strained over the last few weeks as preparations were made for the wedding. Mam made no secret of her concerns that Frank's family wouldn't be happy about the marriage, but Hannah was convinced that once the baby arrived everyone would dote on both the baby and her. Clara hoped she was right.

"We'll be all right as long as Frank ain't had second thoughts," Mam said as she corralled them out of the door on Saturday morning.

It was frosty, which made it much harder for JJ with his crutches.

"He'll be there. His parents'll make sure of that. They've their reputation in the chapel to think of if note else." Dad raised an eyebrow. "Here, son, let me carry you." He lifted JJ and as normal Clara reached for his crutches to carry.

Mam continued to chunter her concerns as they made their way along the road. "An' you be careful with that dress and keep it nice," she said to Hannah. "What Mr and Mrs Carter think about their son marrying the likes of us I don't know. The least we can do is try an' look presentable. You've precious little else that'll fit you in your condition. You're gonna need that dress to make do for a while."

Clara wondered how, with Hannah's increasing size, she would still get into it in a few weeks, but maybe Mrs Carter would help her sort that out.

By now they were arriving at the chapel. Dad stayed with Hannah at the back and Mam led the others inside, with JJ moving himself along with his crutches once again. Mr Carter nodded to them as they reached the front of the chapel and Mam dipped her head in return before moving into the pew. Clara saw Mam's shoulders relax now that she knew Frank and his family had arrived.

The wedding was a small affair, with the two families present, together with the minister, the registrar and a few well-wishers who sat at the rear of the chapel.

Clara had never attended a wedding before. She'd

stood outside their house and watched wedding parties go past from time to time, but the service itself was a mystery to her. At least Frank and Hannah seemed to be smiling. Clara thought that had to be a good start, although with the exception of Frank's sister Mary, all the other adults looked strained.

It was strange to think that after this Clara would see little more of her sister than when attending chapel on Sundays and maybe occasional family gatherings. Although if Hannah didn't have to work, maybe she could bring the baby to see them from time to time. She and Hannah had little enough to say to each other now, it would feel almost as though they were strangers if they rarely saw each other.

Once the service was over, and Hannah and Frank had signed the register, with Dad and Mr Carter acting as witnesses, the whole event seemed very flat. They wished Hannah good luck as they all left the chapel and went their separate ways home. Dad was stony faced as he carried JJ some of the way and Mam remained silent. Grandma took her leave and went straight home, something Clara was quite pleased about. Uncle Jack and family hadn't attended, having made their disapproval of Hannah's behaviour all too clear.

"We'd best get back to work," Dad said as soon as they were through the door. "There's been enough time wasted. These frames won't pay for themselves." He looked around the workroom, shaking his head. "We should be grateful we didn't rent a third frame. It'll be hard enough to meet the cost as it is. Mam and I'll knit, and you and Martha'll have to wind. As to John…"

Dad didn't finish the sentence, but Clara realised that despite him not yet being three years old, without Hannah to help, JJ would be left to his own devices more of the time.

Clara switched between working on the knitting frame when Mam was busy with other things and winding wool when Mam worked the frame. Her days of being able to spend so much time with JJ had come to an end. All of them took turns at doing the household chores, on top of their working day, which was often fifteen hours in itself. It also meant she had less time for reading, as entertaining JJ was her main excuse.

Relations with Grandma seemed to have thawed to some extent, though she was not backward in expressing her disapproval of Hannah's marriage. She came in to help from time to time, for which they were all grateful.

Clara was sad that she couldn't read to her brother, especially when he worked his way over to where she was sitting in the workshop and asked if she would. Sometimes, when she was winding and not working a knitting machine, he would sit near her stool, and she'd try to tell him a story as she wound the wool. She'd read her favourite stories in the Bible so many times, she could almost remember every word, although oddly the old language seemed more strange when she recounted the story than when she read it from the page.

They were still in the workshop in the fading light, one evening in spring, when Clara heard a knock at the workshop door and Hannah came in, tears streaming down her face.

"Whatever's wrong?" Mam asked, stopping what she was doing and going across to her daughter.

"I'm frit," Hannah wailed as her mother took her hand and guided her to the other room.

Clara wanted to stay quiet and listen, but instead Dad called across to her.

"Come and finish this stocking Mam wa' working on, Clara. I need us to have this batch ready for collection."

By the time Dad asked Clara to fetch another candle from the box on the wall in the kitchen, Hannah was looking more composed and the table in the back room was set for them to eat when they finished working.

"Is the baby due soon?" Clara asked her sister, trying to remember how long it was since the wedding.

"Not for a while," Hannah replied and sniffed as though still recovering from crying.

Clara was about to ask if it wasn't that then what was it that Hannah was frightened by, but her mother intervened.

"You'd best take that candle back to Dad or you'll all be in there for the night."

Clara sighed and went back to her work.

When Clara returned to the kitchen, Hannah had gone back to the Carters' house, and no one said a word about what it was which frightened her sister.

A few weeks later they were disturbed not by Hannah, but Frank hammering on the door and calling to them to let him in.

Dad rushed to answer; concern etched on his face. "Whatever is it? Is Hannah all right?"

Frank was clearly agitated and his eyes darted around as though looking for someone. "No, yes, I don't know - it's the baby, it's coming. She wants her mam."

Hettie was already reaching for her coat while issuing instructions of what to do while she was gone. Once she'd followed Frank out of the house and the door was closed it was as though a sudden storm had passed.

Dad sat back at the knitting frame, but instead of starting work, he put his hands together and said a prayer for his daughter.

"Dear Father…"

Clara shot a look to Martha, and they quickly stopped working and put their own hands together in prayer.

"… keep our daughter Hannah safe in this time of great need…" Dad faltered as though wanting to say more but running out of words. "… Amen."

Clara and Martha chorused "Amen," and a moment later, JJ who was sitting in the corner of the room added his own "Amen," although he clearly had little idea what they were doing. Clara wanted to laugh, but the solemnity on Dad's face stopped her.

Dad went back to working and looked over to the girls, nodding that they too should return to work.

Clara was close to winding to the end of the bobbin, so decided to finish that before taking over Mam's knitting frame. She wondered how long it would be before they received news from the Carter house. Frank hadn't stayed long enough to tell them how imminent the birth might be, but then he probably didn't know.

As darkness fell, Mam hadn't returned and Clara prepared supper.

"D'ya think everything's all right?" Dad asked, almost as though he were the child and not Clara.

"I'm sure it is," Clara said, although secretly she too had been wondering.

"Hannah's frit that the baby might be…" Dad hesitated and bit his lip.

"Might be what?" Clara had no idea what her father was thinking.

He took a deep breath and then in a rush said, "Like our John." He nodded toward JJ.

Clara frowned. It hadn't occurred to her that her sister would be thinking that. It wasn't as though any of the rest of them had one leg. Perhaps Dad knew something she didn't.

Clara thought for a little while and then asked, "Dad, why does JJ only 'ave one leg?"

Dad raised both his eyebrows and shook his head but said nothing in reply.

Clara supposed that meant Dad didn't know the answer any more than she did. Perhaps she should ask Mr Cooper. He was, after all, the one who had been trying to help her with JJ's walking, and he seemed to know a great many things.

Clara didn't hear her mother come back that night, but early the following morning, when Clara went downstairs, Mam was already in the kitchen, looking tired. She was talking to Dad and didn't see Clara.

"Frank were off wetting the baby's 'ead wi' his friends as soon as the boy wa' born. Our Hannah wa' asking for him, but he wa' long gone by then. She may as well 'ave married a heathen the way he wa' carrying on." Mam turned and saw Clara and stopped abruptly.

"Are Hannah and the baby well?" Clara asked, wondering what it meant to wet the baby's head.

Mam broke into a broad smile. "Indeed, they are. You 'ave a nephew. They're both doing fine. Thank God for it not being a difficult birth as I don't think your sister could 'ave coped."

Clara couldn't imagine her sister as a mother. "What's 'is name?"

"He's named after his father, Frank Robert, but he'll be called Robert at home to save confusion."

"May I go to see them?" Clara thought she knew the answer, but she did so want to see her nephew for herself.

"When the work's done. We'll be wirrout Mam today, as she's visiting the Carter house to be wi' Hannah. Let's get to it, shall we?" Dad looked at her kindly.

It was hard for Clara to argue as she supposed Dad wanted to meet his grandson but would need to wait just the same.

She ate her breakfast quickly and went straight into the workshop. Perhaps she could work faster than usual and be finished sooner. JJ was playing quietly in the corner. It was strange to think he was an uncle. She wished she could take JJ to see his nephew, but it would be too far for him to manage the whole of the distance with his crutches and Dad wouldn't want to carry him all the way. JJ was beginning to go a little further but if he became tired, all they would be able to do would be to sit at the side of the road until he was ready to carry on, unless a passing cart took pity on them. Maybe she could go with Dad.

"It would p'rhaps be too much for Hannah if we were all to go over an' see the baby," Dad said, late in the afternoon.

Clara held her breath, hoping she would be allowed to go.

"Martha and John had best stay here wi' Grandma and I'll walk over wi' you, Clara."

Clara let out the breath she was holding and jumped up from her chair.

"We won't stay long, mind. I'm sure Frank's family'll have had quite enough of us all traipsing through the house." Dad went through to the kitchen to tell Grandma of their plans.

Mam having been with Hannah all day, was about to leave when Clara and Dad arrived at the Carter house. "I'll wait five minutes and walk back wi' you," she said and looked awkwardly over her shoulder. "I'll be outside. Frank'll show you where to go." She waved toward the front room of the house, before walking briskly out through the back door.

Clara frowned wondering why her mother was in such a hurry to leave.

Dad coughed as he went along the hallway. "Hello, Frank?" No one replied. Dad raised his voice a little louder. "Hello." Dad ran a finger around his collar and moved from foot to foot.

A few moments later, Frank came into the hall, acting as though he hadn't heard them, which Clara found hard to believe.

"Sorry, Mr Phipps, I didn't know you were here. Have you seen Hannah?"

"No. We were…"

"Follow me." Frank didn't wait for Dad's reply and set off up the stairs two at a time.

When they reached the bedroom, Frank didn't stop to check if Hannah was prepared for visitors, but flung open the door and indicated for them to go in. Before they could so much as say thank you, he'd run downstairs as fast as he'd come up.

Dad hesitated in the doorway and indicated for Clara to go ahead of him. Frank's mother in the room, standing by the window, rocking her grandson in her arms. Hannah was propped up in bed looking tired and miserable. Clara thought her sister's face looked tear-stained.

"I thought we were done with visitors at this time of night," Mrs Carter said by way of greeting and made no move to bring Hannah's son over to them.

Clara sat on the edge of the bed and to her surprise Hannah reached over and took her hand tightly in her own.

"It's good to see you." Hannah looked from Clara to Dad, including them both in what she said.

"How are you?" Clara asked, whilst Dad stood awkwardly to the side.

Hannah's eyes darted over to her mother-in-law before answering. "I'm well. And little Robert's fine." A more genuine smile broke over her face as she said it. "Would you like to hold him?" she asked Clara.

"He's not a toy to be passed around," Mrs Carter said, as she rather pointedly laid him down in his cot. "I've got him off to sleep."

"Yes, of course." Dad seemed cowed by Frank's mother.

Clara held tight to Hannah's hand but said nothing. She wondered if Hannah was already regretting her new life, although she was pleased to see the love in her sister's eyes when she spoke of her son.

Mrs Carter stayed in the room. To Clara's eye the older woman was moving things around for the sake of it, as an excuse to remain. It was certainly hard to talk about much with Mrs Carter's watchful eye and ear.

They stayed a few minutes before Dad said it was time to leave. Clara got up from the bed, but Hannah didn't let go of her hand.

"Come again soon." Hannah's eyes held such pleading as she spoke. "Maybe next time you could hold Robert."

Her eyes flitted once more to her mother-in-law and back to Clara. "If he's awake of course."

"Might I bring JJ, if I can help him this far?" Clara asked.

Once again, Hannah's eyes darted across to Mrs Carter before she answered. "I don't think that's a good idea yet."

Clara noticed the smile on Mrs Carter's face at Hannah's answer and shivered.

For Hannah's sake Clara smiled and nodded sadly as she withdrew her hand. Before leaving, she went first to Robert's crib and looked down at her tiny sleeping nephew. Mrs Carter took a step toward her as though defending her grandson. Clara looked her straight in the eye before returning her gaze to her nephew and whispering, "Welcome to the family, Robert." Then she followed her father down the stairs.

No words were exchanged as they left, nor as they met Mam who was still waiting outside. Clara saw a look pass between her parents, but they said nothing while she was there.

None of the family had the opportunity to visit Hannah in the following days, nor did Hannah bring Robert to see them. The first they saw of her was a couple of weeks later in chapel and then it was hard to get close due to all the women cooing over the new baby and Mrs Carter holding court as though she were the only grandmother to be considered.

Clara heard her mother say quietly to Dad, "I knew we weren't good enough for that family. I hope our Hannah can 'old 'er own."

CHAPTER 6

1848- 1849

"Please may I go back inside to see Hannah and Robert?" Clara asked her mother when they came out of chapel a few weeks later.

Clara couldn't understand how, in the small community of the chapel, it was still possible for there to be such separate groups of people.

Mam shook her head, and her shoulders dropped. "You know what Mrs Carter said when we went over to Hannah last week."

Clara did know. She still felt angry whenever she thought about it. Other than herself and Mam, no one else was around to hear Mrs Carter say *'The Carter family might have been tricked into accepting Hannah, but that doesn't mean there is any need for us to accept the rest of the family as well. Robert will be quite well served having one set of grandparents; there'll be no need for any others.'* What Clara didn't understand was how that fitted with all the Bible stories they heard in Sunday school and chapel. Perhaps Mrs Carter didn't listen to them, which made it seem strange to Clara that she chose to attend.

"She wouldn't say that if other people were there," Clara said. "We could go over to her when there are people nearby."

Mam broke into a smile. "And so we could. Although

I'd hate Hannah to suffer in any way for it."

Robert was already a few months old and not once had Clara had the opportunity to hold him. Sometimes she wished Mam or Dad had more fight in them, but she could see how tired and worn down they were. She waved to Hannah when her sister was facing her way; that was better than nothing. One day she'd show Mrs Carter that the Phipps weren't just a poor family who could be looked down upon. Like most of the people she knew, her family were hard-working, good people and deserved to be treated with respect, regardless of the fact they were poor. Respect should never be about money.

Clara worked as hard as she could in the home. She thought there must be something more she could do to help. She didn't have enough hours in the day for their current work and she hadn't learning enough to do anything different. What she needed to do was to gain more education. She'd heard adults saying that's what you needed in order to earn more money and that the likes of the framework knitting families could do no better than their current lot. The only time she had spare was Sunday, and all but the Sunday schools were closed on that day. There was one possibility she could think of.

"Mr Cooper," Clara said quietly at the end of her Sunday school class the following Sunday afternoon.

He looked up, seemingly surprised she was still there. "Is everything all right? Has your John grown again?" He chuckled.

"No, sir, there ain't ote wrong. I were wondering if it might be possible for you to teach me some of my numbers as well as my letters, sir?" She bit her lip, hoping desperately that he would say yes, as she could think of no one else to ask.

He raised an eyebrow as he looked at her. "Well, Miss Phipps, that's a most unusual request. Is there a reason for it?"

Clara looked down, her nerve starting to fail. "I want to earn enough to care for JJ, sir. When we're older and 'e can't work a knitting frame. I don't know how, but I want to get a better job so I can earn enough to care for 'im." She stood on one leg, rubbing her boot against the back of her stocking.

There was silence for a moment and Clara's heart raced. She was thinking of apologising for asking and finding her family when Mr Cooper nodded.

"I see. Well…" he paused appearing thoughtful. "You're certainly capable of learning more, but there's only so much we can do within the Sunday school class. It wouldn't be fair on the other children." He thought for a moment. "If your father were to agree, then perhaps you could stay for half an hour after the class finishes."

Clara looked up for the first time. "Thank you, sir. Thank you." She was delighted and was sure her father would agree. Whilst he couldn't understand her desire to learn, he saw it as doing no harm.

Thanks to Mr Cooper helping her a little after each Sunday school class had finished, Clara began to understand numbers and within a few months could do sums she would never before have imagined. Mr Cooper was generous with his time, and she was quick to learn anything that she could be shown. As she studied, her thirst for knowledge seemed to increase.

"It ain't right they pay us so little for finished stockings now. How can they pay us less and less when our costs are more and more?" Dad looked forlorn as they sat at the table with Clara writing up what they'd spent. Once Clara was capable of her basic arithmetic, Dad had gratefully taken her into his confidence in discussing their finances and she had begun to help in working out where they might save a little money on producing the stockings.

"It's those factories doing it." Mam sighed as she continued to work around them. "Perhaps we should be working in the factories and not have to cover the costs of the frames. I've been working one of these frames since I were a child and never thought I'd see a time that would change."

Clara was thinking the same thing, about them moving to work in the factories, but hadn't been brave enough to say so.

"Mind you. I wouldn't want to do what they're doing. It's criminal. Working the stockings straight up then stretching them, rather than increasing and decreasing the stitches to shape the leg. And as for cutting and sewing the heel to save on work, then passing them off as being as good as properly knitted stockings, well it ain't right and shouldn't be allowed. People buy them thinking they're the same, then wonder why they fall apart."

Dad shook his head. "There were a time you could make a decent living with a knitting frame, but now look at us. I dunno what we can do. We couldn't all take factory work, even if we wanted to and whilst we've the two frames it needs all of us to work 'em and John's four years old, so can't very well be left home all the day."

"They wouldn't give me a job whether I wanted one or not," Mam said, shaking her head.

"Because you're married?" Clara frowned.

"Well yes, but not only that." Mam glanced over to Dad and coloured slightly. "Certainly not when I've got another child on the way."

Clara's eyes opened wide. "Another brother or sister. When?"

"It'll be a while yet thank the Lord. It will make it much harder to feed us all." Mam shook her head.

Clara hadn't noticed that Mam's waist was expanding, but now she came to look more closely she realised how stupid she'd been. She looked back at the numbers she'd written down. They would have to buy in yarn that was ready wound. It would be impossible with Mam breast feeding and caring for another baby for her to work as many hours, and Clara couldn't operate the knitting frame and wind wool at the same time. Martha's winding was good, but she couldn't do all they needed for both frames. JJ would struggle to use the treadle of the spinning wheel. Maybe he could do some winding by hand. He'd be slow, but it would be better than nothing. He wanted to try, but he couldn't work anywhere without risking the yarn being on the floor in the dirt. Perhaps she could find a cloth to place under the wool.

Thankfully, JJ could now move as fast and as far as the other children she saw in the street and, using two crutches, could swing himself to chapel every Sunday and at other times could go out with Clara, on the rare occasions they were free. Much as she loved JJ, she'd still felt a pang of jealousy when the Sunday school superintendent, Mr Preston, had spoken to Dad again last Sunday about the possibility of JJ attending the British School once he was old enough. She presumed it was because of his disability that the place was being offered. Dad had said 'no', but how Clara wished she was being offered the opportunity, paid for by the chapel, and that she could have accepted. Clara wanted to learn so much.

Over the next few weeks Clara spent time thinking of ways they might make the food go a little further but came up with nothing. She could scour the hedgerows for any berries which could be turned into jam, but with so little time and other families struggling to eat, she could find precious few. Besides, jam alone wouldn't fill their bellies. By Thursday each week they were lucky if there was enough bread for them all to have sufficient and they were always relieved when Friday came around again and they received payment for their work. She knew of families where, on a Friday night, the men would go out drinking and spending money they could ill afford. It made Clara sincerely glad that her parents were both tee-total, as it certainly helped them in paying for a full week of groceries.

Clara didn't want the baby to be another brother. JJ was special and she wanted him to stay that way. Now Hannah had left home, the thought of another sister wasn't so bad. Perhaps this time she could have one who was more like herself, sharing in the things she found so interesting.

In the meantime, if she could find a way to keep the wool off the floor, she would begin teaching JJ how to wind by hand. She hoped that by making a game of it, he might apply the same dedication that he'd used with his crutches. The first problem was how it was best for him to sit and where. They needed a place he could be comfortable for long periods of time. She and Martha used the old spinning wheel, carefully letting the wool out from the skein, while using the treadle to wind it evenly onto the bobbin or they sat using both their knees to support their work if they wound by hand. JJ couldn't yet reach the floor with his good leg when sitting at the spinning wheel. Besides, if he used the treadle, he would have no foot on the floor to give him balance.

Much of the time, JJ found sitting on the floor, propped against the wall in the corner of the room was the best place to be, but that wouldn't be any use for winding, unless he had a little table a few inches off the ground, with an edge to prevent the wool rolling off. She wondered if she could ask Mr Cooper about making one but thought it unlikely Dad would be happy if she did. Perhaps JJ would be best sitting at the kitchen table for now. At least that would be a start. She could worry about a little table later.

She showed JJ at the first opportunity. "Like this," she said, winding the wool from the hank and around the bobbin. She passed the bobbin to JJ with her finger over the row of wool she had wound, so that he could carry on.

JJ had his tongue sticking out of the corner of his mouth, just like she used to do, as he concentrated on trying to copy his sister. It made Clara smile.

"That's it. Follow the line of the last piece of wool and work along the bobbin, keeping it tight. That way it unwinds evenly when it's on the machine."

JJ did a few more rows, then let out a breath and put the bobbin down on the table. "My arms ache."

Clara had quickly taken the bobbin so that the preceding rows didn't unwind and become tangled. She could see the problem for JJ. He was too low down, and he was having to hold his arms upwards to rest the wool and bobbin on the table. To work there he would need a higher chair and that was as difficult to find as a lower table. Whether Dad liked it or not, she would talk to Mr Cooper; she knew no one else she could ask.

"Sir," she said, after their class finished the following Sunday. "Please could you help me wi' summat?"

Mr Cooper smiled at her. "I can certainly try. Your reading is almost as good as mine, so I'm guessing it isn't a word you're stuck on."

"No, sir, it's summat much harder than that." Clara explained about trying to teach JJ the process of winding wool, and the difficulties he faced.

Mr Cooper sighed. "I was rather hoping he might take up the place in the school next year, but I dare say that's a lot to ask. A low table would be rather easier than a high chair. I'd need a few pieces of wood…"

By now Mr Cooper seemed to be talking more to himself than he was to Clara, and she waited patiently for him to remember she was there.

Suddenly he came out of his reverie and looked at her almost surprised. "How large a top does the table need to have?"

Clara hadn't thought about that. Big enough for a hank of wool and the bobbin, but not much bigger she thought. "Like this, I think." She held her hands out to indicate the sizes she meant.

Mr Cooper nodded. "Quite so. I'll see what I can do."

Looking at Mr Cooper as she said goodbye to him, it was as though a candle had been lit behind his eyes, for they shone so brightly, and his bushy eyebrows twitched. It made Clara smile. She was about to go, when a thought struck her. "Sir, my dad don't know."

Mr Cooper nodded again and smiled. "This conversation will be our secret."

Clara couldn't see how Mr Cooper could avoid some explanation to her father, but she thanked him all the same.

She spent a little time every day teaching JJ, but each time his arms hurt and although he understood what she wanted him to do, he was able to achieve very little. Clara was becoming concerned about what else they could do to cover the work while Mam had more to take her away from the workshop. She'd begun to wonder about visiting Hannah to see if she could do some of the work for them. However, by all accounts, her sister had found more was expected of her in the Carter household than she'd hoped, so it probably wasn't possible. Whatever Hannah were to say on the matter, Clara doubted that Mrs Carter would agree.

Whilst Clara asked questions about how they would cope, a malaise seemed to have settled over her father as though the thought of another mouth to feed was too much for him to bear. The more she thought about it, the more she worried that he might send JJ away if nothing could be done.

She looked at the skeins of wool. If JJ were to sit on the floor and wind the dark colours, then maybe it would be all right. They kept the brick workshop floor as clean as they could, so maybe a piece of cloth for him to put the wool on would be sufficient. It was strange, but even the darkest of wool seemed to pick up dirt of a different colour. Clara sighed. There seemed to be nothing more she could try.

Clara and her parents were in the workshop the following Saturday when they heard a timid knock at the door.

"Now, who can that be? Go and see, Clara love. It takes me a while to get out from this knitting frame in my condition."

Clara put the skein of wool on the stool and went out

to open the door. "Mr Cooper," she said in surprise.

Her Sunday school teacher broke into a broad grin. "May I come in and see your father?"

Clara held the door wide and ushered him through. Before he entered, he turned back to pick up a large package wrapped in cloth. Clara's heart missed a beat. Could that possibly be what they had talked about last week?

"Mr Phipps." Mr Cooper addressed Clara's father as soon as he was inside the workshop. "I won't disturb you many moments. I've brought something which may help JJ with his studying while he isn't able to attend the school." He unwrapped the package. "Clara explained that he often finds it easier to sit on the floor and I thought if he had a little table that he could work on at the right level, it might be of use to him."

Clara broke into a broad smile. How clever Mr Cooper was. Not only had he made the most perfect little table, complete with a small lip to stop things rolling off, but at exactly the right height to cover JJ's leg and allow him to rest his arms comfortably.

Dad was wringing his hands. "I don't know what to say. You've already bin so kind. Clara, where's John?"

Clara went back out to the kitchen, but he wasn't there either. "I'm not sure, Dad. He won't be far away."

"Never mind. Please give it to him and I hope with all my heart it will be of good use to the boy." Mr Cooper laid the table down at the side of the workshop and bid them farewell.

"Thank you," Dad said, sounding almost stupefied. "Thank you."

Clara went out to show Mr Cooper to the door. "Thank you, sir. I'll make sure to help JJ, as soon as he's around.

I'm very grateful, sir."

Mr Cooper gave her a benevolent smile and patted her shoulder as he left.

JJ had been upstairs and came down step by step on his bottom shortly afterwards. Clara heard him and called. When he saw the table, his face lit up and he obediently sat in the corner of the room so that Clara could place it over his leg. Then she fetched a hank of wool and a bobbin and carefully, he began to wind from one to the other.

After five minutes, he looked up at his sister and broke into the broadest of smiles. "My arms don't hurt." He then looked back to the wool and, with tongue sticking out between his teeth, he concentrated once again.

"Clara." Mam's tone was stern. "Did you ask Mr Cooper to make the table for young John?"

Clara froze. If she were honest then she would be in no end of trouble and she thought Dad would feel he had to pay for the table. But she'd be in trouble if she told a lie too and she knew telling lies was wrong. Was there any way she could explain without actually fibbing to her mother? She was still thinking how to answer when Mam's face contorted, and she clutched her belly.

"Oh, dear God, I think it's the baby. It can't be yet, it's too early."

Clara went to her mother's side to help her as she struggled to move away from her knitting frame. Dad had come to her other side and between them they helped Mam out of the workshop to the kitchen. They were part way there when Mam cried out again.

"We'd best get 'er upstairs, then you need to go for ya grandma." Dad was now half carrying Mam rather than simply supporting her and staggering toward the stairs. Clara ran up ahead of them to her parents' bedroom to arrange the bed covers ready for her.

"Martha, you stay wi' young John," Dad called as they went.

"Should I go for Hannah as well as Grandma?" Clara asked, but Dad shook his head.

"Maybe you should stay 'ere wi' Mam and I'll go," he said as he finally carried Mam into the bedroom.

"I think there's summat wrong," Mam gasped. "The baby shouldn't be 'ere yet and the pain..." She broke off again.

They didn't need her to describe the pain, Clara could see her mother was sweating and from time to time her face was so screwed up as she suffered what was happening.

Dad had already left the room.

"Clara, 'elp me undress. I'll put me nightdress on, that'll be more..." Mam didn't finish the sentence.

As Mam sat on the edge of the bed, Clara untied her apron and then undid the layers of clothing beneath. It felt strange to be doing these things for her mother. She felt pleased to be able to help but she wished fervently that either Grandma or Hannah were here. What if the baby came before they arrived? At twelve years old, she knew so little about childbirth and as Mam thought something was wrong Clara certainly wouldn't know what to do.

She ran through in her mind all the things that happened when JJ was born. It was four years ago now, but she could remember clearly. As soon as she'd helped Mam into her nightdress she went to the doorway and shouted for Martha to come. One of them could sit with Mam and the other do the running around collecting what they needed. Mam wailed again and Clara went back into the room. Normally, she'd shield her younger sister from seeing their mother like this, but she couldn't think like that at the moment. She needed help and whilst Martha might just be nine years old, she was the only one who could give it.

Martha was quickly despatched to put a pan on the stove to boil some water, although Clara wondered how she'd manage the weight on her own. She also told her sister to fetch towels to bring up to the room. Then she sat on the edge of the bed and held her mother's hand while Mam from time-to-time experienced waves of pain which Clara could only imagine.

Clara had never been so glad to see Grandma as when she arrived. She explained what she'd done so far and then moved away as the older woman took over.

"Hettie, dear, it's Mam. Can you 'ear me?" Grandma mopped her daughter's brow. She turned her head to look at Dad who was standing in the doorway. "I don't like this, John. I don't like this at all."

"We've no money for a doctor." Dad's face was grey, and he wrung his hands.

"I know that, son. I ain't gor ote either." Grandma had turned back to her daughter. "We'll have to pray that God'll protect 'er. She may lose the baby, but let's hope she'll be spared. Clara go and make us a pot of tea, I'll need summat to sustain me and maybe your mam'll sip a little."

Dismissed from the room, Clara went downstairs. She was glad to no longer be responsible, but terrified about her mother.

JJ was still sitting exactly where she'd left him, concentrating hard on winding the wool onto the bobbin. He was too young to understand what was happening upstairs, but Martha was in the kitchen crying. Clara sat and put an arm around her sister.

"Grandma's 'ere now. I'm sure everything'll be all right." She wasn't sure at all, but she hated seeing her sister upset.

"Clara." JJ was calling to her from the workshop. "I want to be in the kitchen too."

Clara squeezed her sister to her. "Everything'll be fine." Then she went through to the workshop. Moving JJ was a little more complicated. She needed to hold his position in the winding and move his table at the same time. "Martha." Maybe if she involved Martha in helping, she wouldn't spend so much time worrying what was happening upstairs.

While Clara sorted out the stove and made tea, JJ sat in the corner of the kitchen and continued his winding. He was doing quite a good job, although, winding completely by hand, his progress was much slower than being able to use the old spinning wheel. She tasked Martha with taking the tea upstairs and listening for when Grandma wanted anything.

Clara could do little more to help, so returned to knitting, moving JJ once again to the workshop. Dad, although back at his own frame, was in no fit state to work as fast as usual, but Clara knew how many more stockings they needed to finish that week.

"Martha, check Grandma don't need ote taking up, then go to the Carter house. Tell Hannah what's 'appening. We ain't gonna ger all these finished wi'out help." Under her breath Clara added, 'and please God, let her come.'

For once, Martha didn't argue and set off immediately.

CHAPTER 7

1849

As Clara heard the back door slam shut, she was surprised by how quickly Martha had returned. Her younger sister was out of breath as she came through to the workshop.

"She ain't comin'."

"What?" Clara was on her feet in an instant.

"It ain't her fault. Hannah was all for getting 'er 'at and coat and bringing Robert wir' her, but Mrs Carter stopped 'er and said 'er place wa' there. I ran all the way back. 'ow's Mam?"

"I dunno. There ain't no change as far as I know, but Grandma won't let me go in. When she wants ote she calls for me to leave it at the door. Grandma must be worried; she called for Dad to go up." Clara felt despondent at the prospect of Hannah not being able to help and wondered how far through the order they'd get. If only Martha knew how to use the knitting frame.

Clara was still wondering what to do when she heard raised voices from upstairs.

"We ain't got no way to pay a doctor, so unless you know one who'll come out of charity, I dunno what to do."

Clara was more alarmed by the desperation in Dad's voice than she had been with anything up to that point. Then she heard Grandma and froze.

"And I'm telling ya if we don't gerra doctor, I think

we're gonna lose 'er."

All thoughts of meeting their stocking order went from Clara's mind. Trust in the Lord, that's what she'd been taught. She moved to the side of the knitting frame and sank to her knees in prayer.

"Father God, please save our Mam…" She had no idea what more to say, so recited the Lord's Prayer. "Our Father, who art in Heaven…"

She wasn't ready for her own mother to be in Heaven with God just yet. Perhaps it wasn't wrong to trust in God but also to take matters into her own hands.

"Stay 'ere," she said to JJ and Martha, as she fled from the workshop, took up her coat and hat and headed out of the door. Despite what Martha had said when she returned, surely her best option would be to ask Mrs Carter for help. Maybe they could pay for a doctor for her mother. She ran the whole way to the Carters' house and hammered on the door. "Please, help us. Please," she shouted through the closed door.

It was Mrs Carter who came to open the door.

"Oh, Mrs Carter, please help us."

She'd said no more when Mrs Carter cut in. "I've already told your younger sister that Hannah has responsibilities here. She can't possibly come back to work for you." Mrs Carter closed the door.

"No. Mrs Carter, no." Clara put her hands against the door to give some resistance. "It's not that," she panted. "It's me mam. She needs a doctor. She may die without one."

Mrs Carter opened the door slightly. "And what do you expect me to do? We're not doctors."

Clara swallowed hard before saying the next part. "Mrs Carter, we ain't got no money. We can't pay for a doctor. I came to ask if for Hannah's sake if not for mine, you could help us…"

"With payment for the doctor?" Mrs Carter said with apparent distaste. "I can't help." She began again to close the door.

Clara's shoulders slumped. She resisted any temptation to be rude to Mrs Carter, much as she felt that was what she wanted to do. "Then can you tell me where I can find Mr Cooper, please?"

The door was almost closed when Mrs Carter said, "I don't know."

Clara stood back. She wanted to hammer with her fists, but what was the point if the door wouldn't be answered. How could Hannah let them treat her like this? Did she have no voice in the house?

She knew of no one other than Mr Cooper she could turn to for help, but how might she find him? She could try looking for him at the chapel but could think of no reason he would be there, other than on a Sunday. If nothing else she would say another prayer while she was there. That at least couldn't hurt.

Clara almost tripped over her skirt as she ran to the chapel. She was right. There was no one there. She looked everywhere, just in case. She was about to give up when she saw a carefully written notice saying who to contact if there were any problem. It wasn't Mr Cooper's name, but perhaps the person listed would know where she could find him. The house was a short distance from the chapel, so she set off once again. Under her breath she mumbled, "Please God, let them be in."

By the time she reached the house of Mr Sampson, the gentleman who was listed, Clara was exhausted. She used the door knocker rather than hammering on his door and was grateful when she heard movement within.

It was an older lady who answered. Clara had seen her at chapel, but didn't recall ever having spoken to her.

"Excuse me. I'm sorry to trouble you, but d'you know where Mr Cooper, the Sunday school teacher lives?"

Clara's face must have been written with the woe she was feeling, for the other woman frowned and replied. "Whatever's the matter, child?"

As briefly as she could, Clara explained to this kindly lady why she was in such a hurry to find Mr Cooper.

"Don't worry Mr Cooper, child. Go straight to the doctor. The chapel has a poor fund, I'm sure that can help."

Clara was about to utter her thanks, but the woman interrupted.

"Now don't stand here. Go. God's speed, child. Go."

Clara was struggling to hold back her tears, but nodded to the woman, and despite the stitch in her side, turned and fled along the road to the doctor's house.

By the time she reached the doctor's, Clara was completely out of breath again and barely had the energy to knock the large brass knocker. Once she had, she stood doubled over, trying to recover from her exertions.

A neatly dressed woman in an apron and bonnet opened the door and Clara stood up straight, ready to speak without puffing.

"Can I help you, child?"

Clara wasn't invited in.

"Please, ma'am, we need the doctor. It's me mam."

"The doctor is out on another call at present. What seems to be the problem with your mother?"

Clara's heart sank at the woman's first words, and she felt tears spring unbidden to her eyes. "She's in early labour, ma'am and it ain't going well. I believe she's got a high temperature and Grandma's scared we'll lose her."

The woman nodded and her face relaxed into a comforting smile. "You run along home, and I'll send the doctor just as soon as he returns." She looked at the clock on the wall. "I need some fresh air. Maybe I can meet him on the road and send him straight to you."

"Thank you." Having told the woman their address, Clara turned and ran along the path in the direction of home.

She burst in through the back door and the sight which greeted her stopped her short with confusion. Grandma was sitting at the kitchen table with both Martha and JJ. She had an arm around each of them.

"Oh, thank goodness," Clara said, "is Mam much better now?"

She unbuttoned her coat and wasn't looking at them until Martha let out a howl of anguish. Clara looked up sharply and registered their faces, tear-stained, drawn and vacant. She stopped what she was doing and reached blindly for a chair before she fell down. "Mam?" She wasn't actually sure any sound had come out of her mouth. Grandma looked across to her but closed her eyes and shook her head.

"But…" Clara was struggling to process what this meant. "But I've been for the doctor. He's coming soon." Her voice sounded far away even to herself. "The doctor's coming."

"And he'll be too late to save your mam."

It was her dad's voice, she knew that, but it didn't sound much like him. It was as though he was hoarse and voiceless but forcing out the sound.

"Too late," he said again, as though it needed repeating for the words to sink in with him.

"May I see 'er?" Clara struggled to her feet, floundering through unshed tears to the surface of her grief.

Dad just looked dazed but nodded. Clara turned to Grandma for confirmation.

"I still 'ave to wash 'er and lay 'er out. She don't look good. I 'ad to leave off to comfort these two."

Clara had never heard Grandma sound so gentle that she could remember. The old woman's curmudgeonly ways had been set aside, at least for a while. Clara nodded. Nothing felt real. She should be crying, as Martha was, but instead felt numb. She finished removing her hat and coat and was about to go upstairs when she heard a knock at the front door.

"It'll be the doctor," Clara said. "I'll explain."

It was indeed the doctor, but as Clara opened her mouth to speak, her composure failed, and an utterly visceral sob overcame her.

The doctor must have seen similar reactions all too often. He immediately understood without a word being spoken. In a gentle voice he said, "I'm sorry for your loss. May I see your mother in any case? I'll make no charge."

All Clara could do was nod and lead him up the stairs to her parents' bedroom.

She would barely have recognised the woman lying on the bed. While she knew it to be her mother, it was little more than an empty body, without spirit or energy. The person she saw had an overwhelming hollow greyness - although person seemed far too strong a word.

As the doctor looked over her mother, Clara knelt beside the bed weeping. Weeping for someone who was already gone, she knew not where, wherever Heaven was, but certainly not in that room.

After a few brief moments, the doctor said, "I'm sorry.

Is your father downstairs?"

Clara nodded and made to stand.

"No, don't get up. I'll see myself down. I may not have been able to help if I'd arrived sooner, but you did the right thing calling me. Good day, Miss Phipps." He bowed his head to her and left the room.

'Good day', what a ridiculous phrase it was. How could today be a good day? This was her mother lying here. Now what was she to do?

When Clara eventually went downstairs, she had composed herself. She would have to take over as the woman of the house, unless Grandma Herbert planned to move to live with them. She shuddered at the prospect. She didn't think her father would want that and doubted Grandma would choose to, either. It might have been different if she had been their father's mother, but sadly she died before Clara was born.

Clara took a deep breath and went into the kitchen. Martha and JJ were sitting huddled together, but Grandma was nowhere in sight, nor was their father.

"Are you two all right?" she asked, looking at their crumpled faces. They both nodded bravely.

"Grandma said we wa' to wait 'ere. She's gone to speak to the undertaker," Martha said, obviously trying not to cry.

"And Dad?"

Martha just shrugged.

Clara wondered what she should do next. Someone should tell Hannah, but after her visit earlier she was in no hurry to return to the Carter household. She couldn't go in search of their father and leave her brother and sister in the house, so she took up her apron and began to prepare a meal. None of them had eaten anything all day and they needed to stay strong. For one thing, however upset they were, they had to work. They had to fulfil a quota of stockings and if they couldn't pay their bills sympathy was always in short supply.

As she looked in the cupboard for some food, she thought that keeping Martha and JJ busy might help them, as much as it would the family as a whole.

"We're all gonna have to work very hard or there'll be no food. Martha, JJ, I want you to spend the time 'til supper winding wool. Can you take JJ's table through to the workroom, Martha? The floor's cleaner in there at the moment." Given how quiet her voice was normally, Clara was surprised by the confident tone she managed to bring in speaking to her siblings. Her role in the family had changed, she knew that without anyone spelling it out to her. She had no doubt it would be a hard task, but she'd promised her brother she would care for him, no matter what, and now it seemed she needed to help the rest of the family too.

The others went through to the workshop without complaint and Clara returned to supper preparation, wondering where her father might be. After they'd eaten, she would look at how they could work in order to meet their quota of stockings and pay for the frames. If nothing else, it would stop her thinking about her poor, dear mother.

They were part way through supper in the kitchen when their father returned. Clara had kept some stew hot for him, Grandma having come back soon after Clara started preparations. It was a sombre meal, the words spoken few.

"We've moved Hettie to the back room, so you'll need

to use the kitchen at all times now. We couldn't put her in the parlour, seeing as it's where the frames are." Grandma looked drawn and showed no bluster in her manner.

"I've spoken to the minister." Dad said no more.

Once Clara had cleared away, she sat down to work out how they could afford to live. There'd be the undertaker to pay and as it was, they'd have to beg for help for the current week, or none of them would be fed. With two frames to run she and Dad would need to keep them working all day, but she'd have the household chores to do as well. At nine years old, Martha was old enough to learn the frame or at least take responsibility for more of the chores. If she worked the frame, it would mean buying in wool already wound, which would leave less money to cover the week. She sighed. Perhaps the good Lord would forgive her working on a Sunday, although she suspected Grandma wouldn't.

As it turned out, Martha neither grasped what needed doing at the knitting frame, nor in helping with the chores. If only JJ had two legs. He learned quickly, just as Clara did, but Martha was an altogether different matter. For one thing, Martha simply didn't comprehend that if they didn't all work, there would be no food. Where she thought it came from was anybody's guess. Clara was torn, of course she wanted to take care of the family, but she couldn't do it all herself and she was exhausted. She wished she could talk to Dad about it, but he had become distant since losing Mam and it was as much a challenge to keep him focussed on the work as it was Martha.

Other than when they buried their mother, they saw nothing of Hannah, and it was clear her loyalties now lay solely with the Carter family. Grandma helped when she could, but she had responsibilities with Mam's brother's family who she lived with and was herself tired and arthritic. The more tired Grandma was, the sharper her tongue and none of them appreciated that.

"Dad," Clara said one evening, once they'd finished work. "I think Martha should go to work in a factory."

Dad was dozing but sat bolt upright. "I can't do that. Framework knitting's all I know."

Clara knew the best answer would be for her father to get factory work as well as both herself and Martha, but she'd stopped short of that suggestion, guessing his response.

"No, Dad, I said Martha should do it. She ain't got no wish to learn to knit here and can't wind at the speed we need. She'll earn more than the extra cost of buying in ready wound wool. We might also need to give up renting one of the frames, you could work the one that was left, and I could get factory work too."

Clara presumed her father would slip back into his state of dozing, but he surprised her by asking, "Ain't Martha still too young for factory work? And what of young John?"

She took that as some sort of acceptance of the plan on her father's part. "I know others at Sunday school 'ave started before they were ten. She looks old enough. I think they'll take 'er." She had no idea how she would break the news to Martha.

"John can wind a little, I s'pose, but it ain't much," her father said, clearly more aware of the need for change than he'd admitted previously.

Clara hesitated. "'E could go to school." She paused while her comment sank in. "'E learns fast, and Mr Preston said 'e thought JJ's fees could be paid. It would be 'is best chance of finding a job later." Clara held her breath. If her father saw JJ's fees being paid as charity, he might well refuse, but just maybe he would see the benefit. There would be no opportunity for any of them to spend time with him during the day, except when he was winding wool.

After a long pause, her dad's shoulders dropped, and he nodded. "I'll talk to Mr Preston on Sunday. 'E may still be too young for them to take 'im. D'you think John'd want to attend school? It seems a strange thing to want to do."

Clara broke into a broad smile. "Other than to be able to walk wirrout crutches, there ain't ote JJ'd like more."

Her father shrugged, clearly not understanding. "I'll ask about returning the frame too. Or maybe another household could take over the renting. Maybe wi' JJ out during the day, it would still pay to work the two of 'em."

Clara nodded. "I'll talk to Martha about finding work. If we do return a frame, then I'll look for work as well."

With a plan for their survival in place Clara went upstairs to the bedroom. Neither Martha nor JJ had come up to bed yet, so she knelt by the side of the bed and put her hands together. "Dear God," she paused and thought for a moment. "Take care of our dear mam wherever she is now and have mercy on those of us left behind." Her voice faltered. "Take care of Dad and tell Mam how much I love 'er." Whilst trusting in God gave her some comfort, she could say no more. Clara's throat closed with emotion, and with the force of a breached dam, the tears cascaded down her cheeks.

PART 2

CHAPTER 8

Two years later - 1851

No one had suggested any alternative than for Clara to take on the mantle of their domestic arrangements. While the others helped, it was Clara who planned their food for the week, ensured they had clean clothes to wear and did her best to keep their home in a habitable state.

Martha was eleven now and had been at the factory for two years. She was paid little, but despite having a walk to the factory, on top of her long days, Martha seemed to enjoy working outside the home. She'd always been a far more sociable child than Clara and, in the little time before she fell asleep at night, Martha had many stories to tell of her new friends and workmates. Listening to the tales, Clara felt closer to her sister than she ever had before. Martha made them laugh, mimicking the overseer, a severe spinster who monitored the floor of the factory where Martha worked as a winder.

Clara rose early every morning to prepare breakfast, so that Martha ate before she walked to work. From the moment she awoke, Clara juggled the household chores with running the knitting frame beside her father. He hadn't wanted to work alone and so the second frame had been kept on for Clara to operate. JJ did some winding each day when he came home from school. Whilst it had taken him longer to learn to use the old spinning wheel, he'd eventually managed to sit comfortably and use the treadle. He liked to feel he was helping.

Each day, Clara looked forward to JJ coming into the workshop. "I know I can't go to school myself, but maybe you can tell me what you've done, and I can listen while we work."

Hard as it was to hear over the sound of the machines, JJ was happy to oblige and as he wound the wool, he sat close to Clara's knitting frame and told her everything he could remember of his school day.

Some weeks the work was in short supply, and they could easily knit their required quota of stockings. Those weeks were hardest, for while Clara had time for all her other chores, and occasionally time for herself, they still had to pay the full rent of the frames as well as their living costs, with less money coming in. In those times she spent the extra hours foraging for food along the hedgerows and considering how else they might make savings. Were it not for the regular but small amount which Martha brought home there would have been more hungry days than Clara could count.

Occasionally in those quiet weeks, as long as the weather was good, Clara would head to the British School where JJ studied. Then she found somewhere to sit as close to the window as possible and listened to what went on inside, hoping to learn first-hand.

She was still sitting there one day when classes finished. "JJ," she called as he swung himself out through the doors on his crutches. He came straight over to her.

"Wharra you doin' 'ere?"

Clara had never confessed about the times she sat outside. Usually, she returned home long before the end of day bell rang, so that Dad could take a break too. Today, with the spring sunshine warming her face, she'd been so absorbed in the book, which was being read out to the children nearest the window, that she'd lost track of time.

"Oh, we're short o' work so I thought I'd come an' meet you." She didn't want to spoil him telling her about his day. She loved hearing him explain what he'd learned, and she knew it helped his learning too.

She listened intently to JJ as he recounted hour by hour the activities they had covered, the stories they were told and what they'd done, at least, as much as a six-year-old boy remembered a few hours later.

Clara wished she had a slate or paper to write on. Some days she wished she could keep a diary or write letters to her departed mother. Perhaps in the perfection of Heaven, Mam would be able to read.

With orders still short, Clara couldn't help thinking it would be better for her to find work in one of the factories as well as Martha, but they were just about managing and Dad said he didn't think he'd cope at home during the day without her. But her opportunities to sit beneath the school window were becoming too regular and that worried Clara.

"Miss Phipps."

Clara turned her head sharply and stood up from where she was sitting.

"Sorry, I didn't mean to startle you. I'm Mr Ward, I teach in the school."

Clara nodded. She knew his name from JJ. "I don't mean any harm, sir. I sit 'ere listenin'."

He smiled and frowned at the same time. "No, I didn't think for a moment you were doing anything wrong. Mr Cooper has told me about how well you've done over the years in Sunday school. Why don't you enrol in the school? I'm sure you'd be welcome."

Clara looked down as she spoke. "We can't afford it, sir. Nor can we afford my time to be 'ere. It's only 'cause work's so short this week that I've 'ad the time to sit listenin'. Besides, JJ - that is John James tells me what 'e's learned each day which 'elps with my learnin'."

Mr Ward nodded sadly. "Would you wish to learn more if it were possible?"

"Oh yes, sir, more than ote in the world. I love learnin', but there ain't ote to be done."

"Leave that with me, Miss Phipps. I have half an idea that it might be possible."

Clara put the idea out of her mind as she walked home with JJ. If she couldn't afford the material to mend her own dress, they certainly had none for her to pay to improve her education. She was glad that JJ loved learning and was as eager to share his knowledge with her.

When they returned to the house, she worked on the knitting frame so her father could take a break too. The little that Martha brought in wouldn't be enough to stop them starving if they had many more weeks of short working.

Martha came in exhausted, but still happy for the time she spent in other company. It suited her far better to be amongst so many people her own age and older, than it did to be confined to home-working.

Clara was now one of the eldest in the Sunday school classes and enjoyed the opportunities she had to help some of the younger children. She was a good reader and could read the Bible stories with the same competence as the teachers. Over the years Mr Cooper had been a real friend to her family and was always willing to spend a little time at the end of the Sunday school lesson teaching Clara a wider range of subjects. Consequently, at the end of class the following Sunday it was no surprise to her to hear him saying, "Miss Phipps, do you have a moment?"

"Yes, sir." Clara went to the desk where he was seated.

"Mr Ward asked me to speak with you. I believe you met him last week."

"Why, yes. I were sitting outside the school… waiting for John James, sir."

"And listening to the lesson."

Clara felt her face colour.

"Yes, sir, I was. I hoped to learn more myself."

Mr Cooper was smiling. "Mr Ward is delighted you are so keen to learn. He's sorry not to be able to enrol you in the school. Your brother is doing well I hear."

"Thank you, sir." Clara swelled with pride on hearing JJ being praised.

"Mr Ward asked if I would speak to you about an idea. You may know of Mrs Frances Langham. She is a widow who lives alone most of the time. I believe her young nephew spends his school holidays with her but is away at boarding school during the terms. Mrs Langham is a highly educated woman who used to provide young ladies with private tuition. She would be welcoming of a visit or two from you during your spare hours on a Sunday, or any other day for that matter, and would be glad to try to further your education should you so wish."

Clara's eyes were wide. Had she understood what Mr Cooper had said to her correctly? "Oh, sir, I'd love to visit her, but I ain't got no means to pay."

"I'm sorry, I didn't make myself clear. Her husband left her well provided for, so she has no need to charge a fee.

She would be happy to have the company and would see that as more than sufficient recompense for her time. Perhaps you in turn could become a Sunday school teacher yourself, if there are enough hours in the day for both things."

Clara felt tears springing to her eyes. "Sir, I dunno what to say. I'd love to teach the children 'ere and d'you think Mrs Langham means what she says?"

"I know she does. It's lonely for her sometimes stuck in that big house on her own, but her brother's instructions when he died were that his son, that is her nephew, should remain in boarding school until at least the age of sixteen when he might choose for himself. When both her brother and his wife died, her nephew's care rested with Mrs Langham, and she has been more than happy to carry out her duties."

"Then I'll go as soon as my father allows it." Clara hoped more than anything that her father's pride wouldn't get in the way.

"I will speak with him now. Leave it to me." Mr Cooper stood up and strode toward the door, leaving Clara trying to keep up.

She suddenly realised it was Mr Cooper's intention to reach her father ahead of her and for it not to look as though he had already spoken with her. She fell back a little, but still wanting to hear what was said, continued in that direction. By the time she arrived at her father's side, their greetings had been dispensed with, and Mr Cooper was in the middle of speaking.

"… and so it would be a great favour to Mrs Langham if perhaps Clara were able to call in occasionally to read to her. Your daughter reads so well that I can't think of anyone better to ask."

Clara held back her smile. Mr Cooper had so cleverly presented it that it would be the Phipps family doing the favour and not the other way around. She hoped her father accepted the story, but he had no reason to disbelieve Mr Cooper.

Mr Phipps was nodding. "It can't be easy being all alone as she is. My Clara ain't got much time when she ain't working, but I dare say she'd be willing to call up there to see Mrs Langham."

"She might go some Sundays after Sunday school. There's not much more she'll learn here so I've asked if she would take on teaching some of the younger children." Mr Cooper smiled at Clara.

Had Clara not known the real purpose for the visits to Mrs Langham, she would have been disappointed by the suggestion of taking away the one time in the week when she had no work, but the thought of continuing her learning filled her with excitement.

Much as Clara wished she could visit Mrs Langham that same Sunday there was no time available. Nor was there during the following week, when thankfully the order for stockings was far greater than it had been recently. Clara didn't have a moment to think about going until the following Sunday. As soon as Sunday school finished, she donned her hat and coat and still full of the pleasure of teaching her own class, under the guidance of a more experienced teacher, she turned in the direction of Mrs Langham's house.

Clara could feel the flutterings of anxiety in her belly as she walked away from the centre of Wigston Magna. She rarely had cause to walk in this direction and it felt strange. She distracted herself by looking at each of the buildings she passed and was struck by the number of public houses there were. She wondered what they were like inside, having only heard of them talked about by those who disapproved of their existence. She knew that Hannah's Frank was a regular visitor at one or other of the inns but would never have asked him to tell her about them.

She turned onto Bull Head Street and returned her thoughts to the afternoon. She was trying to think what to say to Mrs Langham. Should she offer to read as Mr Cooper had suggested? Clara had no idea what conversation had passed between Mr Ward and Mrs Langham and how much the older lady knew of her. She walked up the steps to the front door and took a deep breath. With the summer sun glinting on the highly polished knocker, the front of the house gave off an air of grandeur which Clara had never before experienced. She suddenly felt her dress might be considered shabby, even though it was her Sunday best, but she could do nothing about that now, unless she turned and went home without knocking. She was still considering that possibility when, to her surprise, the front door was opened before she had so much as knocked.

"Oh, I, er…" Clara suddenly pulled herself together and remembered her manners. "Mrs Langham? I'm Miss Phipps, Mr Cooper said I should…"

As she registered the beaming smile which broke across Mrs Langham's face, Clara let out a long breath of relief. Her fear that the older lady wouldn't be expecting her or wouldn't welcome her visit was banished.

Mrs Langham opened the door wide, revealing a large airy hall, with a round mahogany table in the middle, and a perfectly clean tiled floor in a pattern of black and white. Clara almost gasped. She didn't think she'd ever seen anywhere as beautiful and had never imagined that someone could live like this - and this was only the entrance hall.

"Come in, Miss Phipps, or may I call you Clara as I believe that is your Christian name?" Mrs Langham's eyes twinkled as though this were all some wonderful conspiracy and they were both on the same side. "Come through to the library."

Clara wondered if she'd heard correctly. Were there really houses that had libraries inside them? When Mrs Langham opened the doors into a room of double height with bookshelves around every wall, Clara couldn't hold back the gasp. It wasn't that they could fit the whole of the Phipps family home into this one room; nor even that the high windows let in so much light around three sides. It was the books. There were hundreds or maybe thousands of them lining every single wall. For a moment, Clara completely forgot she was in company. It was as though she were in a dream, and she pirouetted around the room, gazing from shelf to shelf as she turned.

"Both my late husband and I were avid readers, and he was a great scholar." Mrs Langham broke into Clara's thoughts.

Clara jumped and stood wide-eyed facing Mrs Langham and fidgeting with her dress sleeve. "I'm sorry. I quite forgot myself. I ain't never seen anywhere like this. It's...it's... "

Mrs Langham was smiling again. "That was what I hoped you'd think."

Clara hadn't actually managed to voice what it was she thought, but Mrs Langham did seem to understand. "Are they real?"

Mrs Langham's laugh was a hearty one. "Why don't

you take one off the shelf to see?"

Clara tiptoed to the nearest bookcase and held her breath as she withdrew a volume called *Shakespeare's Sonnets*. The book fell open easily to a page about a third of the way through and it was clear to see this must be a favourite page. She looked from the book to Mrs Langham and back to the book.

"Take a moment or two to have a look around and then join me for some tea."

It was then that Clara noticed a tray with two cups and saucers, a pot of tea and some biscuits, was already laid out. She frowned. 'Ow did you know that I'd come today at this time?"

"Mr Ward said this would be your usual time if you could make it, so I was prepared and hoped that he would prove to be right." Mrs Langham beckoned Clara over to the seating at the far end of the library and poured the tea. "Now, why don't you start by telling me a little about yourself?"

Clara blinked. She had never been asked to do that by anyone and didn't know what to say. "There ain't ote to tell, ma'am."

"Now don't call me ma'am, you're not here as staff. I'm Mrs Langham to you."

Clara wondered exactly why she was here, but took a deep breath and hoped she could find something to say. Trying hard to speak properly, like Mr Cooper did, she began. "My family are framework knitters, ma... Mrs Langham. We lost my dear mother a couple of years ago and Hannah, that's me eldest sister, had already left home by then. There's Dad, Martha, JJ - that is John James, and meself at home."

"Ah yes, and he's the crippled boy?"

"JJ? Well, he only has one leg if that's what you mean, but he gets about well otherwise." She'd never thought of her brother as crippled. It was the way he was.

"Mr Ward tells me that Master Phipps is almost as clever as you are. Perhaps he could come with you to see me sometime?"

"Oh, yes please, Mrs Langham, he'd like that very much."

"Do drink your tea while it's still warm."

Clara was feeling utterly overawed and shifted uneasily in the leather chair. She was being invited to drink tea from a china cup and saucer. Her hand trembled as she reached to pick up her drink and she decided that perhaps two hands would be better so as not to end up dropping the cup. What on earth was she doing here?

CHAPTER 9

1851

That first week, Clara did no more than answer questions from Mrs Langham about her life and family. Mrs Langham didn't ask her to read, and she didn't say anything about what would happen if Clara were to visit again, leaving Clara wondering how she would learn.

As she walked home, she pondered some of the questions Mrs Langham had asked but could find no sensible answers. If she could do anything with her life, what would it be? She'd grown up not expecting to have such choices. Her parents were framework knitters and so were their parents before them. She knew it was much harder to make a living from the work now than it had been years ago, but they knew no different. She could, of course, move to work in a factory. At fourteen years of age, she was more than old enough, but she didn't think that was the sort of thing Mrs Langham meant. She sighed and gave up thinking.

As she continued to walk, her mind wandered to how much she was enjoying teaching in the Sunday school. She felt such joy when some of the children asked her questions about the story she'd read to them, and she had been able to answer. Mrs Langham had asked if she ever thought about the different ways people around her spoke, the words they used and how they were pronounced. She was conscious that Mr Cooper spoke what her mam would describe as 'proper', but she'd never thought that she could speak like that too. Mrs Langham had said that making her words clear would help the children she taught in Sunday school, which seemed obvious when she said it, but had never occurred to Clara.

She frowned, struggling to grasp a thought that was forming in her mind. She had loved teaching JJ his letters and helping him before he started school too. Next to learning, she thought teaching others about what she'd learned was the best thing she'd ever done, but Mrs Langham couldn't mean something like that. Clara would never be able to be a proper teacher, would she?

Walking back along Moat Street, Clara's step quickened. She was excited to tell the rest of the family about the wonder she'd felt in the grandeur of the library. She wished she could share it with all of them. One day she would at least take JJ to see for himself.

To her disappointment, when she arrived home, Martha was full of her own day and didn't so much as ask what Clara had done, and their father was fast asleep in the back room. Only JJ wanted to know what it was like.

"Mrs Langham asked if maybe one day you'd like to come wi' me when I go. Then you can see for yourself." She paused a moment and added "with me," quietly to herself.

"Me?" JJ's eyes were wide. "Go to 'er big 'ouse?"

"One day," Clara replied.

"Well, my dear," Mrs Langham said, when Clara visited next, "I didn't ask you here so that you could drink tea. Mr Cooper tells me you're a quick learner and would like more of an education than you can achieve in the Sunday school. Is that so?"

"I've enjoyed attending Sunday school very much indeed. Now I can help with the younger ones." Clara hesitated and thought for a moment. "But there ain't...isn't time for Mr Cooper or Mr Preston to spend teaching me no more."

"And there is no opportunity for you to attend the school, I believe?"

Clara shook her head. "No, Mrs Langham. Me brother's allowed to attend. He ain't...isn't able to work the knitting frames, so Dad agreed it would be best for 'im to go. His place is paid for."

Mrs Langham smiled as though she were well aware of the finances for JJ's place at the school.

"Well then, my dear, with your agreement, I'd like to spend your visits here doing what I can to further your education. If that is agreeable to you?"

Clara's mouth opened and closed and then again as she tried to form words but for a moment could get nothing out. She coughed slightly covering her mouth with her hand as she did so and tried again. "I would like that, but you do know I can't pay ote... anything, even a small amount?"

"There is no need for a but. I enjoy sharing knowledge and from all Mr Cooper has told me, I think I will find in you a ready pupil and that makes it all the more enjoyable. May I ask you something, Miss Phipps?"

"Anything."

"What will you do with your new learning?"

Clara's shoulders dropped. If she could do nothing with the learning, would Mrs Langham say she shouldn't come? She took a deep breath. She had to be honest. "I 'ave to work the frames to earn enough money to feed our family and I've promised JJ I'll take care of 'im always. It may be harder for 'im to earn a living and there will be things 'e can't manage around the house. There's few hours spare beyond those I 'ave to work. I ain't sure what I can do with any learning I receive, except 'elp in Sunday school and I'm already willing to do that."

Mrs Langham nodded. A smile was playing over the older woman's lips. "I think I might ask you that question again in the future. Don't look so sad, child. I'm not about to turn you out if you can't immediately see a use for the teaching I will provide. Now, why don't you take a book down from the shelf and read to me? Pick out any book you choose. We can talk about what you read, and I can start to understand where we should start with your lessons."

Clara let out a long slow breath and felt her mouth twitch upwards again as she went over to the bookcase. She could choose from so many books in all shapes and sizes, but one caught her eye. The spine was standing proud of the shelf as though asking to be taken out. It was slimmer than the others around it. She drew the volume forward and brought it across to where they were sitting.

"And which is it that you have selected? Read me the title and the author's name and then let us start at the beginning."

"It's called *A Christmas Carol* and it's written by a Mr Charles Dickens." Clara read from the cover of the book.

"Ah yes, I do love his work. Have you read any before, Clara?"

Clara shook her head. "I've only ever read the Bible." She stopped suddenly. "Grandma Herbert says that's the only book I should read on a Sunday. Should I put this one back?"

Mrs Langham had a twinkle in her eye as she said, "Well, I'm not going to tell your grandmother if you don't. Now, why don't you open the book by Mr Dickens. I rather think that the story is as good a lesson as any in the Bible."

Clara opened the book with the reverence she would have shown if it had been the Bible and turned to the opening page. Her first surprise was to find that the language in which it was written was much more familiar to her than that of her Bible. It was almost as though someone were in the room with them, reciting a story. As she read of Marley's ghost and Scrooge's life, her wonder grew, but when she reached the description of Tiny Tim, the tears rolling down her cheeks meant she could read no further.

"I suspect that might be a good place to stop for today." Mrs Langham's voice was tender. "He has reminded you of your brother John."

Clara nodded, the lump in her throat preventing her from saying anything in reply.

"I'm not giving away the whole of the book, but I think you should know that Tiny Tim has a happy ending, and all goes well for him."

Clara looked up, searching Mrs Langham's face for more.

"I won't tell you more now, but I can promise you will like the rest of the book. You may take it home with you to read if you wish, or you can read it to me when you next visit."

"Take it home?" Clara couldn't believe what she was hearing. Then she thought about how much she'd enjoyed having someone listening to her, much as when she'd read to JJ before he was at school, and the fact she had nowhere to keep the book safe. "No. I'll wait. I promise to come back as soon as I can."

"I know you will, child." Mrs Langham smiled broadly. "And I shall look forward to it too."

From then onwards Clara visited almost every Sunday and occasionally at other times if she was able. She not only read books to Mrs Langham but talked about them and discussed what they were about. Clara took books home and read at every opportunity she could find, both fiction and non-fiction titles. The natural history books with their pen and ink drawings were her particular favourites. Mrs Langham also instructed her in writing her own projects for homework and without asking if Clara had such items at home, took the trouble of providing her with pen, ink and paper on which to write. She also gave her a candle to use especially for her homework.

As they talked about how difficult it was to earn enough as a family in framework knitting, Clara looked at her own life differently, as well as the lives of those around her. Mrs Langham asked her many questions which made her think.

"Your frames are rented I believe?"

"Yes, they are."

"And do you always have full work for both of them?" Mrs Langham looked deep in thought as she asked.

"No, indeed we don't. The rent is the same however many stockings the Master instructs us to knit. The amount we're paid per pair o' stockings is lower than before the factories started too, from what Dad 'as said."

Mrs Langham nodded. "I have heard that some families are tied to buying their food from a particular shop. Is that the case for yourselves?"

Clara shook her head. "That at least ain't... is not the case. In the past me dad said he 'ad to take part o' the money in bread, but that is not so now."

"You don't have to spend your whole life as a framework knitter." Mrs Langham sounded cautious as she spoke.

"But I know no other." Clara frowned. "What else is there? I could go into service, but me dad needs me at home. I couldn't live in."

"I rather wondered…" Mrs Langham seemed to be choosing her words carefully. "…if you might like to be a teacher."

Clara gasped. "But how could I do any such thing when I ain't… have not been to school myself and know so little? And look at me. Whoever would employ such a ragged child as I am?"

"And that my dear girl is where I come in. I rather think that may have been what was in Mr Ward's mind when he first asked if I would help. You already know much more than you realise and the rest I am sure you could learn with little difficulty."

Clara sat perfectly still, trying to absorb what Mrs Langham had said. Surely, such a step could never be possible for someone such as herself. "I need to be at 'ome. I couldn't possibly go to school now and not earn money for the family."

"What if I could teach you enough for you to start as a pupil teacher in a couple of years? If you could secure a position of that nature, you would be paid a small salary in return for teaching the younger children and then you would continue your own learning at the end of the school day."

"I… but… Oh, Mrs Langham, do you think I could?"

"You won't know unless you try and, in the meantime, learning is never wasted. I should of course speak with your father. It wouldn't be proper for me to do this without his blessing. Should I call to see him this afternoon?"

"No. I mean..." Clara's mind was racing. How could Mrs Langham possibly come to their humble cottage? Clara kept the house clean enough, but they had nowhere like this for her to sit and their cups and saucers were of the ordinary type, not of fine bone china.

As though reading Clara's mind, Mrs Langham smiled. "I have visited many houses around Great Wigston and am as happy in the smallest as in the grandest. You have no need for concern."

Clara wondered if that last part were really the case.

"Besides, you're already fourteen, so if we are to put this plan in place, we have no time to lose. Should we say that I will call an hour from now?"

At least that would give Clara a little time to forewarn her father and make the house, and for that matter her brother, as presentable as possible. She smiled as she said goodbye, realising that had been Mrs Langham's intention and feeling grateful for her sensitivity.

When Mrs Langham called later that afternoon, Clara was relieved by how at ease the lady seemed in their cottage. She spoke to Clara's father about her idea and left him in complete agreement. She also took the time to talk with JJ and ask about his schooling and what he enjoyed. Clara was delighted and began to believe that some improvement in her situation might be possible.

As Mrs Langham had explained to her father, if Clara could become a teacher, then her wage would be far more reliable than when framework knitting. It would also mean she could do something she loved which she had never dreamed was possible. Helping at Sunday school had opened her eyes, and she'd always enjoyed teaching JJ.

The following weeks sped past and every moment that Clara could find free time she would go to Mrs Langham's house. If the older lady was busy, she showed Clara into the library and left her alone to study a passage from a book. They would then look at it together later. Clara was doing that one Tuesday afternoon in late autumn when they had little work for the knitting frame. She was sitting at the small desk which Mrs Langham had set up close to her own at the end of the library and was reading *A Midsummer Night's Dream* by Mr William Shakespeare. She was still in awe that such books existed, let alone that she was able to read them. While some of the words in this were less familiar than those used by Mr Dickens, she was nevertheless lost in the beauty of the language and the fairy world held within. A cough made her jump. When she saw a boy about her own age behind her, she scrambled to her feet and the book went clattering to the floor.

"I'm so sorry," the boy said politely and stooped down to pick up the book at the same time that Clara did, their heads banging in the process.

The bang wasn't hard, but Clara felt a little dazed, more out of the confusion she found herself in as she stood up again than for the bang itself.

"I'm so sorry. I seem to be saying that a lot."

Something about his grimace made Clara laugh and before they knew it, they were both in fits of laughter. Clara could feel the tears of mirth running down her cheeks and wondered if she'd ever stop. It was Mrs Langham coming into the library which brought Clara quickly to her senses.

"Ah, there you are, Samuel. I see you have introduced yourself to Miss Phipps."

Clara blinked. She saw something familiar about the boy, but she couldn't quite place what it was. So, this was Master Samuel Hurst, Mrs Langham's nephew and ward. He was normally away at boarding school and during the last holidays had travelled with the family of a school friend to Florence so hadn't been home. Mrs Langham had shown her both the school and the route they would take on a map, but Clara had found it hard to comprehend.

"I'm pleased to meet you, Miss Phipps," Samuel said, clearly stifling further laughter. "Aunt Frances has written to me a great deal about you."

What could Mrs Langham possibly have had to say about her? She suddenly felt her best clothes scruffy next to this well-dressed boy and felt awkward and shy. She chose her words carefully, desperate to speak properly and create a good impression. "Master Hurst, how do you do?" She held out her hand to shake his, thinking this was perhaps the proper course of action.

"I was doing well until I blundered in here."

Clara's smile fell away. So, he had noticed her shabbiness.

"Oh no," Samuel said, "I didn't mean to imply I wasn't pleased to see you. I meant I seem to have done everything wrong since I have. Shall we start again?" A grin spread across his face which was infectious. "What is it you're reading, Miss Phipps?"

She turned the book cover so he could see.

Samuel struck a dramatic pose as though on a stage and recited;

"*Over hill, over dale,*

Thorough bush, thorough brier,
Over park, over pale,
Thorough flood, thorough fire,
I do wander every where,
Swifter than the moon's sphere;
And I serve the fairy queen,
To dew her orbs upon the green:
The cowslips tall her pensioners be;
In their gold coats spots you see;
Those be rubies, fairy favours,
In those freckles live their savours:
I must go seek some dew-drops here
And hang a pearl in every cowslip's ear.
Farewell, thou lob of spirits: I'll be gone;
Our queen and all her elves come here anon."

Clara was aware she was gaping at him but couldn't stop herself. She had never in her life heard a dramatic reading of any sort and was mesmerised. She came to her senses and applauded. "Bravo. How wonderful."

Samuel laughed and dropped into an armchair which was near the desks. "We performed the play last term at school. That was the part I played. It was great fun. I tried telling Aunty that I'd like to be an actor, but she said that wasn't appropriate. I'm actually hoping to become a teacher like you."

Clara blinked. Obviously, Mrs Langham had talked in her letters to Samuel of what Clara was doing.

"We could read it together if you like. Take different parts. There's another copy in here somewhere I believe."

Clara wasn't used to having company while she studied, but reading the play with Samuel brought the whole story to life and she wished she could have seen it performed. How much more fun it must be in a classroom of children, all eager to learn and working together. Mind you, from talking to JJ it seemed some of the children didn't seem as keen to learn as he was, and she wondered why their parents paid for them to go to school if that were the case. If only they knew how lucky they were and how much she would like to have taken one of their places.

She walked home that day with a lightness of step, wishing she could return to Mrs Langham's the following day, but knowing it would not be so. By the time she could go back, Samuel was due to have returned to school, which seemed a shame. Perhaps he would visit again in his next holiday, whenever that might be.

CHAPTER 10

1851 - 1852

With any hours Clara wasn't working being spent studying, she rarely had time to visit her mother's grave, but she couldn't let Christmas pass without doing so. She cut holly in berry to lay on the site and carried it wrapped in a cloth, to avoid being pricked by the points of the leaves. The wind was a bitter northerly as she walked along Welford Road toward Leicester, and she was glad of the scarf around her face to shield her from the worst of it.

Clara was alone in the windswept cemetery as she laid the branches on the unmarked ground.

"How do I get Dad to tell me what's wrong?" she asked her mother. "I know he misses you. We all do, but there's something apart from that and I don't know what. Some days he works well and produces many stockings. Other days he completes few or makes mistakes on the ones he does. He doesn't have arthritic hands like Grandma, but I can't help thinking something is stopping him working." Clara sighed heavily. She could find the answer from her mother no more easily than she could from her father himself. When she had asked, he simply put on a smile and said everything was fine and she shouldn't worry. She never told him about the mistakes she corrected, although he saw the extra hours she put in on the frame to help finish each order.

Walking home, the wind was behind her and carried her along. She wished she could stop off to see Hannah on her way back. Perhaps her sister could shed light on how their father was. She might at least have some ideas. However, they were still no more welcome at the Carter household than they had been in the early days of Hannah's marriage. Perhaps she should talk about her worries with Mrs Langham, yet it felt disloyal to talk to someone outside of the family about such a private matter.

Clara's competence with the knitting frame had increased as she'd grown stronger. She still had to concentrate to make sure she made no errors and dropped no stitches. Now, as she worked the bars rhythmically forward and backward her thoughts now turned to other things. She'd seen Mrs Langham's nephew a couple of times since their first meeting and thought that he was that same boy who had stopped to help with JJ several years ago and who had left the sticks on their doorstep. He never said anything about it or showed his recognition, so she still thought she might be mistaken and didn't feel comfortable to ask.

When Clara went to Mrs Langham's house shortly after Christmas, a blanket of snow carpeted the ground. It was Mrs Langham's housekeeper, Stubbs, who showed her into the library and rather than sitting waiting for Mrs Langham, Clara stood at the window looking into the garden. She had never been out there and thought it looked beautiful draped as it was in a layer of white. She wondered what it must be like to have such a space all to yourselves.

"I wanted to build a snowman, but it's not so much fun on my own."

Samuel's voice made Clara jump and she turned to

realise he'd joined her looking out.

"I've never built a snowman. I don't think I'd know how."

"Come on, let me show you."

Samuel's enthusiasm was infectious, and Clara smiled. She was starting to follow him, when Mrs Langham came in. "And where are you two off to?"

Clara stopped where she was and remembered why she was there.

"I'm sorry Mrs Langham, I had quite forgotten myself."

"Miss Phipps has never built a snowman, Aunty. I thought as part of her education I should show her." Samuel winked at Clara.

Mrs Langham smiled. "One moment." She rang the bell and with a brief pause Stubbs appeared. "Please fetch some overshoes for Miss Phipps and a spare pair of my gloves."

Stubbs nodded and went straight out.

"We can't have you freezing or ending up wet through. Now, run along you two and we'll have tea when you come back in half an hour."

They waited in the hall for Stubbs to bring the clothing and once Clara was suitably dressed Samuel led the way out of a side door to the garden.

He rolled a snowball along the ground, picking up layers of snow as he went. "You do one too. We need a large one for his body and a small one for his head."

Clara formed a ball of compacted snow as Samuel had done and then rolled it, copying what he was doing. She laughed with the sheer joy of seeing the ball pick up more snow and grow into a large orb. She stopped where Samuel was standing catching his breath under a large oak tree.

"This is where I found the branches I brought you," he said, looking up at the tree.

"So, it was you. And you do remember. I thought it was, but when you said nothing about it, I thought I was mistaken. Why did you do it?"

"Because I wanted to help, and I admired both yours and your brother's determination." Samuel looked suddenly shy and embarrassed. "Come on, let's get his head on his body and decorate him so we can go in and get warm."

At the sight of their finished snowman, with his coal pieces for buttons and eyes, and his carrot nose, Clara couldn't stop smiling. Although, she found it hard to imagine being able to spare a whole carrot simply for the pleasure of bringing a snowman to life. Her own smile was mirrored by that of Mrs Langham who, Clara saw as they returned to the house, was watching them from the window. She raised her hands in applause as Samuel pointed to their snowman. Clara wished she could capture the moment to keep forever.

Clara was ready for tea once she'd removed her outer garments and was glad of the fire to sit beside.

"I think today's lesson has been a different one," Mrs Langham, said as she took a biscuit.

"Oh, but I haven't studied today at all." Clara felt a pang at the thought they would not be reading or discussing one of the books.

"My dear, Clara, you have learnt how to build a snowman, and from the smile on your face I think you may also have learnt that sometimes doing something for yourself is the most important."

Clara realised that Mrs Langham was right and that none of the things which had been troubling her felt quite as impossible as they had done an hour previously.

The following Sunday, to Clara's delight, Samuel was still at Mrs Langham's and this time the three of them read different parts from Mr William Shakespeare's *The Tempest*. As always, Samuel insisted on acting out the part he was taking. Clara couldn't help thinking he might make a fine actor.

The more Clara read in her sessions with Mrs Langham, the wider her world became. As a child, she had thought no further than their own community in Great Wigston and the immediate problems faced by her family and neighbours. Now Clara understood that ensuring families had enough bread to feed them and could stay healthy throughout their lives was not always something they could control themselves. The more answers she received, the more her questions multiplied.

How could anyone change their life if they didn't have access to education and how could they access education if they had to work all hours simply to feed themselves? Clara realised how lucky she was and didn't want to waste any of the opportunity. What she wanted to do was find ways to help others as Mrs Langham was helping her.

She wished that she could talk about her ideas with her family, but none of them had enjoyed the opportunity to see further than their own situation. Martha was happy at the factory and saw no need of education for herself. And whilst JJ was keen to learn, he was still too young to understand many of the things which Clara wanted to discuss. As for Dad, he was lost in his own world. It was only on her visits to Mrs Langham that she could share her excitement on reading in the newspaper that libraries would be set up across the country, which would be available to any reader, with books that were free to borrow. With Mrs Langham she could also talk about the ideas she had and her own hopes for making a difference. For the other six days in the week, Clara's thoughts remained her own as she worked night and day to complete the orders for stockings.

"Whatever's the matter?" Clara realised that JJ had tears running down his face as he worked one afternoon after his return from school. She stopped at the end of the row she was knitting and gave him her full attention. "JJ, what's wrong?"

JJ wiped his eyes on his sleeve and sniffed hard. "I don't want to go to school."

Clara got down from where she was sitting and went over to him. "Why ever not?"

"I'm different and the other boys laugh at me, because of my leg."

Clara sighed. This was something she'd feared might happen. She wrapped JJ in her arms. What could she say to him? He was different. He would always be different. She couldn't argue against that. The world was a hard and cruel place. Even if JJ's teacher could stop what was happening in the classroom, it was still likely to come from elsewhere. How did you protect a child from such problems? Or was it more about preparing him for how to deal with such situations?

Clara thought carefully about what words to use. She didn't want to give her brother false hopes, or ignore his concerns, as she believed them to be very real.

"We are all different, just not in the same way. Some people find writing easy; some are better at running. There are people with blue eyes and others with brown. We are each special and individual. Being different isn't a bad thing if we use what talents we have. I know it's easy for me to say that you need to ignore the taunts and instead find the things you are good at and that you enjoy. Use the talents that you do have. Hard as it is now, you will be the happier person by looking for all that is good, than by letting other boys bring you down to their level."

JJ held tightly to her and nodded. "How do I stop them laughing at me?"

Clara sighed. "I don't know, my darling boy. I don't know. I think maybe you need to be brave and show them that you are as capable as any of them. Learning is so important. Don't let them spoil it for you."

Over the following days, Clara watched JJ carefully, but he said no more about the trouble at school. He was still only seven years of age, and she hated the thought of the effect the other boys might have on him. Much as she'd wondered about calling at the school to speak with his teacher, she wasn't sure they would listen to his sister and besides, what could be done?

When work was busy, Clara didn't have time to meet JJ out of school and would instead look forward to his return. He never dallied nor had other places to go, so when he wasn't home by four in the afternoon, Clara began to worry. The weather had been icy that morning, but the sun had been out and whilst it would be dark again soon, she didn't think anywhere had frozen. Another hour passed and there was still no sign of him.

"Dad," Clara said, interrupting her father concentrating on the row he was knitting.

He looked across to her, blinking.

"JJ should be back by now. I think I should go to look

for him."

"Should I go?" he asked, already getting up from the frame.

Clara shook her head. "No, you're much faster at knitting than I am. I'll go."

Her father nodded and sat down again.

As Clara got up and went to fetch the lantern, the sounds of her father's knitting frame followed her from the room.

As she stepped out into Moat Street Clara called out, "JJ, are you there?" She didn't know if he'd have walked through the lanes or round by the roads, as she knew he switched between the two. She'd start with the roads. Surely, he couldn't have been involved in any accident there or someone would have come for them.

"JJ. Where are you?" She picked her way carefully, avoiding the deeper ruts as she went. Thankfully at this time of day there was little passing traffic to be mindful of.

"JJ. JJ."

Of course, if he'd gone the other way, he might be home already and this might be nothing more than a wild goose chase, but Clara was feeling uneasy. He was rarely late and never as late as this.

By the time Clara reached the British School, it must have been after six o' clock. There was still light coming from the classroom. She felt uncomfortable entering, so knocked loudly on the outer door and waited. It was Mr Ward who answered.

"Oh, sir, I'm sorry to disturb you. My brother has not yet returned, and I wondered if he might still be here."

Mr Ward shook his head. "He left at the same time as the other children." Then he frowned. "There had been some trouble earlier, but I thought the boys were friends again."

"What kind of trouble, sir?"

"The usual jostling of growing boys. Nothing more as far as I know."

Clara nodded but inwardly her heart sank. Why hadn't she talked to the school about her concerns?

"Thank you, sir." She turned and left the school, walking more quickly than she had done earlier and headed for the route home through the lanes. In her haste, she almost tripped over a piece of wood lying across her path. When she held her lantern out to see what it was, she gasped in horror. Broken in two in front of her was one of JJ's crutches. He could manage with one. Perhaps he was ok. Her heart was thumping in her chest as she called out again. "JJ. I'm here, JJ. Where are you?" There was no reply in the darkness. Clara listened but heard nothing. She continued moving forward holding her lantern first to one side of the path and then to the other. She had no idea if she was looking for JJ himself or expected to find his other crutch. She swallowed hard. He had to be all right. Maybe the one crutch had been an accident.

Clara's mouth was dry as she made slow progress in the dark. Then to her horror, there he was, doubled over and lying on the ground.

"JJ." She sank to the ground beside him.

JJ groaned.

Clara held the lantern to see his face, tear-stained and bloodied. He was at least conscious. His other crutch was nowhere in sight.

"Oh, JJ, what happened?" Without waiting for him to answer she said, "I need to get help. I can't carry you on my own."

"No." JJ croaked. "Don't tell anyone. It'll make it worse.

Just bring my old crutches. I can get home with them."

The school was much nearer to find help than going home. Clara looked back the way she'd come. She should get Mr Ward. He'd know what to do.

"Clara, no."

It was as though JJ could read her thoughts.

"But…"

"No, Clara. Please."

Even in the lamplight Clara could see the desperation in his face. She sighed heavily.

"You can't stay here."

JJ snorted. "And where else am I going to go if I ain't got my crutches? I tried crawling, but I'm seven not two."

"Then let me leave the lantern with you. My eyes will adjust to the dark soon enough." Clara got up before he could argue with her. She would bring another lantern on her return. She only had to make her way along the lanes to home. That would be safer than going by the road without light.

Clara began to pick her way along the narrow path. An overhanging branch caught her face, and she jumped. From then she bent her head, hoping that by staying lower she was less likely to walk into anything hanging down from above. Although moving slowly, she was breathing hard and was out of breath when she entered the house. Dad was still working at the knitting frame. She made to open the door to the workroom then stopped. If JJ didn't want any fuss, then it was best not to tell their father. She went upstairs and took the old crutches from under the bed. It would be awkward for JJ using them, but he had little choice until she could ask for Mr Cooper's help. She stopped. She'd have to tell Mr Cooper, but what if he spoke to the school? There was nothing she could do about that. For now, she needed to get back to JJ as soon as possible.

With the benefit of the lantern and knowing where she was heading, Clara reached her brother in little over ten minutes. He was still exactly where she'd left him, although at least now sitting rather than curled up in a ball.

As he raised himself up with the crutches he gave a sharp intake of breath.

"Are you hurt bad?" Clara asked.

"I'm ok."

JJ's voice was quiet, and Clara suspected he wasn't telling her the whole truth, but there was little she could do.

When Samuel was at home that summer, they ventured out into the garden once again, to look at the plants and learn about them. Clara was amazed to find Mrs Langham was growing flowers she had never seen in any hedgerow and was eager to learn their names.

"It would be far better for my brother to come than for me and for me to attend school in his place. Then we could both learn as happily."

"Why so?" Samuel asked.

Clara poured out to him all that had happened. Talking to someone her own age felt good.

"Aunt Frances feared that might happen."

Clara stopped walking and frowned. "Whatever do you mean?"

Samuel looked pale as he turned to her. "Please, forget I said anything."

"Samuel, I thought you were my friend. Please tell me what you mean. What has this to do with your aunt?"

"Come let's go inside. I think it better that I allow my

aunt to explain."

Clara was still frowning as she sat in the library waiting for Mrs Langham to join them. Samuel was unusually silent. He'd left Clara for a few minutes while he went to find his aunt and was now sitting opposite her pulling at a thread on the chair.

"Now don't look like that. There's nothing to be concerned about." Mrs Langham came into the library exuding a no-nonsense energy that couldn't help but make Clara smile.

Mrs Langham indicated to Samuel that he should pour the tea. "Whilst you drink, I will explain what Samuel doesn't know how to tell you. I believe you have already worked out for yourself that it was Samuel who stopped to help you with your brother when he was young. He came home that day and told me all about the determination of the two of you. He said how inspiring you were and how he wished he could do more to help."

Clara felt herself blush and didn't dare look at Samuel. She could see out of the corner of her eye that he was fidgeting with the tea things on the table, despite having finished pouring.

"It was Samuel's idea to see what branches in the garden might be suitable to help you and to bring them to you. After that he came to me and asked whether we might help in other ways. That was when I first raised the subject of your brother with Mr Farmer and said that if a place could be found for Master Phipps, then I would cover the costs of his schooling, as I do a number of other children."

Clara nodded as some of what had happened began to make sense. "And that is how you already knew of me."

Mrs Langham smiled. "It was indeed, but you have Mr Cooper to thank there. He was the one who spoke with Mr

Farmer about how capable you were. Initially, he hoped you could be enrolled in the school."

Clara sat quietly for a moment, taking in what she had heard. "It is indeed kind of you, but why us?"

Mrs Langham smiled. "I would help everyone if I could, but that is not possible. Helping you made Samuel happy and that in turn makes me happy. Besides, once I'd met you, I could fully understand why my nephew admired your spirit." As Mrs Langham spoke, Samuel stood up from his seat and went over to the far window. He stood with his back toward them, fiddling with a pile of books on the table.

Clara didn't know what to say, other than to thank these kind people.

"Nonsense," Mrs Langham said, "you are an able pupil, and I enjoy teaching you. Which reminds me, we need to get on with some work. Now, where were we?"

With that the matter was closed and Clara felt unable to raise JJ's unhappiness at school and wished she'd said nothing to Samuel.

Clara was relieved that Samuel had gone back to school before her next visit to Mrs Langham. She had no idea what to say to him after learning that he was behind all the kindness which had been shown to both herself and JJ. Simply thanking him seemed inadequate and when she had, he seemed embarrassed about her mentioning it. It seemed far better to continue as though nothing had happened, and that was all the easier if she didn't see him.

It made Clara still more determined to do well. If Samuel had had such faith in her, it was the least she could do. She wished she could protect JJ from the bullying he faced at school, although in reality she presumed it was a reflection of attitudes he might face throughout his life. Much as she did her best to take care of him, she hated that she couldn't fix his problems or shield him from being hurt. She could only do her best to ensure that he had a stable and happy home to go back to at the end of each day.

CHAPTER 11

1853

Although Clara visited Mrs Langham at least once a week over the next few months, she rarely saw Samuel, which both saddened her and left her grateful. The disappointment was that she had such fun studying when he was around. Occasionally he would be there and join their session but Clara, despite his friendship, now felt a little nervous in his presence, although Samuel always had a twinkle in his eye which could make Clara smile.

"I cannot believe that there could be schools like the one in *Nicholas Nickleby*," Clara said, when they stopped reading a passage.

"It is the art of the writer to make things larger than life to illustrate his point," Samuel said, looking to his aunt for her agreement. "But can you imagine if you found yourself teaching in a school even half as bad as that?"

Clara gasped.

"I should have to come to rescue you at dead of night." Samuel stood up from his chair and pretended to parry a sword.

Clara laughed and Mrs Langham raised an eyebrow in the direction of her nephew.

"When you have quite finished scaring Miss Phipps witless, perhaps we could return to reading?"

Clara could tell by the curl upwards at the edge of Mrs

Langham's lips that she wasn't cross at Samuel digressing from the book and she supposed the point he made was part of their discussion on the subject.

As he had no siblings or other young people regularly in the house, Mrs Langham often encouraged Samuel to accept the invitations of school friends to spend some of the holidays staying with them.

"It does a boy good to see a little more of how others live, whether or not those others are his school friends," she said to Clara one day when she was opening a letter from Samuel while Clara was struggling with some more difficult arithmetic.

Sometimes Mrs Langham would read Samuel's letters to her and Clara sat eagerly waiting, hoping that might be the case today. He wrote with such levity about the antics of his classmates, and it made her laugh. She wished she could write to him as well, but it felt too forward to suggest such a thing.

"Samuel will attend college once he leaves school." Mrs Langham sighed heavily. "I wish you could do the same, my dear. If anyone deserved that opportunity, you do. Alas, as a young lady that would be more difficult regardless of the other complications."

Mrs Langham seemed careful to make little mention of the Phipps family's financial situation. At Christmas she had given Clara a parcel with fabric enough to make new dresses for herself and Martha and long trousers for JJ, but she had never made Clara feel shabby, or poor. The gift was simply because each had outgrown the clothes they were wearing, and the fabric was appropriate to their needs. Clara was grateful. Here, despite the beautiful surroundings, she felt accepted and welcomed just as she was.

She tried hard to keep her learning and home life separate, although she loved to find more time to read if she could. She borrowed books from Mrs Langham every week now but kept them carefully out of harm's way in the house. None of them had much space they could call their own, but her father said she could use the end of a shelf in the workshop where the finished stockings were kept before they were collected.

Martha showed not the least interest in reading and JJ couldn't reach the shelf yet, so for the time being the books were perfectly safe.

The others had teased her at first about trying to improve the way she spoke, but over time they seemed to have grown used to that.

JJ was still growing as fast as ever and every few months outgrew the latest crutches that Mr Cooper had made. The difference now was that at eight years of age, JJ was old enough to help in their making.

"We're going to Mr Bailey's workshop to find some wood. Mr Cooper says Mr Bailey might 'ave some old tools I could use to 'elp." JJ's excitement was infectious.

He spent hours in the workshop at home winding wool but fetching and carrying anything that couldn't be carried in a bag across his body or with the use of one hand, was difficult, as he always needed at least one crutch to move about. No one talked about what he might do when he was older. Much as he still liked learning, he no longer enjoyed being at school. It certainly meant that his own interest didn't lean toward teaching and Clara doubted he would be able to work in a factory, as from what Martha said, they had their pick of able-bodied people. Clara didn't know enough about other jobs to think what else he might be able to do. Winding wool would never be enough to pay the bills.

When JJ came back from his first visit to Mr Bailey's workshop, he started telling Clara about it almost before he was through the kitchen door. "'is tools are 'anging all round the walls. You ain't never seen so many different things. I couldn't reach any of 'em, but 'e took some down and showed me how to use 'em. Mr Cooper stayed to 'elp me. He was showing me 'ow to make the wood smooth so I wouldn't get no splinters." He showed Clara a block of wood he'd been using for practice. One edge was perfectly smooth and the other still rough. "Eliza Bailey goes to the school too, but she's in the girls' class. I saw 'er watching us, but she didn't come in the workshop. She ain't allowed in there."

JJ continued to go to Mr Bailey's workshop when he wasn't at school or helping to wind wool. He didn't do all the work for his next pair of crutches, but he'd played a part in making them and was proud of the result. "They're even better than the ones Mr Cooper made wi'out my help," he said, showing them off to Clara and their father.

"You'll make 'em on your own before you know it," Dad said. "If Mr Bailey continues to be so kind as to give you offcuts of wood."

Clara suspected Mr Cooper was using more than offcuts in making the crutches, but it was better for her father to believe otherwise. His pride and refusal of charity could go too far on occasions.

"It's time we looked for a student teacher position for you, Clara Phipps," Mrs Langham said when Clara visited her next.

"Oh, but what will Dad do without me to help every day?" Much as Clara wanted this for herself, she wouldn't want to leave her father to work alone.

"I've spoken with Mr Cooper and he in turn has been to see your father."

Clara gasped. Except for her visits to Mrs Langham, she could think of few times that she hadn't been there, and besides, why hadn't her father told her?

"Your father finds being alone in the house hard. He's asking if there's a journeyman looking to work the second frame and if not, Martha may leave her job in the factory to do so. You will have an income from teaching as long as a role can be found. Mr Cooper will be speaking with the school board on your behalf about that too."

Clara blinked several times but sat silently. She had no idea what to say. Here she was, wondering how she could ever be ready for such a step, especially with not having attended the school herself and yet those around her had such faith in her capabilities. Eventually she came out with the only thing she could think to say. "But I've got no suitable dress to wear to teach."

Mrs Langham laughed as heartily as ever. "If that's all there is left to worry about then I'm sure we can do something about it. I rather think your Sunday best will do just fine for the interview, and we can find you some material to make something else for when you start working at the school. I'm not offering you an old dress of mine, except that you could alter it to your own taste. I'm sure it would be much too old fashioned. I don't suppose for one moment that anything I might wear would meet with your approval."

Clara had never in her life had the opportunity to consider the style or fashion of a dress but had simply made alterations to whatever might be available such that it best fit her size. She opened her mouth to say she was sure that any of Mrs Langham's dresses would be gratefully received but thought better of it and remained silent.

Until then she had thought she would always work a knitting frame, together with keeping house. She had been content knitting, but Clara now worried that if she didn't secure the teaching post, she would always wonder what might have been and maybe wish her life had turned out a little differently. She sighed. Her parents had brought her up to do her best and that is exactly what she would do. If she didn't succeed, she could at least hold her head up and know that she'd tried.

It wasn't many weeks before Mrs Langham said, "You are to attend the British School for an interview on Tuesday at 10 o' clock."

Clara gasped. "Whatever will I say to them? I have never before had an interview. I…"

"Calm yourself, child. Firstly, you have had an interview. You just didn't realise that was what it was. When you came to me two years ago our first meeting was exactly that. I asked you questions about yourself in order to understand whether teaching you would be a productive use of my time. You answered honestly and sincerely. If you do the same on Tuesday, then I have no doubt Mr and Mrs Farmer will be just as happy with your answers as I was. Secondly, I thought today we could go through some questions which might leave you better prepared."

Clara let out the breath she was holding. How grateful she was for having been introduced to Mrs Langham. She sat on her usual seat but still feeling anxious perched on the front of the chair rather than sitting right back. Mrs Langham gave her an understanding smile but made no comment.

"Miss Phipps, why do you wish to train as a teacher?"

Clara smiled. That one was easy to answer. "I love learning and want to share that knowledge with others. It is wonderful to see the change that can be wrought in a person when they can write their own name and read what is put before them."

Mrs Langham nodded. "And what experience do you have of teaching children?"

Clara's face dropped. Other than sitting beneath the window when JJ was in class, she had never attended the school for so much as one day. "I have none."

"Oh, dear child." Mrs Langham sounded exasperated. "You most certainly do have experience. What about all the work you've done with your brother at home? And before you came to me you were teaching in the Sunday school."

"Oh, but I thought you meant in a school and I've never so much as stepped inside."

Mrs Langham smiled and said gently, "They know that, and they know the reasons for it. Tell them all you can of the things you have done, not the things you haven't. Now, answer that question again."

The afternoon proceeded with questions about her home and family which Clara would never have expected to be relevant, but little by little she gained confidence and hoped that she might still feel a little of that when she went to the school on Tuesday.

It hadn't occurred to Clara that there would be other applicants for the pupil teacher position and, finding herself waiting with another girl about the same age as herself, or maybe a little younger, came as a surprise. She wondered if this girl had already been a pupil in the school and so would be known to the master and mistress already. A sense of impending disappointment washed over her and she tried to remind herself that she would be no worse off than she was at present and that maybe there would be the opportunity at another time. Except to say, "Good morning," she didn't try to engage the girl in conversation.

The girl smiled shyly. She had seemed about to speak when she was called through to see Mr and Mrs Farmer and Clara was left waiting alone.

Clara's palms were damp with perspiration. It was a long time since she'd done anything which made her nervous. Her life was lived within such a limited circle of activity. She looked around the room at the whitewashed walls, noticing tiny details that would normally have passed her by. She spent a while watching the dust motes dancing in a shaft of light from the window where a draught caught them. Eventually, the door opened, and the smiling girl walked out.

"Good luck," she said quietly to Clara as she passed out of the room.

Clara was confused. If they were both trying to be appointed to the same position, why was the girl wishing her luck? The door was closed again, but she presumed she wouldn't be waiting much longer. She swallowed, realising she needed to breathe more deeply to slow her rising panic.

The door opened and into the waiting area came a stout woman, dressed in a stiff black dress, which looked for all the world as though it might have a life of its own when not being worn. In other circumstances that thought might have amused Clara.

The woman spoke. "Miss Phipps, come through."

Clara stumbled to her feet. Why was she always so clumsy when she was anxious? That thought did make her smile, remembering back to her prize giving at Sunday school all those years ago. If it hadn't been for that day, then she wouldn't be here. The thought made her stand taller as she walked into the office.

Mr Farmer was seated behind the desk.

"Sit down, Miss Phipps." He waved her to a chair.

Without the time spent in Mrs Langham's house, she might have been overawed by these surroundings with the grand wooden desk. Instead, she took a long slow breath to steady her nerves.

"As you may be aware, we have two positions available."

Two positions. That was why the other girl had wished her luck. They could both be appointed. Clara's heart skipped a beat, but she said nothing, presuming that she should only answer any direct questions.

"Now, first of all, your brother, Master Phipps..."

Clara held her breath wondering what they were about to say.

"... is a credit to you."

Clara blinked rapidly. That was not what she had been expecting. "Thank you, sir."

Mr Farmer nodded. "He is one of our brighter pupils and he has often told his teacher how you go through his work with him every day. Whilst I know you have not attended our classes, that does mean you will be familiar with the curriculum we cover. I also believe from Mr Preston that you were rather a star pupil in the Sunday school and now help with the younger children there."

Clara was no longer feeling as anxious and so when Mrs Farmer took over from her husband and asked her why she wanted to become a teacher, she was able to explain almost as easily as she had to Mrs Langham.

"You will earn three shillings and sixpence a week, with an increase each year of your pupillage. If you are successful in your examination at the end of your pupillage then you will become a qualified teacher."

Clara was thinking what 3s and 6d would mean to them. On a good week she could earn more than that with the knitting frame, but those weeks weren't often these days. It wouldn't be easy, but the work and money could be relied on.

"As a teacher you may not marry and must conduct yourself in a manner becoming of your position."

Clara blinked. Not be allowed to marry, well she couldn't imagine doing so, but still it seemed odd, as what of Mrs Farmer herself? But perhaps she didn't teach. She simply replied, "Yes ma'am, I understand."

It wasn't as though Hannah seemed happy with her married life, although Clara rarely saw her sister or her nephew for that matter. Besides, she had promised she would always be there to take care of JJ and that would make any idea of marriage impossible.

"You will yourself receive tuition at the end of each day. You may start at the beginning of next term. Thank you, Miss Phipps."

"Thank you." Clara could hardly believe what she was hearing. "Good day and thank you." She wanted to say so much more. She wanted to skip out of the room and along the corridor. She wanted to run to break the news to Mrs Langham and then to her father. Instead, she inclined her head in a slight nod and demurely left the room.

It was right that she should start by telling her father.

"Will you be my teacher?" JJ asked when she broke the news at home.

"No, silly. I'll be helping with the girls." Except for her own sister Martha, she didn't know many of the local girls. She thought maybe one or two from the Sunday school attended, but she wasn't sure.

"You might teach Eliza," JJ said with a groan.

"And who might Eliza be?" Clara frowned. She couldn't think where he might know this Eliza from.

"She's Mr Bailey's daughter. I see 'er sometimes when I go to the workshop. She's mean."

Clara raised an eyebrow. Wasn't it usually boys who were mean to girls? At least that's what she thought at the age JJ was now. "How exactly is she mean?"

"She hid my crutches."

Clara realised that JJ wasn't looking annoyed. "And had you done anything to Eliza first?"

"I might 'ave pulled 'er pig tail," he said grinning broadly.

Clara smiled. It was good to think that JJ had friends of his own, even if it was just a girl who he teased and who teased him back. Being without his crutches made getting about difficult for JJ. It was hard for him to stay balanced and hop far. Although he was quite proficient with a single crutch these days.

Her father said little beyond his first few words, "If only your mother were alive today." Then he sank into his own thoughts and went back to the workshop to continue knitting.

"I will miss you," were Mrs Langham's first words when Clara broke the news to her.

"Can I not still come to see you?" It hadn't occurred to Clara that she might not see the old lady when she started at the school.

"I would like that. I would like that very much." Mrs Langham dabbed her eyes surreptitiously.

"And I should like it too. May I still borrow books to read?"

"Oh, my dear child, of course you may. We need to sort another dress for you to wear as well. We'll go upstairs and look through my wardrobe."

Clara was well aware she needed a dress and given her other option was to go to Hannah for help, she would not turn down Mrs Langham's offer, although she would need to find something plain to wear as a pupil teacher.

By the time the autumn term began, Clara was torn between excitement and terror. What if she couldn't do it? She knew she could still fall back on the framework knitting, but as they'd decided in the end that the best option would be to give up one of the frames, leaving her father working alone, that would not be so easy to accomplish.

At the start of term, she walked to the school with JJ, glad of his company. In future she would start earlier than her brother, but not on that first day. As he left her at the entrance to the school, she remembered fondly the times she'd sat beneath the class window trying to listen from outside. She wished that was all she needed to do today.

"You're here too. Oh, I am pleased. I didn't want to be the only new girl."

Clara turned wondering who was addressing her. She

broke into a smile. It was the girl from the day of her interview looking as anxious as she felt. She held out her hand to shake that of the girl. "Miss Clara Phipps, how do you do?"

"Miss Millie Dowson. I'm well, if I don't think about how terrified I am."

The girls both broke into relieved laughter.

"Shall we?" Clara said, taking a deep breath.

Millie nodded and the two girls headed into the building together.

CHAPTER 12

1853

"The last girl never finished her years as a pupil teacher," Millie whispered as they went in. "She had to get married." Millie gave Clara a knowing look.

Clara thought of Hannah and hoped the girl from the school had made a better marriage.

"Ah, Miss Dowson, Miss Phipps, good morning." It was Mrs Farmer who greeted them. "Follow me, please."

She led them through to a large room where the girls of the school were already sitting at their desks, separated from where the boys' area was set out. Mrs Farmer went to the front of the class and silence fell in the room.

"Good morning, Mr Ward. Good morning, girls."

"Good morning, Mrs Farmer," the girls chimed as one voice.

Mr Ward nodded and gave Clara and Millie what felt to Clara to be a reassuring smile. It gave her a little courage to realise that Mr Ward would be the teacher they were working for and learning from.

Mrs Farmer continued to address the entire room of girls. "We have two new teachers starting with you today."

Clara noticed the absence of the word 'pupil' and gulped.

"Miss Dowson and Miss Phipps will be working with

the younger girls. I hope that you will make them most welcome." She beckoned for the two to go forward and join her. "This is Miss Dowson."

Like a well-trained choir, the girls chorused "Good morning, Miss Dowson."

Millie looked across at Clara and blinked and then took an obvious deep breath and turned back to the class. "Good morning, girls."

From the satisfied look on Mrs Farmer's face that seemed to be the right response and Clara was grateful that she had not been the one to go first.

Once the introductions were out of the way, Mr Ward addressed the room and in so doing gave his new pupil teachers their initial roles within the classroom.

As Clara listened to children practise their reading and in turn read to them, she soon forgot the newness of the situation. But for the fact that the story being read was not from the Bible, she could as easily have been with a class of Sunday school children. Later, working with some of the younger children, teaching them the letters of the alphabet reminded her of doing the same with JJ when he first began learning.

Clara thought there were at least fifty girls in the room, although she hadn't had a moment to count properly, but the desks were laid out in neat rows so she couldn't be far out. She was grateful she wouldn't need to remember the names of all of them to begin with, just the younger ones who she was assigned to work with. Millie was helping the youngest girls and Clara the ones a year or two older. Mr Ward split his time between giving the two of them instructions on what he would like them to cover with their charges and teaching the eldest of the girls in the school. With them all being in the same room, Clara had to concentrate hard on the basic addition and subtraction she was teaching, while hearing Millie trying to teach counting to ten and Mr Ward teaching multiplication.

The time soon passed. When the children left at the end of the day to return to their homes, Clara and Millie became the pupils and spent time learning from Mr Ward about what was expected of them in teaching the children.

By the time she went home, Clara was sure that she would thoroughly enjoy her new role. She was already thinking about the following day and how she might give more help to the girls who found learning hard.

Her father was quiet when she entered the house. Grandma Herbert was there for part of the day and had left food prepared for their supper, but she'd made clear that wouldn't be happening every day and it would only be while Clara found her feet. Their father had worked alone until JJ joined him in the workshop on his return from school.

"It's so quiet in there," JJ said to Clara. "Dad don't say ote to me other than telling me what wool needs to be wound next." As Clara served out their meal, JJ was keen to talk to his sister about his own day of studies, as he always had done.

It made Clara smile to wonder what the girls she taught were saying in their own homes and hoped they had had a good day too.

During their meals each evening, Dad asked about both hers and Martha's days but said little about his own. The orders to be fulfilled were steady enough to keep the one frame running and for the time being, he would be unlikely to have times being idle, but she learnt more of that from JJ and by keeping the family's finances, than from her father himself.

Over time, Clara and Millie became firm friends. Millie's family had been able to afford to send her to school, although that was before moving to Great Wigston. Millie was fourteen now, two years younger than Clara. She'd had the choice of applying for factory work or for a position as a pupil teacher. "Dad's working on some of the new buildings that are going up. I didn't see myself carrying bricks."

Millie had said it with a straight face and Clara wasn't completely sure if the other girl was joking. No one would employ a woman to do building work; or at least she didn't think so.

It didn't take many weeks before the new routine of working at the school felt normal. The playground was split in two, with half for the boys and half for the girls, much as the large classroom was. It meant that although she caught glimpses of JJ when she was outside supervising breaks, their paths never crossed. As she watched the children, she saw enough to know he had few friends and was more often to be found sitting quietly trying to keep out of harm's way, than mixing with the other boys. It made her sad, but she knew that he wouldn't want her to fight his battles.

"Is school any better?" she asked JJ one evening.

"'S'alright." He shrugged but said no more about himself. "Eliza says you're a good teacher."

Clara felt herself blushing.

"She says, she can understand things when you show her."

Clara thought it was perhaps one of the biggest compliments she'd ever been paid. "Thank you. She's a nice girl."

Eliza Bailey, Mr Bailey's daughter was eight years old,

the same as JJ, but had been slower with her reading than JJ. Perhaps no one had spent any time with her outside of school, reading to her and listening to her read. Now she seemed to be gaining confidence as much as anything and enjoying her schoolwork.

As often as she could, Clara would visit Mrs Langham. Each time borrowing a small number of books to read between visits. While she no longer read the books aloud to her friend, they discussed each one after Clara had finished reading and she was always amazed to find whichever book she had chosen from that beautiful library, Mrs Langham seemed to have both read and completely remembered.

The weeks passed and just before Christmas, Clara wrapped the shawl she had knitted for Mrs Langham and set off for the house. Term had finished and she had some precious time to catch up on all the things at home which were left undone from week to week and in preparing for their own Christmas. JJ was busy in the workshop winding wool most of the time, which would save them a little money whilst he was on holiday from school. If he had time free, other than helping Clara with what household chores he could manage, he would go to Mr Bailey's workshop to work on his next crutches or other small projects.

Clara had spent the previous day scouring the hedgerows for branches of holly in berry, and other boughs which might decorate their tiny home.

As she walked, she was thinking of her father and how distant he was becoming. He seemed to spend much of the time in his own private world and his grief seemed as fresh now as it had four years ago when her mother died. She'd tried talking to him, but he always closed the conversation down, never willing to talk about how he felt or for that matter how she might feel, either. Clara could do little, but that thought didn't make it easier. She did her best to answer JJ's questions about their mother. He was four when Mam died, and he was frightened of forgetting her. Martha seemed to have few recollections although she had been nine years old at the time.

For her own part, Clara at least had Mrs Langham she could talk to occasionally.

She was still lost in thought when she arrived on the steps to Mrs Langham's front door and rapped the knocker. Being Sunday, she was expecting Mrs Langham to open the door herself and was surprised when it was Samuel standing there.

"Oh, I…" She felt out of place and confused. She'd seen nothing of him since the summer. He'd grown taller in the intervening time with a shock of dark hair which curled around his ear.

"Do come in, Miss Phipps." He was grinning as he spoke. "Aunty and I were about to have tea in the library. Your timing is perfect."

As it was the time that Clara so often called, she had a fleeting thought that this was deliberate on Mrs Langham's part.

Mrs Langham was sitting in the armchair, the picture of innocence. "How lovely that you could join us my dear. Samuel, please pour tea for Miss Phipps."

Clara smiled seeing they already had three cups on the tray and took a seat opposite Mrs Langham.

"As Samuel is still thinking of teaching when he finishes school, I thought he might be interested to hear your experiences."

Clara sat wide-eyed. "I am a lowly pupil teacher and have been so for one term. I can't claim any great knowledge of teaching."

Samuel's laugh made her feel comfortable and Clara remembered the happy times when he joined her study sessions.

"And the experience I have is that of sitting in a classroom with boys my own age, so I have rather less knowledge."

Clara enjoyed discussing all that she'd learned, including the lengths Mr Ward would go to in order to hold the attention of the children who wished they were elsewhere. She was so engrossed in telling Samuel about her own charges, that she almost forgot to give Mrs Langham her present. It was as she stood to leave that she found she still had it by her side.

"Oh, my dear, how kind of you. Thank you. I shall save it to open on Christmas Day. I have a little something for you too, and Samuel will find it for you as he shows you out."

"Will you come again before I return to school?" Samuel asked as they went along the hall. "I should like it very much. It's the first holiday I will have spent much time here for a long time and I don't know anyone apart from you and Aunty."

She looked up at his eager face and felt herself blush. With her duties at home, it was almost impossible for her to commit to a visit in the next week, but she would do so as soon as she was able. "I shall certainly try."

As Clara worked at home that week, her thoughts kept returning to Samuel and every time they did, she found herself smiling. It was interesting talking to a boy of her own age, especially when it came to their both following the path of teaching. He knew about so much more than she had learned. He spoke French and Latin and knew more of geography and history than she ever would. She supposed he would teach in a boarding school like the one he attended, rather than in a church school for local children. Such a place must be quite different. She wished she could see what a boarding school was like, but his was over sixty miles away, a distance she could not imagine travelling, besides which, she doubted girls would be allowed to look around.

Part way through the week her father developed a head cold. While he sat at the frame trying to fulfil his quota of stockings it was clear to Clara that he would be better in bed for a day or two, where he could stay warm.

"Let me do that," she said, taking over in the workshop. "You rest up."

He was unprotesting, which made Clara realise his illness was worse than he had shown. All thoughts of another visit to Mrs Langham went from her mind as she applied herself to knitting the stockings which were due by the end of the week. At first, she was slow, having had a few months away from the work, but she soon found her hands remembering what they must do. Her muscles ached from working the frame. She had become used to the lighter work of teaching without realising the strength she was losing as a result. She and JJ worked in companionable silence, each concentrating on their own task.

Dad was ill for the whole of the Christmas holidays and Christmas itself passed quietly. He missed attending chapel with the children and Clara for once forgave Martha for not wanting to attend, so that one of them stayed at home to keep him company.

Between going up and down stairs with things for their father and cooking their Christmas meal, it was late afternoon before Clara had the opportunity to open her gift from Mrs Langham. When she did so she gasped. It was an exquisite leather-bound pocketbook, together with a letter.

'My dearest Clara,

I thought you should have somewhere to note all the new things you are learning in your teaching,

with much love

Frances Langham'

Clara drew it to her face and breathed deeply the smell of leather. Whilst she still loved the Bible she had been given by the Sunday school for attendance, she didn't think she had ever owned anything half as beautiful as this journal. She ran her finger over the hand stitching of the leather and smiled. She might not yet have the opportunity to thank her friend in person, but she would write to her without delay. She would also explain, for Samuel's benefit, why she wasn't able to return as they had planned.

It was almost New Year before their father was strong enough to get out of bed and Clara was relieved to see him improve.

"Thanks, love," he said when Clara took him some breakfast on New Year's morning.

Clara sat on the edge of his bed. This was the best chance she would have to talk about how losing her mother had affected him. She sat quietly as he propped himself up and took the tray.

"Dad, I miss Mam too. It must be hard for you." She bit her lip, waiting to see if he would reply.

He pushed the porridge away from him slightly and reached his arms out to embrace Clara. "It is, love. It is."

151

He fell silent holding her to him. Then said, "I never want to burden you with my troubles. You're a good daughter and your mam would be so proud of what you're doing. I guess I'd grown tired." He held Clara away from him so he could look at her. "I thought it might be my time to join your mam, but with your care I seem to be on the mend. Thank you." He gave a weak smile. "And now I must eat me porridge or me daughter'll be telling me off again."

Clara realised that was his way of saying the conversation was over. It was far more than he'd said of any personal nature in the whole of the years since Mam had died. Clara kissed his cheek before she went back downstairs to continue on the knitting frame. She hoped he would be back on his feet before she had to return to school.

When term began, Clara felt as though she were returning to school for a rest. Her father was much improved and had started back in the workshop the previous Thursday, but for half the day. That had at least given Clara the opportunity to complete the household chores which were still to be done before the first day of term.

"Good Christmas?" Millie asked as she caught up with Clara by the school gate.

Clara was about to say that it wasn't, but then she thought of her leather notebook and the brief time she had properly spoken with her father and smiled. "Yes, thank you it was. How about you?"

"I've got five brothers, what do you think?" Millie raised an eyebrow and they both laughed.

While Clara loved having a brother, she couldn't imagine having five of them, all still at home. She guessed Millie was probably glad to get back to school too.

She quickly settled into her usual term-time routine and on the Sunday, once Sunday school finished, went to see Mrs Langham.

When her friend opened the door, Clara was delighted to see she was wearing the shawl which Clara had knitted.

"I think it rather suits me," Mrs Langham said as they went through to the library. "Samuel was so disappointed not to see you again. Sadly, he had to return to school last weekend, so isn't here now, but he left this for you." Mrs Langham handed a letter to her.

Clara wondered if she should open it while she was with Mrs Langham or wait until she was on her own, but Mrs Langham answered the question by handing her a letter opener.

The envelope, written in a scrawling hand, was addressed to *'Miss Clara Phipps'*.

'My dearest Clara,

I hope I am not being too bold in calling you such.

I was sorry not to have seen you again over Christmas as I would have liked very much to ask you more about your time teaching. I asked my aunt if she thought it would be acceptable to write to you and she seemed to think it a splendid idea. Would you mind awfully exchanging letters with me from time to time and answering questions about the work you are doing?

your loyal friend

Samuel Hurst'

Clara could feel her cheeks colour as she read it through a second time.

"Well, my dear?"

Mrs Langham was looking impatient to know the contents, which made Clara smile.

"He's asked whether I might write to him from time to time."

"And will you?"

Clara nodded slowly. "I rather think I might." She would be able to find a penny for postage once in a while. Then she tucked the letter carefully into her bag and rose before Mrs Langham could say anything further. "Shall I pour the tea and bring it over to you and you can tell me all about your Christmas?"

CHAPTER 13

eighteen months later
1855

Clara didn't mind that she was a little older than if she had progressed from school pupil to class monitor at the age of thirteen, and then into pupillage. It did mean that by the time she'd served as a pupil teacher for seven years she would already be twenty-three when she fully qualified. The time passed quickly, and she and Millie had already worked well together for the last two years.

Millie was adept with the youngest children. Coming as she did from a large family, she was used to their ways. Clara was happiest when teaching children to read and write. Seeing her own sisters' lack of competence, brought home the grim reality of the difference a basic education might make.

Martha at fifteen, was happy enough working in the factory. Without any education behind her, she would never be able to make any progress; not that she wanted to. All she dreamed of was a future with a family of her own. That was something Clara wondered if she herself could ever have if she were to keep her promise to JJ, as well as taking care of her father when he could no longer work.

Over the last couple of years, there had been a number of times when her father needed help to finish an order and Clara would work late into the night when he could work no more. As a result, her visits to Mrs Langham had become less regular. When she did visit, they seemed to talk almost as much of Samuel's news and progress as they did about the works of Mr Dickens or Mr Shakespeare. Samuel and Clara still wrote letters every few weeks but had seen almost nothing of each other in that time. She would have written more frequently had she been able to spare more money for postage.

Samuel's letters always made Clara laugh. Despite asking her about the serious matter of teaching and discussing problems she found in the classroom; Samuel would save some of the page to tell of events at the boarding school. He wrote with such vivid description that Clara almost wondered if he should become a writer instead of a teacher.

"I rather hoped Samuel would study at Oxford, but he has his heart set on Cambridge. I dare say his school is the influence there. I suppose with Mr Langham not being his father they have paid no attention to where my husband studied. It was a whim on my part. The school was specified in his father's will, despite my preferring the idea of him not boarding." Mrs Langham sighed. "Some of that was selfishness on my part. I do so enjoy the company of you young people."

"Will he go to Cambridge next term?" By that time, he too would be eighteen years of age. Clara couldn't imagine what it must be like to study somewhere so grand. She'd seen sketches of the colleges in one of the books in Mrs Langham's library.

"No." Mrs Langham paused. "His father stipulated that he should spend at least some of the year travelling before taking up his college place. He'll go up to

Cambridge next year. He has asked me to accompany him for part of his travels." Mrs Langham sighed. "Of course I'd like to go, but it's a long while since I've been away from home for any length of time. I've grown somewhat set in my ways."

Clara smiled. Of all the older people she knew, she thought Mrs Langham to be the most willing to try new things.

"I also think he plans to spend a term teaching at the British School to gain some experience as well."

Clara's heart skipped a beat. She looked up. Had she heard correctly what Mrs Langham had said? Samuel hadn't said anything of that in his letters to her. Clara's voice was surprisingly unsteady as she asked, "The British School, surely he would be found a place at the National School more easily?" She presumed with his Anglican connections he was far more likely to teach in a church-based school than one attached to the chapels.

"I said much the same, but I think after the two of you writing about the school so much he's keen to see it for himself. I've spoken with Mr Ward about the idea, and I believe he has already discussed it with Mr Farmer, who is amenable to the suggestion."

Clara didn't know what to think. Her mouth had gone dry. She cleared her throat. "And which term would that be?" To see Samuel at the school on a regular basis would be strange.

"He has in mind that we will travel through the autumn and winter months and that he will spend the final term teaching, if they will find a place for him then. He will of course be in the boys' part of the school." Mrs Langham shook her head. "I'd much rather travel in the better weather. Spring is rather beautiful in the southern parts of

Europe, but I dare say I will go along with his plan."

Clara wished she could see Samuel again. She would much rather talk about some of the issues than write about them in a letter. If he taught at the British School then he might teach JJ, which felt strange. She would ask him more about his plans when she next wrote, if he didn't tell her first. The next letter she received went some way toward that.

'My dearest Clara,

I'm sure my aunt has told you of our plans to travel this autumn and winter. We both wish that you could accompany us but understand that is not possible with your own work and family.'

Clara blinked. Oh, what a lovely thought it was that they had even considered her going. She couldn't imagine visiting such distant places, the images of which she'd only seen as illustrations in books.

She read on.

'I hope upon our return to spend some time in Great Wigston before going up to university next year. It will be good to see you again.'

He then included his usual passages about the day-to-day activities at school, before signing off.

'I will send you news of our travels if I am able to do so.

your loyal friend

Samuel Hurst'

Clara sat back and read the letter through again, smiling. He was planning to spend some time in Wigston. She could at least look forward to seeing him on his return from travelling, although that was nearly a year away.

The summer days stretched out before her. As her father seemed to be working longer hours, Clara had some time to herself during the school holidays. She and JJ wound the wool between them at those times and could easily supply all their father needed, leaving some time once housework was complete to sit outdoors reading. JJ often headed to Mr Bailey's workshop, leaving Clara free to wander where she chose. It was a luxury she was unused to, and as she sat in the shade of an ash tree near the river, she felt utterly content.

Since writing to Samuel, Clara had thought more about some of the issues which affected people locally. Both the lack of education and the difficulties faced by framework knitters, had become topics they discussed at length. As a result, from time to time she would buy a newspaper and try to understand more of what happened within government, locally and for the country as a whole. Clara didn't understand some of what the paper reported and would have loved to discuss with Samuel in person, but the more she learned, the more she realised the unfairness of some of the privations suffered by those around her and how entrenched into their way of life the problems were.

She put today's paper down and sat watching the river as the sun twinkled on the rippling surface. Where, she wondered, did you start in making any kind of difference? For her it had been the Sunday school which gave her an opportunity, but on its own that wouldn't have been enough. She wished she could help some of the children who couldn't afford either the money or the time to go to school, as Mr Cooper and then Mrs Langham had helped her.

By the time Mrs Langham set off on her travels with Samuel, Clara was starting her third year as a pupil teacher and was still enjoying it as much as when she began. She would have described herself as happy were it not for worrying over her father. Although Clara, Martha and JJ all still lived at home with him, their father was becoming increasingly distant and from his manner, the smell on his breath and the small amounts of money missing from the housekeeping, Clara suspected he had started drinking. He wasn't a drunkard and nor did he spend all his nights in public houses, but until recently he was teetotal and that certainly no longer seemed to be the case. She wished she could speak of her concerns with him, but he changed the subject of conversation. She would have liked to talk of her concerns with Hannah but saw her so rarely and never on her own.

The autumn nights drew in and Clara found herself wondering where Mrs Langham and Samuel were visiting. She had never thought of people travelling much beyond Leicester until Mrs Langham talked about their trip. Of course, Clara knew that the school at which Samuel boarded was much further away than Leicester, but she had no precise idea of where that was, despite looking in an atlas. But Paris, Geneva and Florence sounded so very far. The travelling would take them a good deal of time. She hoped that Mrs Langham would bear the journeys well. Some of the miles were to be travelled by train, some by boat, and others by horse and carriage. Clara had looked at a map with Mrs Langham before she went and was in awe of the whole of what lay ahead. Their trip seemed to have been carefully planned, with Samuel writing on ahead to make each of the arrangements. How much you must learn on such a trip.

Clara went and stood beside the railway lines in Great Wigston one day, to watch the trains go by and smell the smoke from the engines as they passed. They looked so powerful and magnificent, their steam billowing like a bull snorting on a winter's day, as they pulled their carriages and wagons along the track. One day she would travel by train, even if it was on a local journey. There were many people now that made the journey into Leicester by train, but she had never had cause to do so.

All she could hope was that Samuel might write and tell her how he and his aunt were progressing.

Arriving home one day in late November, Clara was surprised to find Hannah in the back room talking with Dad. Robert was with her and was now about eight years of age.

"Hello," Clara said, the surprise clear in her voice.

Hannah stood up and greeted her awkwardly.

Clara moved to hug her sister, but Hannah pulled back to avoid the contact. Clara looked more closely at Hannah. Were they bruises on the side of her face? She couldn't be certain, but it looked that way.

"I thought I should tell you we're moving away from Wigston."

Clara gasped. She didn't know why, but the thought of Hannah moving alarmed her. "Where to?"

"Oh, not that far. Frank's dad is starting building houses in Blaby. Now Frank's finished 'is apprenticeship we're to move to live in one of the 'ouses they're building there. We'll be the first people to live in it." That last part she said with awkward pride as though she knew it to be something which might be envied but still needed to convince herself.

Clara nodded. Blaby was a few miles away; far enough for there to be more reason for Hannah not to see her family. Except for a Sunday, none of them could afford the time to walk the hour or more it would take to get there and the same to return.

"It'll be all right," Hannah said in a faraway voice that made Clara think her sister thought it to be anything but all right.

"I'm 'aving another baby as well." Hannah added it almost as an afterthought. "It'll be good for Robert to have a brother or sister won't it, love?"

The boy, who had remained quiet through the whole exchange, scowled and shook his head.

"What do you think of that then?" Clara asked her father after Hannah left.

John Phipps looked sad. "What would your mother say? All Hannah's high ideas and where've they got 'er? There ain't much I can do. It ain't as though there's ote here for 'er." Then without another word he picked up his coat and hat and went out into the night.

Where he went Clara had little idea, but he seemed now to go out with increasing regularity, often missing dinner and not returning to the house until the others were in bed. Meanwhile, Clara prepared supper for herself, JJ and Martha and left Dad's for him to eat when he came in if he was hungry, though he rarely seemed to be.

Clara's first travel letter from Samuel arrived in late November. He'd written it over a number of days having had to give up trying to write while moving, as the ink kept blotting. The post mark on the envelope said Florence, but as it was posted on the day he arrived in that city the news was of their stay in Paris and thence to Marseille and onwards by steamship to Genoa.

As she read, Clara was sincerely glad to have seen

drawings of the sorts of ships involved as it enabled her to picture the travellers on board. She imagined what it might be like to be with them, but when she read that it had left Mrs Langham fatigued, she hoped that Samuel was taking good care of his aunt. The travellers would be staying in Florence for two weeks and Samuel hoped to write again before they left.

Clara looked at the address at the top of the letter and wondered if two weeks would give long enough for her to send a reply. Then she laughed, realising some of that time had already passed and she would need to be patient until they returned.

Christmas came and went with little by way of celebration beyond the few branches of decoration which Clara had brought in. As the new year arrived, Clara looked forward to Mrs Langham's return. She'd missed the older lady more than she could have imagined. With her own mother no longer around and Grandma Herbert growing more cantankerous as the years went by, it was nice to have a woman she could talk to, even if most of their conversation was about the books in the library and now Clara's teaching. As she didn't know the exact date when Mrs Langham was due home, Clara took to walking past the house once or twice a week to see if the drapes to the front windows had been rearranged. She found she was looking forward to seeing Samuel with a strange sense of excitement that she was unused to.

February slipped icily into March and there was still no sign of the travellers. As Mrs Langham had said she was going for only part of the trip, Clara had expected her arrival home ahead of Samuel, but if he planned to spend a term teaching, he would need to be back within no more than a few weeks himself.

In the middle of March, Clara saw a lamp flickering in the drawing room and quickened her step. Was it too late in the day to call? She thought it probably was, but waiting until Sunday felt impossible. Surely, she would be forgiven the excitement of seeing her friend once again.

Clara was ready to ask the housekeeper if Mrs Langham were home and whether she might see her, when to her surprise it was Samuel who answered the door.

"Oh, I… it was just…" She felt herself colour as she searched for words to cover her confusion.

"Miss Phipps, what a delight. Please do come in."

Despite daylight having long since faded and Samuel being lit by only lamplight, his face appeared to have a ruddy glow that suggested travelling might have suited him rather well.

Clara's awkwardness and embarrassment was lost in the warmth of his greeting. He led her into the drawing room where Mrs Langham immediately stood from her seat by the fire to welcome their guest.

"My dear girl, come in, come in."

"I may not stay long, as I need to prepare supper for my family, but I've been longing to see how you are and welcome you home." Clara sat in the chair on the other side of the hearth as indicated to her by Mrs Langham.

Mrs Langham smiled. "Then we shall not begin our description in earnest, shall we, Samuel? That will wait for another day. I rather think our friend Mr Dickens might turn some of our adventures into tales if he had half the opportunity. We've met characters equally larger than life and twice as witless. But I'm tired of travelling for a while and longing for the comfort of home. Tell me what has happened here while I was away."

There seemed precious little worth telling as far as Clara could think, but Mrs Langham listened intently, especially when Clara told of Hannah moving to Blaby.

"And now I feel quite as though I'm back where I belong and am happy to be home." Mrs Langham sighed deeply and sat back in her chair. "If you can spare a little time on Sunday, I'm sure Samuel would be delighted to help me tell you of our escapades."

With that, Clara bade them goodnight and left with a lighter tread than the one with which she had arrived.

She was quite determined that she would have time on Sunday and so took the unusual step of excusing herself from eating with her own family at teatime and asking Martha to prepare the meal for her father and JJ.

"I s'pose so," said Martha pouting. Then she laughed. "You know I'm jealous that I have nowhere else to be. At least I see my friends during the week at work. How you can bear to spend all day surrounded by children is beyond me."

Clara frowned. She'd never thought of it in those terms. Of course, she would never regard the children as her friends in the way Martha saw others working at the factory, but Clara loved watching them grow into the people they could become and saw learning as an important part of that.

"Can I come wi' you?" JJ asked. "I'd like to 'ear about the places Mrs Langham and Mr Hurst visited too."

Clara felt a pang, realising how much she wanted to keep the day all to herself, but she saw the eager look on JJ's face and smiled. How could she ever say 'no' to her brother? She was certain Mrs Langham wouldn't mind, and she had always promised that one day she would take

JJ.

As Clara and JJ walked to Mrs Langham's house after Sunday school, Clara couldn't stop herself from fretting. "Remember to say please and thank you and you should call Samuel 'Mr Hurst'."

"You are funny. I do know how to be'ave. Mrs Bailey says I'm very polite."

Clara smiled. "You're growing up so fast. Sometimes I forget you're already ten years old." In her heart she was most anxious that Mrs Langham should think as well of her brother as she herself did, for he meant the world to her.

Her heart was racing as she knocked at the front door.

Samuel opened the door with a flourish as though greeting honoured guests and bowed low. "Miss Phipps, Master Phipps, do come through."

He was so comical it was impossible for both Clara and JJ not to laugh as he showed them along the hall to the library. As they went through the door, JJ stopped suddenly, and Clara almost knocked him over. He simply stood with his mouth open, gazing around the room.

"JJ," Clara hissed to him. "Greet Mrs Langham." She watched him shake his head as though checking what he was seeing was real, before swinging himself further forward into the room and stopping again.

"But it's so big."

"JJ." Clara's heart was thumping. She thought she'd prepared him for how to behave.

Mrs Langham laughed and spoke to JJ as though it were a great secret, "I remember the first time your sister came into this room. She quite forgot herself and pirouetted as though she were a ballerina."

Clara smiled remembering back and, realising how understanding Mrs Langham had been of her own reaction to this strange environment, relaxed.

The afternoon passed by all too quickly as Mrs Langham and Samuel recounted their travels and Clara and JJ asked them questions.

"Do tell me about all the wonderful paintings you saw," Clara said, as they talked of Paris and Florence.

"What's it like going on a steam train? How fast do steam ships go?"

JJ's questions were so different to her own and that made her smile. The answering bounced from Mrs Langham to Samuel and back. When he was talking of the travel to JJ, Samuel would get up and almost act out what had gone on and JJ sat in rapt attention throughout. Clara thought what a wonderful teacher he would make if he took the same approach with the boys in the classroom.

Eventually Mrs Langham coughed and said that was quite enough for one day. She was tired and would like to rest.

Clara would have felt disappointed but knowing that Samuel would be there for the whole of the next term lifted her spirits and she looked forward to returning the following week.

CHAPTER 14

1856 -1857

Clara saw occasional glimpses of Samuel the following term at school. Rules were such that he had no choice but to stay within the boys' side of the school and she the girls' side. Had she not done so her own position would have been terminated without question. They both stayed at the school late to receive further tuition but were with different teachers and rarely left at the same time. It would have been frowned on for them to walk out together. But they exchanged an occasional smile when supervising breaks in their respective parts of the playground. Even then, they didn't want the children or other teachers to notice their friendship.

Clara's evenings and weekends were now almost entirely devoted to framework knitting once again. Her father was increasingly wandering from home, rather than working, and the orders still needed to be fulfilled.

"Dad, where do you go of an evening?" she asked when he came home late one night. She could smell no alcohol on him these days, which at least was a mercy.

"Never you mind, child. Never you mind."

She'd asked JJ if he knew where their father went, but he just shrugged. Martha simply said she was sure everything was fine, but she didn't offer to help make up the difference in the orders, partly because she was too tired after a long day at the factory.

How could Clara tell her father he needed to work harder and spend less time away? All she could do was try to complete the work he missed, however little sleep that meant she could have and even if it meant she worked on the Sabbath. She just hoped that no one outside of the house could hear the knitting frame running all hours of day and night, but if they did, thankfully there were no complaints.

Things didn't improve as summer approached and JJ said, "I'll finish school in June."

Clara stopped what she was doing and stared at JJ. "Won't you stay on longer? You'll be only eleven years of age."

JJ shook his head. "I ain't like you, Clara. I like learning, but it's hard to sit there and I ain't got what you'd call real friends amongst the other boys."

"But what will you do? If you stayed you might teach, or maybe become a clerk?" Of late, Clara had thought that with an education behind him there might be many jobs which JJ could do.

"I don't think so. I couldn't bear more years in school. Besides, Mr Bailey says he'll take me on."

"As a carpenter's apprentice?" Clara frowned. How could JJ possibly do all that would be needed of a carpenter? She was almost reluctant to ask the next question. "And, will he pay you?"

JJ shrugged as though it had not occurred to him to ask about money. "A little, but he says I can have as many offcuts of wood as I want to use."

Clara shook her head. Offcuts of wood might provide the crutches he needed, but they wouldn't put food on the table. "Have you spoken to Dad about this?"

"I've tried," JJ said.

That was probably about the sum of it. Clara managed to get so little sense in talking to their father that she didn't suppose JJ would fare any better. She wondered if perhaps Samuel could talk to JJ about continuing his education. There must be something they could do.

On Sunday, Clara prepared to visit Mrs Langham. The week's order for stockings was worryingly low and her father seemed to have worked well in the last couple of days. At worst she would have to work in the evenings when she came in from school that week.

"I'm sorry to say Samuel isn't here at present. He received an invitation from an old school friend who doesn't live too far away and has gone for the weekend. I can certainly talk to him about Master Phipps when he's home," Mrs Langham said after Clara had poured out all her concerns.

Clara felt disappointed not to see Samuel in person. Of course, she told herself, it was because she wanted to talk to him about JJ, but her heart felt heavy as she walked home thinking that Samuel would soon go up to Cambridge and she'd miss him very much.

JJ said no more about leaving the school and Clara forbore from asking. She had no idea whether Samuel had spoken with him and was reluctant to ask, as JJ would be unhappy to think she had talked about him in that way.

She saw nothing of Samuel outside of school in the last few weeks of term and on the last day he was packed, ready to travel once again. This time he was travelling to Paris with the family of a friend, before heading straight to university. For once he had waited for her after school, so he could say goodbye in person.

"And will you write to me again?" he asked, taking her hands earnestly in his.

Clara felt a blush rise to her cheeks. "I should like that, as long as you have an address."

"I will write just as soon as I do. Farewell, dearest Clara. I hope I shall see you soon."

As Samuel let go of her hands to leave, Clara felt a lump in her throat and tears threatening to spring to her eyes. She swallowed hard, mumbled a final goodbye and rushed from the school, before Samuel could look at her face too closely.

When she arrived home, Clara presumed JJ's better mood and broad grin was because school was over for another term. That changed, when he told her that it was not only the term that was finished, but that his formal school education was now at an end. Clara sighed wondering what lay ahead.

Every day, after Samuel's departure, Clara felt that life was rather less bright. But she had little time to think with all the work she needed to do.

JJ began working with Mr Bailey immediately. He left the house at a regular early hour and didn't return until the end of the working day. He seemed happier than Clara had ever seen him and when he proudly presented her with his small recompense at the end of the week Clara shared some of that delight, as it was more than she was expecting him to bring home.

"I said I had an apprenticeship," JJ sounded annoyed.

"I know, but…"

"Even you don't believe I can do things." JJ almost spat the words at his sister before manoeuvring himself out of the kitchen.

Clara sank into a chair. Was JJ right? Of course she

believed in him, but how could he ever earn a proper living as he was? There was so much he couldn't do. She would apologise to him later and ask him to tell her about all that he was doing. She'd been so busy building her own career so that she might provide a home for him, that she hardly knew him anymore.

The money JJ brought home would certainly help. He seemed to eat so much and, when their father didn't appear for a meal and his was left cold the following morning, JJ would often take it to eat for his lunch. Clara hoped that her father was eating sufficient, but watching him day by day, as he became increasingly distant and withdrawn, she doubted that was the case. She asked him several times if he had a particular problem that she might be able to help with, but he was never forthcoming and told her she needn't worry about him. She knew that not to be true, but nothing she said led to her father saying more.

As the bright days of autumn with their blue skies and heavy dew gave way to November's dense grey fog, Clara had little opportunity for anything other than working. Between her teaching, her own continuing learning, fulfilling the orders for stockings that her father couldn't keep up with and caring for the family, she barely knew what day it was. On the rare occasions she was able to visit Mrs Langham, as soon as she sank into the easy chair by the fire it was all she could do to stay awake.

Although Samuel wrote to them both, he included different stories in his letters, and they exchanged the tales he had written to them. As they recounted his adventures, Clara wondered if in some ways they weren't both trying to live vicariously through things they couldn't have. For her it was the college place and the life that went with it that she envied, but for Mrs Langham it was as much the youth and vitality that she wished to reclaim through her nephew.

"Samuel seems to be having a grand time at Cambridge," Mrs Langham said one day the following spring. "He still manages to write to his old aunt, but I've not seen him since Christmas and can only hope he will come in the summer."

Clara thought how much she would like to see him but said nothing.

"I see from your face that you miss him too." Mrs Langham was smiling at Clara.

Clara sat bolt upright in her chair. "Why yes, for the conversation about books and teaching of course."

Mrs Langham nodded, but the wry smile suggested she didn't altogether believe Clara's protestations. "Maybe we will see him in June. Shall I send word to you if I hear when he's coming home? Although I dare say he'll write that news to you as well."

"Oh, no. I wouldn't want you to go to any trouble. I'll try my best to call on you whether Samuel's home or not." Clara felt flustered and as though she were tying herself up with string.

Mrs Langham nodded but said no more.

With term at an end, although her father was not spending the hours needed at the knitting frame, Clara could complete his work and still have time on a Sunday to visit Mrs Langham. It was on her third such visit that summer when Samuel opened the door with a flourish and grinning made a slight bow.

"Miss Phipps, how nice to see you. Pray, do come in."

Clara could feel herself blushing as she went in ahead of Samuel.

"We're taking tea in the library," he said, in order to direct her along the hall.

The afternoon passed pleasantly, with Samuel asking as much about her family and life at the British School as recounting tales of his days at Cambridge.

As the mantle clock struck the hour for the second time, Clara looked up surprised. "Oh my. I must be getting back. The time has rather run away from me."

"May I walk you home?" Samuel asked, getting up as she did.

"No." The word was out of her mouth without thinking. How could she possibly let Samuel see where she lived? Of course, logically he already knew where it was and most likely had passed by many more times than when they met as children, but oh the shame she would feel at their poverty now. "I'm sorry, I should have said, that is kind of you, but I'd rather walk alone." Clara's heart sank as she saw the look of dejection which crossed Samuel's face. It was no good, she couldn't undo what she'd said.

She bid Mrs Langham farewell and held her head high as she left the room. She wondered what they would say once she'd left. Mrs Langham had been to the house and perhaps might understand. She hadn't meant to be rude to Samuel and now thought her own discomfort at him coming to the house might have been better than how her rudeness had left her feeling.

She looked at their shabby home as she arrived back. It had deteriorated so much since her mother died. She could think of a long list of things which needed fixing, but her father never had the time or the inclination to attend to them and they certainly had no money left at the end of the week to pay for anyone else to do the work. She wished they were on better terms with Hannah's family. Then maybe her Frank could have helped, but unless Clara was to do the repairs herself, they would probably remain undone. What did she know about replacing a cracked pane of glass, or repainting the window frames? When she entered the house, she went through to the empty workroom and wept.

All week Clara worried about the upset she had caused to Samuel, but she wanted to see him in person and with the amount of knitting and housework she needed to do, could do nothing until the following Sunday. However, by her next visit to Mrs Langham, Samuel had already left. Clara felt an overwhelming sadness that she couldn't give him a full and proper explanation and apology. All she could do was write to him, but how could she explain her fear that he would think less of her, when in writing it seemed such a silly notion and suggested she trusted so little in their friendship? Several times she took up her pen to write but could find no way to explain to him. His friendship meant the world to her and losing it would be unbearable. She took another sheet of paper and began.

'My dearest Samuel,

I can do nothing but apologise for my rudeness to you when you offered to walk me home. We have always been honest with each other, as friends should be, so I will endeavour to explain.

Your home is such a beautiful place, well cared for and tended. Where I call home is so different. It is not the smallness which concerns me, and God knows I do all I can to keep it clean and tidy, but we are a poor family, and our house is in need of much repair.

When I visit your aunt, she treats me with such respect that I sometimes forget my own background, but seeing my own home through your eyes, I fear you would think less of me. It reminded me how unworthy of your friendship I am and so I reacted without thought.

There, it is said. I'm sorry.

Your humble servant and friend

Clara Phipps.'

Clara reread the words she had written and sighed. Whatever would Samuel think when he read it? Perhaps she should simply burn it on the fire, but she had to do something. She took a deep breath and placed it in an envelope. If she posted it immediately and didn't allow herself further thought maybe she would sleep better again.

Every day, Clara waited and hoped for a reply from Samuel. When two weeks had elapsed and she still hadn't heard, Clara convinced herself that maybe it was for the best. Hers and Samuel's backgrounds were different, and it may be less painful to part now, than at some point in the future when he found a suitable woman to be his wife. The thought of how much she would miss him and his letters felt unbearable, but if she concentrated on her work, she knew the pain would lessen in time.

Having reconciled herself to a future without hearing from Samuel, she was taken by surprise when a letter in his scrawling hand arrived the following week. A shock ran through her as she picked it up and despite being about to start preparing dinner, she took it to the back room to open with some privacy.

'My very dearest Clara,

Oh, how I wish I had understood your concern so that I could have taken away the pain you were feeling. I would have replied sooner but was away for a week and have today returned to my lodgings.

In all our conversations about the importance of education and about giving people equal opportunities, have you not understood that I do not judge a person by their station in life, when they have had no chance to make it otherwise? I do not think of you in terms of where you live or of your background, but of the person you are and the wonderful times we spend together. Do you not know me well enough to know my friendship is sincere?

We have talked a little about my wanting to make a real difference, but this shows me exactly why I must do so. I know there is more than education which needs to be fixed and that children cannot both go to school and work to help support their family. However, in my mind they should not have to work in such a manner.

If I was insensitive to how you might feel, then forgive me and let us remain friends. There is so much I should like to share with you of my ideas and your letter has made me the more determined that I want my teaching to be to help those who need it, not only those who can pay.

Your loyal friend and servant
Samuel Hurst.'

Clara read it through a second time. She wished Samuel were there so they could talk about the things he'd written. Recently they had discussed the changes needed in education provision. As far as the wider issues were concerned, she wanted time to think about them. She could see no way that any major change could be made, but she wanted to hear what Samuel thought. Then a smile broke across her face. However important those things were, right now, what meant most to her was that she had not lost his friendship. She put the letter away carefully, wanting time to think before replying.

CHAPTER 15

1857

As summer turned to autumn, their father was absent more and more often. Clara thought they'd be better without a knitting frame to pay rent on, as it was almost impossible for her to find the hours to finish the outstanding work, but she knew her father wouldn't hear of it.

"Maybe you should leave the factory and work at home," she said to Martha one night when her sister finally came in. She could earn more than she was doing at the factory, certainly at full speed of working anyway.

"And be 'ere on me own all day? Why would I want to do that?"

Clara took a deep breath. Now wasn't the time to get into an argument with her sister. "Because Dad isn't coping being here on his own. He'd be here too."

Martha snorted. "If Dad were 'ere, I wouldn't need to be. Besides, he's no company, as well you know. Why don't you do it?"

Because she could earn more as a teacher, now that she'd had some of her annual increments. But what was the use in trying to explain? It was clear Martha was determined not to change her employment. Clara decided to try a different tack. "You wouldn't have to get up as early or finish so late. There wouldn't be the walk every day."

"I like the walk. Stan walks wi' me and we 'ave a real laugh together."

"Stan? Who's Stan?" Clara hadn't heard him mentioned before, but then she didn't often have any length of conversation with Martha these days.

"Stan's me boyfriend."

Clara almost gasped. The shock must have shown on her face.

"Don't worry, I won't be as stupid as Hannah."

Clara raised an eyebrow. That was easy enough to say, but Martha was already as old as Hannah had been when she'd married Frank. Clara forced a smile and said, "And do we get to meet him sometime?"

Martha's face softened and, in the lamplight, Clara could see the blush spread across her cheeks.

"Maybe."

Over the following months, Clara continued to struggle to complete all the work that needed doing. She approached her father again in the hope he would tell her what the problem was. Some days he produced almost a full quantity of stockings, but others he completed almost none.

"Dad."

John Phipps looked up absently at his daughter.

"I'm worried about you."

John blinked as though trying to focus and then squinted.

"Dad," Clara said, wondering if this might in part be the problem. "Can you see properly?"

Clara's father seemed to deflate in front of her. He ran his hand through his remaining hair and stood up from where he was sitting.

Suddenly, Clara understood. It wasn't only that her father was still grieving for their mother, though he obviously was. When the daylight was dim, he couldn't see well enough to work the frame properly. From the times he fell most behind, Clara realised that he struggled less with the plain stockings, but as soon as the order demanded a pattern, he was floundering. Candles and lanterns couldn't provide him with enough light to see clearly. Why had she never worked that out before? Not that it was a problem that was easy to fix, but she could have talked to him and found a solution together.

She went to his side. "Oh, Dad, why didn't you say something?"

When he turned toward her, he had tears in his eyes. "What could I say, the useless, broken man that I've become? I can't provide for me own family. I see you working all hours God sends and there's note I can do to help."

"We should give up the frame entirely," Clara said with a degree of certainty that surprised herself. "We would be better off without the cost and worry of it, and I can't keep going like this."

Her father shook his head. "Without the knitting, I'm nothing. I 'ave to be able to work." His next words were said with more force than she thought she'd ever heard from her father. "If I can't work and can't do ote for me family, I'd be better dead."

Clara gasped. "No, Dad. No. Never. Oh Dad, you don't need to provide for us now. We're adults. You have provided for us all the years of being children. You've done your work. Your youngest child is out at work. Now allow us to care for you. We can manage. Somehow, we can manage."

John Phipps didn't reply to his daughter. He picked up his hat and coat and went out into the night.

Clara sat in the kitchen and sobbed like she never had before, not even when their mother died. She felt as though the weight of their lives rested on her and she wanted to help her father, but how? She needed someone she could talk to, but her father would be mortified if he thought she'd told anyone about his problems. Who could she trust? Who would be there for her?

For a fleeting moment she thought of Samuel, but he was away at college. Perhaps Mrs Langham might be possible. She knew she could trust her friend. But what could she say and what could anyone do?

Clara didn't complain that winter, as the amount of work she needed to finish to meet her father's quota increased. Now she knew what the problem was, she made plans for the work as soon as she saw that the requirement was for patterned stockings, or if the weather meant the light was particularly dim. She worked by candlelight before she left for her own job, and in the afternoon if her father wasn't at the frame she would continue as soon as she came home. It meant she had no time to visit Mrs Langham, but she did her best to complete everything at home and wrote occasional letters to Samuel when she could spare the penny for postage and when she didn't fall asleep with the pen in her hand.

Mornings were the hardest. She dragged herself out of bed in the early hours to get breakfast for Martha and the rest of the family, and to get a head start on the stockings before leaving for the school. By nighttime, Clara fell into bed exhausted and slept soundly until the next day's chores began.

Never before had she counted the weeks off to midwinter and the days starting to lengthen. She thanked God for every bright sunny day when her father could work more easily and stay longer at the frame. How she wished that she could go to Hannah for help, but that wasn't an option. Nor was there anyone else who Clara could turn to. Her respite in the week was the chapel services and those stood out like a pool of calm in an otherwise turbulent river.

February was especially dismal. Clara arrived home many days to find her father's work undone and him having gone out, she knew not where. When she asked him, he simply waved a hand dismissively, as much as to say he went nowhere in particular.

As Clara was up late knitting the stockings, she was normally still awake when he came home. She was later than normal one Thursday night, as the order would be collected the following morning, and she was behind. She was surprised her father had not returned as the mantel clock struck midnight. This was unusual and when, half an hour later, Clara went up to bed she wondered if she should stay up waiting, but she was far too tired. He'd be home when he was good and ready and wouldn't thank her for treating him like a child.

When he hadn't returned the following morning, Clara felt sick with worry. She said nothing to JJ or Martha, after all, what could they do? They all needed to be about their work. He would return in his own good time. He always had.

She left a note with the stockings to be collected by the master who issued their orders, in case her father still hadn't returned and set off for school.

Clara was reading a story to her group of children in the far corner of the room and had her back to the classroom door. In unison all the children stood from their desks and chorused, "Good morning, Mrs Farmer."

Clara scrambled up from her chair and turned toward Mrs Farmer. She was waving for the children to be seated but beckoning for Clara to follow her.

"Miss Dowson, take over please."

Millie moved so she was in front of the larger group of children. After their several years of working together, she was able to pick up the class with little difficulty.

Clara followed Mrs Farmer to the office wondering what could possibly be so urgent. She was surprised to find both Mr Cooper and Mr Farmer in the office and they stood as she entered. She looked around the group and froze. All she registered, as he held his hat in his hands before him, was the grave expression on Mr Cooper's face.

"Whatever's happened? Dear God, not JJ." She didn't sit but reached for Mr Cooper's arm.

He gently took her hand in his. "Sit down, Miss Phipps, please." He led her gently to the chair but continued to stand and hold her hand in his. "It's your father."

"My father?" She was flooded with confusion. "But he'll be at home now, working. I left his breakfast for when he came in."

"Miss Phipps, I'm sorry to have to tell you, your father was found in the river this morning. He must have fallen in last night."

Clara stared up into Mr Cooper's face. This couldn't be true. Why would her father be in the river? He couldn't swim. Whatever was he doing? Then she looked again at Mr Cooper, and it hit her. This was no mistake, and she crumpled. A thought struck her. "I should have called a search party when he didn't come home last night. This is my fault. We could have saved him. If only I hadn't gone to bed."

"Miss Phipps, none of this is your fault. I don't suppose there would have been any chance of finding him last night. None of us would have known where to look."

Clara registered that Mr and Mrs Farmer were sitting like spectators of some tragic play unfolding before them. Except the play was her life.

"Whatever shall we do?" She stood up suddenly. "I must go to Martha and JJ."

"I think you should have some tea before doing anything. You're in a state of shock. Then I will go with you." Mr Cooper looked pointedly at Mrs Farmer.

"Yes, of course. Tea." She seemed almost disappointed as she left the room.

A thought hit Clara. "Was it…? Did he…? Was it an accident?"

"It doesn't look as though anyone else was involved, if that is what you mean. There were no signs of a struggle."

Clara shook her head. That hadn't occurred to her, but she had no idea how to say what was on her mind. "I'm sorry, I meant…"

But Mr Cooper seemed to understand. "There's no reason to think it was anything other than an accident. You may put your mind at ease, Miss Phipps."

Clara nodded, but still she wondered.

The funeral of John Phipps was not a large affair. Although Hannah was present, her family were not, which saddened Clara almost as much as the day itself. She thought how hard life must be for her sister and worried for her.

"Are you happy with your life, Hannah?" It seemed all

the more important to ask her, after having lost their father.

"Of course," Hannah replied, rather too quickly.

Clara squeezed her sister's hand. She wanted Hannah to know she was there if she was needed but could say no more.

Grandma Herbert's arthritis was now so bad, that the walk was too much for her and they saw her rarely. A number of people from the chapel attended, including Mr Cooper, but other than that the people in attendance were Mr Bailey to whom JJ was apprenticed and, sitting quietly at the back of the chapel, Mrs Langham. Seeing her there, Clara didn't want to be the one coping for everyone else. She wanted to fall into Mrs Langham's arms as though Mrs Langham were her mother and sob for all she had lost.

With three, instead of four, of them now working, they could ill afford to lose more money than was necessary and Martha returned to work the afternoon of the funeral. Thankfully neither the school nor Mr Bailey were docking Clara or JJ's wages for the hours they would miss that day, which at least gave them the afternoon to reflect on the life which lay ahead. Clara couldn't possibly burden JJ with too much of her concern. He might be apprenticed, but at still less than thirteen years of age, he was little more than a child.

"I think we shall have to move house," she said, testing for a reaction.

"Can we move closer to where Mr Bailey lives? I'd find it easier not to go so far."

Having expected JJ not to want to move, she was delighted by his response. "If there is anywhere we can afford. Otherwise, we might have to move in with others of our family. I don't suppose Hannah…" She didn't finish the sentence. Of course, Hannah and Frank would not welcome them. Besides, moving to Blaby would make the distance much too far for JJ, even if she could walk to Wigston for the school. Then she had Martha to think about. She'd talk with her later.

She had already approached the Master to return the knitting frame, although if they were to move, maybe the house would be taken by another framework knitter. Her pay had increased each year that she had been a pupil teacher, but despite that, none of them were on full adult wages and although they lived frugally, it would be hard to make ends meet. She did her sums again and thought they might be able to manage.

Sorting out their father's meagre belongings took little time. He still had a dress of their mother's. She drew it close to her and breathed in the smell of the fabric. Nothing but moth balls and damp. Had she expected to still smell her mother after the years that had passed? She would alter the dress and make it wearable by either herself or Martha. With a good wash and airing it should be passable.

On her return from school the following day, she was delighted to find a letter addressed to herself in a handwriting both familiar and dear to her. She opened it carefully with a knife from the kitchen.

"Samuel," she said aloud, holding the letter to her, before drawing it from the envelope.

The letter was brief, expressing his condolences and hoping that he might see Clara when he was home next. He would write a longer letter soon but was thinking of her the previous day.

She sat back and sighed. How kind of him to write, but she realised her feelings were more than simple gratitude and the prospect of seeing him when he came home was one which appealed to her very much.

CHAPTER 16

1858

To Clara's surprise, it was the Master of the knitting frame who presented a possible solution to their problem.

"If you'd permit me to make a suggestion, young lady? There's a journeyman knitter in need of both frame and accommodation. Might I be so bold as to suggest he lodges here and takes over the frame?"

Clara was dumbstruck. She had never thought to have a stranger living with them in the house, but she could see the merit in the suggestion. If he paid his board and lodging it would give her no more work than she'd had previously, but a steady contribution which would solve their immediate financial problems.

Except for no longer having access to the workshop, apart from to keep it clean, it was by far the best arrangement for them all, although it meant JJ had the same distance to go to Mr Bailey's workshop.

Their lodger, a middle-aged gentleman who had moved to the area from Nottingham, worked all hours and kept himself to himself, other than for mealtimes, which he normally took back to his own room. Were it not for the sound of the knitting frame they would barely have known he was there.

They were a quiet household. Her father's childhood nickname for her of 'mouse', could be applied to any of them, save for Martha. But Martha was seldom home and when she was, she had little to say to her sister. As a result, Clara was surprised when a few months after their father died, Martha asked if the two of them could go for a walk one Sunday afternoon.

Clara had wondered about paying a visit to Mrs Langham, but as it was so unusual, she was intrigued by her sister's request.

Other than pleasantries, they said little until they were into the country lanes.

"Clara."

"Yes." Clara knew better than to try to push the conversation along.

"How will I know when the time's right?"

Clara had not understood her sister's question. "Right for what?"

"You know, with Stan."

Clara gasped and turned to face her sister. It wasn't that she had no experience of these matters, nor that the Bible clearly taught it was something she shouldn't do before being wed, it was their elder sister who came to mind. "Have you learnt nothing from what happened to Hannah?" She wanted to say Martha was much too young, but she was eighteen. She was older than Hannah was when Robert was born.

"I'd be careful," Martha said, as though trying to convince herself.

Clara felt a rush of tenderness toward her sister and caught Martha's hands in her own. "Martha dear, if it was so easy to be careful there wouldn't be so many weddings in haste."

"But Hannah did it deliberately. She said so."

Clara nodded. She'd realised that was likely the case,

but Hannah would probably make a different choice if she could go back now.

"Do you love him?"

Martha nodded, her lips twitching at the corners.

"Then why not marry him?" Although desperately wanting her sister to be happy, Clara hoped it wouldn't happen too soon. For one thing, she wanted Martha to be sure she was doing it for the right reasons.

Martha sank down onto the grass of the meadow. "Because 'e ain't asked me. I don't s'pose 'e's thought about it."

"And this isn't the way to make him think about it. Oh Martha, please don't make the same mistake as Hannah and end up unhappy."

"But I've got to marry someone, and it may as well be Stan."

What would their mother say if she were alive now? Clara even wondered what Grandma Herbert might say, but she didn't want to ask her. How could she counsel her sister when she had absolutely no experience of these things and never expected to marry? It was no good her imploring Martha to be patient. That was something Martha had never been. She briefly wondered how many people would marry if there wasn't already a baby on the way.

"You must make your own choices," Clara said to her sister. Most important was that Martha should be happy.

It was a fair walk to the cemetery where her parents were buried, but, as often as she could, Clara picked flowers from the hedgerow and took them to the grave. Her parent's grave had no headstone. That was a luxury they couldn't afford, but Clara knew the plot and sat a while wondering how different things might be if they were still alive. What advice would they give to Martha? They weren't able to prevent the mistakes Hannah had made, so maybe not much.

Perhaps of all the siblings it was Clara's life that would be most changed if they were still here, but except for their loss she wasn't unhappy. She loved teaching and hoped that as soon as she was fully qualified, she might be taken on. It would be hard to move to find a position elsewhere, especially with JJ spending so much time with Mr Bailey.

"It's kind of him," she said to her deceased parents, "to take such trouble with JJ. I don't suppose JJ can use all of the tools to do useful work. It's hard for him to stand without support and use both hands to work. I suppose if I have to move to find employment, JJ will simply have to come." It was no good worrying about that now, she still had another couple of years until her pupillage would be finished.

She said her farewells to the silent grave and walked away, turning once as though to wave goodbye to a departing friend, but instead weighed down with the sadness the visits always brought. Clara walked back along Welford Road toward Wigston. Her thoughts were distant, and her steps took her to Mrs Langham's without any conscious thought.

"Come in, come in."

Samuel's face beamed as he opened the door to her, and it immediately lifted her spirits. "Why, I had no idea you were home."

"I arrived yesterday. I have a great deal of studying to do before my final year and I can do that as easily in the library here as I can anywhere. We're in Aunt Frances's study. Come through."

Clara had never entered Mrs Langham's study in all the times she'd visited. In fact, she didn't know Mrs Langham had such a room. As she entered, Clara gasped. It was the most beautiful room, overlooking the garden and had sunlight flooding in. She admired the wood panelling around the walls and the mahogany desk with green leather inlaid into the surface.

Mrs Langham waived a hand dismissively. "This was my husband's," she said by way of explanation. "I took it over when he died. I'd have chosen something rather more simple."

"But it's perfect," Clara said, still looking around her in awe. "If I were ever to have a study, I'd want it to be exactly like this."

Mrs Langham smiled as though she appreciated the comment. "Now, sit down child and Samuel will fetch us both tea. I'd say to look at you that might be needed and then perhaps you'll tell me what's troubling you. I can send Samuel on some errand to give us time." She looked pointedly at her nephew.

"Oh but, Aunty, I would like to talk to Miss Phipps too."

He sounded like a petulant child and Clara smiled.

"And you may do so afterwards, when you walk her home."

Clara frowned. She remembered her former rebuff to Samuel and was still anxious lest he think poorly of her for where she lived, but this time she would not refuse.

Clara found Mrs Langham to be a good listener. When she outlined what Martha had raised with her, the older lady laughed heartily.

"Oh, excuse me," Mrs Langham said, wiping a tear from her eye. "The problems of the young never change a great deal. It was no better in my day. In my experience, there is almost nothing you can say to Martha which will influence the decisions she takes where a young man is concerned. You will have to let her make her own choices, and hope they are the right ones."

Clara found Mrs Langham's words soothing and was in far better spirits by the time that she and Samuel set off for her home later in the afternoon. As they walked, they talked of teaching and he of all his future plans. Other than getting by day to day, it had never occurred to Clara that she could plan any kind of future. She simply wished to earn sufficient to provide a home for her and JJ in the years to come.

"You've put yourself out quite enough," Clara said as they reached the corner of Moat Street. "I shall be fine from here." She said it not because she was tired of Samuel's company, but because she still couldn't bear the thought of him coming into the house and seeing how shabby it was compared to his own home, despite all he'd said.

Samuel looked chastened. "I'm sorry, I shouldn't have let my aunt talk you into allowing me to walk with you. I hoped, however, that my words might have given you reassurance."

"Oh, they have." She couldn't snub him again. She took a deep breath. "I'm sorry, I've never been walked home before. I don't want to put you out."

Samuel's face brightened. "I don't think you could if you tried, unless you were to say that we were no longer friends. In that case I would be very put out indeed."

He laughed and she realised he was teasing her. She wanted to say that he should come back to the house after all but couldn't find the words.

Then he put his arm through hers as they continued to

walk along Moat Street. Clara's mouth was dry, and she could feel her heartbeat fluttering.

As they reached her home, he stopped and turned to her. "Good day, dear Clara," he said, taking her hand and bestowing a kiss upon it. "I sincerely hope that I shall see you soon."

"And I too."

As Samuel gave her a little wave and turned to go back to his aunt's house, Clara was at once disappointed that he'd gone.

Clara visited Mrs Langham again the following week as much in the hope of seeing Samuel as to see his aunt.

"I wanted to talk to you on your own," Mrs Langham said quite pointedly. "I rather think you're keeping Samuel at arm's length and I'm wondering why?"

The older lady sat waiting patiently, giving Clara the sort of look which said that one way or another she intended to have to answer.

Clara blinked. She was used to Mrs Langham being straight talking, but this had rather taken her by surprise. How could she tell this lovely lady that despite knowing it meant nothing to Mrs Langham; Clara was still ashamed of her family's poverty and the state of their tiny home when compared to this one? How could she explain that she was frightened of her own feelings toward Samuel, when it could never lead to more than friendship not only because of their difference in class, but because of the life Clara had chosen.

"Will you tell me, or do I have to say what I think may be the problem?"

"Oh, Mrs Langham." Clara sighed heavily. "It's just…"

"My dear," Mrs Langham said. "I'm not getting any

younger. I would like to see my nephew settled before I depart this world. Do you love him?"

Clara gasped. That was something she had not expected to be asked, and she had no idea how to answer. She felt her cheeks flush. Clara wished she could say nothing, but there was something about her friend that always demanded answers, and honest ones at that.

"How can I know? I have never loved any man to know what those feelings are and besides, what is the point? I can do nothing about it even if I do."

Mrs Langham nodded and was quiet for a moment. "You can call me fanciful if you wish, and maybe it comes of reading too much fiction, but there are certain notions I find quite ridiculous. Whether someone is born rich or born into poverty is an accident of birth and need not define them. I am more concerned about what lies in their soul than whether they think they are deserving of unmerited recognition. Or for that matter deserve recognition that they do not believe is due to them. And that is how I have brought Samuel up, I hope."

As abruptly as she had begun, Mrs Langham stopped her lecture and Clara was dumbstruck, with no idea either how to respond or if she was expected to. They sat drinking tea in silence for a short while, her mind in a whirl. The silence was broken by Samuel returning from the errand he had been on and, having clearly had no idea of the discussion which had taken place in his absence, he launched into a story of an encounter he had had minutes ago with a cart whose driver had little control of his horse.

Once again Samuel walked Clara home and, on the doorstep, bid her farewell.

Clara felt a pang. She had intended to invite him in but could say nothing. The things Mrs Langham had said ran through her head, but what was the point? She couldn't give up teaching and lose her way to provide a home for her brother and sister, even if the disparity in their positions could be overlooked.

By Clara's next visit to Mrs Langham, two weeks later, Samuel had left in a hurry on the invite of a friend to study together. The friend's family had taken a house in London for the summer and Samuel was to meet them there. Clara sighed, thinking how much she might like to visit London, quite apart from how she'd miss Samuel.

A week later she received a letter from him, telling her of Tower Bridge, The British Museum and the Houses of Parliament.

'One day, I should like to sit in that great house and work to make our country a better place.'

She read his words and smiled. She'd never thought about the work politicians must do, certainly not in terms of high ideals and improving lives. She thought of all the people around her, and wondered how many of their concerns could be made better. As far as she knew, while there had been much talk of a House of Lords Commission report on framework knitting, it had done nothing to ease the problems that existed in the industry. Samuel was a good man. Perhaps one day he would be able to do as he said in his letter.

He didn't return before the start of the autumn term, but they exchanged further letters, and their discussions turned increasingly to wider world issues, some of which until now Clara had never given any thought. Of course, they talked of education and the need for it to be more widely available, but Clara couldn't see how that could ever be the case while children needed to earn money to help their families pay for food. She wondered what Mr

Charles Dickens thought could be done. He was undertaking a tour of towns of England, and she would like to have gone to hear him speak, but she had no spare money to cover such frivolity.

On her return to school that autumn, Clara was called into the office, where Mrs Farmer was waiting for her.

"I'm sorry to have to say that Miss Dowson will not be returning to the school."

Clara was wide-eyed and was glad she was already seated. "Why ever not?" The words were out before she considered if it was appropriate for her to ask the question.

"She is with child." Mrs Farmer spat the words out as though it was the worst thing she could say about anyone. "And I don't need to tell you that any relations with the opposite sex are not acceptable if you are to be a mistress at this school."

Clara felt herself blushing, though she'd done nothing to cause concern. "Yes, Ma'am," she said and tried to prevent herself frowning as the thought occurred to her that it had clearly been acceptable at some point for Mr and Mrs Farmer themselves, but that was a thought she would not be sharing.

"You are a considerable way through your pupillage, Miss Phipps. It would be a shame for anything to prevent you from becoming a qualified teacher."

Mrs Farmer stood up and Clara realised with that general warning she was dismissed from the meeting. She wanted to ask if anyone was to be taken on in Miss Dowson's place, but she would have to wait to find that out. Clara would need to work harder until the school recruited a new pupil teacher. The school had grown in numbers each year so there was more to do. Beside that, she and Millie had worked together so long that they knew each other's ways. She thought they were close, but clearly not close enough for Millie to have told her about her young man. Clara sighed.

By Sunday, Clara was exhausted and grateful for the partial rest it bestowed. She still enjoyed the quiet time of contemplation which the services at chapel afforded in her busy week, but most of all she enjoyed the few short hours of freedom from responsibility that came in the afternoon, once teaching in the Sunday school was over. The weather was bright, and she planned a walk out into the country lanes and then to call at Mrs Langham's house on her way back. She was preparing to go out when she realised Martha was sitting at the table with tears streaming down her cheeks.

Clara's first thought was that Martha had found herself in the same position as Millie Dowson and as Hannah years before. She braced herself for her sister's revelation. "Whatever's the matter?" She sat down next to Martha and drew her sister toward her.

"Stan don't want to see me anymore."

Clara gasped. "You're not... you know?" If the answer was yes, this would be a thousand times worse than Hannah.

Martha shook her head and tears splashed onto the table. "I wouldn't. That's why 'e don't want to see me. I thought 'e loved me."

Clara let out a long slow breath of relief, while trying to find words of comfort for Martha. "Then perhaps if he isn't interested in how you feel, he isn't the right man for you."

"I listened to what you said and decided you were right."

Clara blinked. She certainly hadn't expected her sister

199

to say that. She didn't think Martha had ever listened to her before. She thanked God that she had chosen to do so when it mattered most. Clara wished she could find words of wisdom now, but all she could do was hold Martha close and let her cry out her grief at losing Stan.

CHAPTER 17

1858

Clara hated seeing Martha's distress at losing Stan and hoped they would resolve their differences. Much as knowing her sister wouldn't be marrying soon eased some of Clara's worries about money, she would much rather have seen her sister happy. As long as Clara could qualify as a teacher, she would be able to support both herself and JJ with comparatively little difficulty. Although she would earn less than a man in the same position, she thought they could manage. Until then she depended on both Martha's money and that of their lodger. If Martha were to move out, they could yet have to find a cheaper place to live, but of course they'd do that if it were needed.

With her own final examination getting ever nearer, Clara wanted all the help she could get with studying. Mr Farmer had told her that she was well prepared, but she wasn't so sure. In every spare moment she could find, she visited Mrs Langham, who was delighted to go through things with her in the same way they used to study.

"Samuel will be applying for positions as a schoolmaster himself soon," Mrs Langham said on one such visit. "There are a couple more terms until he graduates." She threw her hands up as she said, "Where all those years have gone, I have no idea. I would like it if he were to be local, but I'm not sure if there will be schools close by with suitable positions."

Mrs Langham looked as though waiting for a reaction, but Clara said nothing on the subject. She had no idea what to say. She had resigned herself to the fact that Samuel would have to go wherever he could find an appointment and that may not be local to Great Wigston.

"Will he be home for Christmas?"

Mrs Langham paused, looking as though she were thinking. "Indeed, he will, so why don't I arrange something special? It has been a long time since I've organised a little gathering."

Clara wondered what she had in mind, but didn't feel she could ask.

Clara was surprised to find Martha singing when she arrived home that afternoon. It was so unusual these days that it made her smile.

"What's put you in such a good mood?" she asked her sister, who was also preparing a meal for them all.

"Stan says 'e's missed me and don't want us ever to fall out again."

Clara sat down heavily, her thoughts racing. Did that mean Martha had given in? Would Stan ask Martha to marry him? Tentatively she said. "How lovely. What brought that about?"

"I went to see Hannah and asked 'er advice."

Clara's heart sank.

"She said I should make 'im jealous. I made sure 'e saw me talking and laughing wi' Charlie Shepherd. Before I knew it, Stan wa' standing between us and askin' if we could go for a walk."

Clara sighed. It sounded as though Martha might not

be being fair to either man, but what did Clara know about romance? She had so little experience. All she could do was hope that Martha was more sensible than Hannah had been.

"How is Hannah?"

"She seems all right. 'Er Frank weren't there. I saw 'im go in the pub, so thought it would be safe to visit."

"Does she still have bruises on her face?"

Martha shook her head. "Note wa' showing, but she didn't say much, 'cause Robert wa' there."

Clara nodded. She hoped sincerely that her older sister was safe and well.

A few days later, Clara was surprised to receive a written invitation from Mrs Langham. It asked her to take tea on the Sunday before Christmas. Her surprise was soon replaced with a thrill of excitement, realising this was Mrs Langham's way to ensure she visited when Samuel would be there. It would be lovely to see him again and to be able to discuss in person some of the ideas they shared in their letters.

Perhaps this time Clara would invite him into her home if he walked her back. She looked around. The house was clean enough, as well as she could keep it, but she had little to furnish the rooms, and they gave off the overwhelming sense of tiredness. Looking about made her want to fetch flowers from the hedgerows to brighten the room, but at this time of year she'd find precious little that wasn't green save for any holly she could find in berry. She could at least make more effort to decorate their home for Christmas than she had done in a while.

"How do I look?" Clara asked Martha before setting off for

Mrs Langham's on the appointed Sunday.

"Clara?" Martha put her head on one side and looked at her sister. "You're twenty-one nearly twenty-two and you've never asked me that before. What's going on?"

Clara felt as a wild animal must do when caught in a snare. "I'm having tea with Mrs Langham, but she especially invited me so I'm making more of an effort."

Martha pursed her lips. "If I didn't know you better, I'd think there wa' a man involved. Oh, Clara, there in't is there? I ain't never known you say anything about a man."

Clara could feel her cheeks heating and wished she'd asked JJ instead of Martha. She couldn't lie to her sister. She couldn't lie to anyone. But she certainly didn't want to give her the impression that Samuel was, or ever could be, anything more than a friend.

"I think Mrs Langham may have invited a larger party for the afternoon. I don't know exactly who will be there." That much was true. She was guessing Samuel, but there could well be others present.

"Wait there."

Martha ran upstairs leaving Clara frowning.

When her sister returned, she pinned a small flower brooch onto Clara's dress. Clara recognised it immediately and gasped.

"Wherever did you get that from?"

"I found it in Mam's things," Martha replied in an off-hand manner.

Clara didn't know whether to be delighted to be wearing something so beautiful that had belonged to their mother, or whether to be angry with her sister for not mentioning it before. "Why did you never say you had it?"

Martha pouted. "Don't be cross. I found it in the wardrobe when Dad died. You and Hannah had your own memories of Mam, but I couldn't remember what she looked like anymore. I wanted something I could 'old and know she'd worn. Something I could 'ave in place of the memories."

"Oh, Martha dear, I'm so sorry. It must be hard not to remember her." She took the brooch from her dress. "Please, you keep it. I don't need to wear any adornment on my dress. I'm sure it will look fine as it is."

Martha pushed her hand away. "Please wear it. Mam would like us to share it."

Clara kissed her sister on the cheek and returned the brooch to her dress.

It was a maid who opened the door to Clara, which was unusual for a Sunday, when even Mrs Langham's housekeeper had a day off. From the sound of voices coming along the hallway, Clara realised that Mrs Langham had invited a number of other people and felt oddly disappointed. Maybe Samuel wouldn't be there at all, but either way she was glad she'd taken care with her appearance.

"Clara, my dear." Mrs Langham was quick to greet her as she entered the room.

Clara looked around to see who she might recognise and was surprised to see Mr and Mrs Farmer among the guests.

"Samuel." Mrs Langham called her nephew over from where he was standing looking out of the window.

"You look about as lost as I'm feeling," Samuel said as he led Clara to a quieter corner. "I had no idea my aunt knew so many people, never mind planned to invite them."

Clara blinked feeling suddenly shy and lost for words.

"I'm home for a couple of weeks for Christmas but need to get back then to study for my finals. It's a busy year. I say, what a beautiful brooch. Was it a present?"

Samuel seemed to be babbling slightly, which Clara put down to his nervousness being surrounded by so many people.

"It was my mother's." She found herself wanting to tell him about how hard Martha found it to remember their mother, but stopped herself, wondering how difficult those thoughts might be for Samuel himself, having lost his own parents so young.

He nodded and fell quiet for a while.

Clara stood with him companionably surveying the room.

Quite suddenly Samuel asked, "Is it strange having the journeyman living in your home?"

Clara blinked. "How odd that you ask. I think little of it, save for the fact that we had to do that in order to pay the rent. They say beggars can't be choosers, and whilst we aren't by any means beggars, we had to accept him being there as the best way to pay our bills." Clara frowned. She didn't normally talk about such matters, even to Samuel, but suddenly she wanted to explain so much more to him. "Whilst our house is small, we're all quite used to sharing it and have never had space that is our own, so it doesn't feel to be a hardship. My home is so different to yours. I'm not sure what you would make of it."

For a moment he looked pained. "I thought you understood that I don't judge people by what they have. We have talked of so much of what is wrong in our country when we write, don't you know that I want to work toward better opportunities for children whatever their backgrounds?"

Clara sighed. They were fine words, but she thought it would take much more than that to bridge the gulf between them. Both Samuel and Mrs Langham might think nothing of their difference, but she knew that others would and whatever she felt, that would surely be enough to keep them apart.

Mrs Langham introduced Clara to other guests. They were mainly much older than she was, and the conversations didn't flow so easily as they did with Samuel, but she was pleased to find that she wasn't nearly as nervous as she had expected to be. She was glad when Samuel came over and offered to walk her home when she was ready.

Although not lengthy, Samuel's letters over the following months were regular. They were filled with tales of the things he needed to study for his examinations and his thoughts on where he might take up an initial teaching appointment to gain experience. He had made no suggestion that he would return to Great Wigston and Clara accepted that their meetings would be infrequent. From time to time, he asked her questions on what she thought about political issues.

'Have you heard that for the first time a woman has been registered as a qualified doctor?'

Clara had not heard of Elizabeth Blackwell, but the importance of the event was clear to her. She was used to the idea that only men undertook such responsible jobs and despite all her time learning with Mrs Langham, found the idea of that not being the case quite strange. But why couldn't women do many of the things which had been the preserve of men? JJ having one leg no more affected the capability of his brain than being a woman did for her. What was missing for them and others to fulfil their potential was education. She smiled. It wasn't only the education of those who were currently excluded that was needed, but in other ways it was equally those who sought to exclude them who needed to be educated. She hoped in the future that might be where Samuel's life would lead.

She in turn wrote telling Samuel of all that went on at home. She gave occasional news of his aunt, but presumed that Mrs Langham would write to him herself, so Clara kept her news mainly to her own family and teaching.

To her surprise, Martha was still walking out with Stan and had, as yet, neither married nor fallen pregnant. She left that part out in writing to Samuel. She couldn't imagine saying such a thing to a man, however well she was getting to know him. She did tell Samuel how proud she was of JJ. He now made his own crutches when replacements were needed and occasionally asked for help to bring back other small items he'd made to help him at home. They served their purposes and considering he was fourteen years old, they were rather good, in Clara's eyes. One of the things JJ made from odd pieces of timber was a small single bed for himself to sleep apart from his sisters. Mr Bailey had brought it home for him in his cart. There was room in their bedroom to squeeze in both that and the one which Clara and Martha shared.

Clara and Samuel's writing continued through to the following summer. Samuel wrote with the news that he had gained his degree, but shortly afterwards was to travel once again and would not be home before starting his new position as a junior teacher in a school outside Cambridge.

"I rather hoped he would seek a position here, so he could be near us both," Mrs Langham said with a sigh, the next time Clara visited.

"Us? Surely it is you he would wish to be close to." Clara frowned.

Mrs Langham let out a hearty laugh. "My dear Clara, haven't you realised he's sweet on you?"

Clara blinked. The thought felt ridiculous. She had never known anyone be sweet on her. Besides, he knew she had to stay in her own teaching position. Why would he ever think otherwise? Perhaps it was a passing fancy and the fact he had moved away showed his feelings were not strong.

With Samuel travelling, their letters became less frequent, and Clara worked hard toward her own examination the following year. This would be her final year as a pupil teacher and Mr Farmer had already intimated that they were likely to have a position for her at the British School once she qualified.

It was the following Christmas when Clara saw Samuel next, a full year since their last meeting and two months since their last letter. Clara felt oddly shy in his company again. It wasn't only that she hadn't seen him. In the intervening time he had become a man and the change in him was considerable. Gone were the youthful looks and ways of his student days and in their place a more serious countenance.

"My dear Clara," he said, taking her hand, "how lovely to see you. You never told me that teaching was such hard work."

Clara laughed, seeing his furrowed brow. "The difference is perhaps that you have a class to yourself, whereas I work still under Mr Ward's guidance."

Samuel nodded. "Simply keeping the boys in order can

take all my energy. Some of them are of a mind that because their parents are paying such high fees, I am in some way their servant rather than their teacher. I should much rather teach less privileged children, I think."

"And sometimes they don't want to be there at all," she said, smiling.

"I know I owe you a letter, but every evening when I return to my lodgings and pick up the pen to write, I find myself dozing long before I have reached the point of writing your name."

His boyhood grin returned to his face, and Clara melted. "I was tired when I started working at the school. It is quite different to working at home, and more so from being a pupil yourself."

Samuel nodded. "Does it get any easier?"

"A little," Clara said, laughing.

Clara was still thinking of her afternoon at Mrs Langham's when she arrived home.

"He's asked me."

Martha was in a great state of agitation when Clara went through the back door.

Clara's thoughts were on Samuel, and she could think of nothing he could possibly be asking her sister. "He's asked you what?"

"To marry 'im, of course."

Clara's eyes widened in surprise. "Who has?"

Martha was shaking her head in exasperation. "Stan of course. Stan has asked me to be 'is wife."

Clara sank into a chair, a smile crossing her face. "Congratulations, that's lovely news. I hope you'll both be very happy." The reality of the situation dawned more slowly. "When will the wedding be?"

"As soon as it can be arranged." Martha jumped up and

down like a child in excitement. "We're going to live with 'is family until we can find somewhere of our own. It's nearer to the factory than 'ere."

Clara nodded. As they had no spare bedroom, with the lodger taking up the second room, that would also prevent having to ask the lodger to leave. However, it would mean less money coming in.

Standing in the chapel for Martha's wedding a few weeks later, Clara was overwhelmed by the sense of having lost most of her family. When Hannah married, both her parents were present, now, Hannah was unable to be there to support her sister, and both their parents were dead and buried. Clara was grateful that despite her arthritis, Grandma Herbert had managed to attend. On the other side of the chapel, Stan's family gathered in a larger group. Unlike Hannah's wedding, Stan's family seemed welcoming and had greetings for them all. Perhaps at least this meant she wouldn't lose Martha as she had Hannah.

Martha looked so happy and as Clara watched her sister walk down the aisle, with JJ giving her away, she felt such pride in both her brother and sister and her mood lifted. They would miss Martha at home, but at least she wouldn't be living far away and maybe she and Stan could join them for a meal from time to time.

Walking back into their home that afternoon seemed strange. Suddenly, the house felt empty. Of course, they still had the lodger, but they rarely saw him. There was just herself and JJ now. She'd known it would come to that at some point, but perhaps she hadn't expected it to happen quite so soon.

When JJ returned from Mr Bailey's workshop in an evening, they ate together and then most often sat by the fireside to read for a while before bed.

It felt strange to Clara to have a bed to herself for the first time in her life and took a little getting used to. Being able to stretch out was a luxury and, all the time, she expected to come into contact with the arm or leg of one of her siblings.

It would be better now if JJ could make her a smaller bed, so they would have more space in the room than they had at present. She didn't think she should suggest it, as whilst JJ could do the work, she couldn't afford to pay for the materials.

The next few months were absorbed in her final examination preparations. She wished her father could see her now. How proud he would be of his little mouse. She held on to that thought through the moments of doubt, when she could see no likelihood of qualifying. He would have been proud of her no matter what and she imagined him quietly saying she could only do her best.

That was the thought that carried her into her examination and which she clung to as she awaited the result. And it was thoughts of her father's pride that made the tears flow when Mr Farmer called her to the office to break the glad tidings to her that she was now a fully qualified teacher.

She immediately went to Mrs Langham with the news. For the first time her dear friend embraced her.

"I had no doubt that you would, but I am nevertheless pleased to hear the news made official. You have made an old lady very proud indeed."

They both had tears in their eyes and Clara struggled to find words. "I will never forget how kind to me you have been. I wish I could repay you in some way."

"You already have a thousand-fold, child. You already have." Mrs Langham seemed far away as she spoke.

After her visit to Mrs Langham, Clara picked some flowers from the hedgerows and took them to her parents' graves where she wept openly. "I loved my brother from the moment I first saw him. The promise I made when he was born has always been important to me and now as long as I have work, I will be able to support him as much as he needs me to. Although he does seem to be doing rather well himself. He needn't be in want."

She stood a long while at the foot of the graves and wondered if she were to start saving now that her salary would increase, whether it would be too late to pay for a stone to mark the place where her parents lay. Perhaps no outward marker was necessary as the place was marked in her heart as clearly as any stone could show it.

PART 3

CHAPTER 18

1861 (Two years later)

Clara set the summer flowers down on the front window ledge of what was now the parlour. She couldn't imagine being happier than she was now they had the house to themselves. Qualifying as a teacher and being able to take up a regular teaching position, had enabled her to start putting aside a little money each week in the Penny Bank. Finally, she had felt they could afford to give notice to their lodger.

"Which bedroom would you like?" she asked JJ, when she broke the news to him.

"After sixteen years of sharing, I ain't never thought of having a room of my own. I think I'd like to stay in the one where we've slept. If you don't mind?"

Clara didn't mind at all. At twenty-four, it felt strange to her too. She had always liked what had once been their parents' bedroom and moving into that one was no hardship. She would ask Martha and Stan to help her move everything around.

Strangely, seeing the knitting frame taken away was more emotional than addressing the bedrooms. With the frame, went a big part of their lives and a link to her parents which Clara still treasured. But go it must. Home-working was reducing as the factories grew, which was hard for the families who still depended on that way of life. Quite apart from anything else, reducing home-working took away opportunities for married women, who found it hard to secure other types of employment.

Their landlord did nothing to repair their house, but with Stan's help the outside of the cottage was newly painted and the broken panes of glass repaired. He might never have served an apprenticeship, but he could do pretty well with some help from JJ making new window frames and a front door. The house looked a good deal better for it. As she looked around the room that she had so carefully begun to brighten into a welcoming living space, small as it was, she no longer felt embarrassed by their home.

She visited Mrs Langham most weeks, and they still compared the stories which Samuel told in his letters to each of them. He included less frivolity in his tales now his classroom time was as a teacher and not as a student, but he also wrote of work he was doing with local people outside of the private school which employed him. He had become involved in organising educational lectures for any in the community to attend, as well as offering some private help with reading and writing to those who, whilst now adult, had never had the opportunity to learn.

He was still living close to Cambridge, and his many activities made it difficult to come back to Great Wigston with any regularity, even during the holidays. Clara hoped that he was happy and cherished the times she saw him at his aunt's house.

She was gazing out of the parlour window into the road when she saw JJ approaching, at the end of his day working with Mr Bailey. The satchel he carried over his shoulder looked heavier than usual, and she went out to greet him.

"Shall I?" she said offering to take the bag.

JJ stopped to take the satchel from around his neck. "It's for you anyway. At least for your parlour."

JJ was amused by her excitement at having a room for best, but his words were said without teasing. Clara took the bag from him.

"Then I shall open it inside," she said, as much to give JJ the opportunity to find somewhere more comfortable to rest as anything.

The satchel held the most beautifully crafted wooden bowl. The grain of the oak breathtaking even in the dim light of the cottage. "JJ," Clara gasped. "Did you...?"

"'Ow else d'ya think I got it?" he said with a snort of laughter.

"Oh no, I didn't mean did you make it. I was asking if you'd really done it for me? It is simply beautiful. Mam and Dad would be so proud of all you've achieved. It's perfect."

JJ smiled. "Thank you. I enjoyed learning how to get the best from the wood. I think oak is my favourite, although I do like the colour of cherry."

Of course, as JJ explained to her, some of the work was more difficult for him to do, but he had found ways to adapt how he worked to make almost everything possible, and he played as full a role as any apprentice.

"Thank you," she said and kissed her brother's cheek. "It's perfect." She placed it in the centre of the sideboard and stood back to look at it. In that moment, Clara thought she might possibly be the luckiest person in the world to have so much.

On her next visit to Mrs Langham, Clara was looking forward to telling her friend of all the changes she'd made to the house. Amongst other things, JJ had built a small bookshelf for the wall in the parlour and along it was a row of Clara's own books. Pride of place was given to the Bible she'd been presented with for Sunday school attendance all those years ago and the journal which Mrs Langham had herself given to Clara.

When Mrs Langham greeted her, the old lady was full of her own news, which quite put the bookshelf out of Clara's mind.

"Samuel is coming for a visit this Christmas. He's planning to stay for the whole of the holiday and says he has an important matter to discuss with me. As a schoolmaster they will prefer him to have a wife sooner rather than later."

Clara was well aware of how old he was; they were the same age. Her heart sank at Mrs Langham's words.

"It seems odd," Clara began but wasn't sure whether to finish the sentence, but Mrs Langham seemed to read her mind.

"That the same isn't true for women who teach?" She nodded sagely. "I've often thought that myself. There are many inequalities when it comes to being a woman. Very many." Mrs Langham sighed. "I rather hope that it is you he wishes to discuss with me."

Clara felt her cheeks colour but shook her head sadly. "How could it be? Our backgrounds are so different, I doubt the school he is teaching at would be happy. And besides, I will always have JJ to think of." Clara bit her lip. Her thoughts and feelings were whirling in confusion. That Mrs Langham could think such a thing, was incomprehensible. And why would Mrs Langham help her to qualify as a teacher if she expected her to throw it all away and marry. She realised Mrs Langham was still talking.

"That's as maybe." Mrs Langham looked distant, "but I do believe you could make my nephew happy. And, if I'm not mistaken, you have strong feelings for him."

Clara couldn't look at Mrs Langham. Of course she had feelings for Samuel, how could she not? But she should put such ideas firmly from her mind. She had her teaching to concentrate on. She would be quite happy with that and JJ's companionship at home.

Because Clara was so happy with their little house now that she had finished the work she wanted to do, she wished for the rest of the family to see it. She saw Martha and Stan often enough, but it was less frequent that she saw Hannah and her family.

"What do you think of inviting everyone here for Christmas dinner?" she asked JJ, before putting her plans into action.

"Who's everyone?" he asked, looking up from a small piece of wood he was whittling into the shape of a bird.

"Martha, Stan and their two." She counted the numbers on her fingers. Martha's twins were eighteen months old, so barely needed to be counted. "Hannah, Frank and Robert." Robert was thirteen now.

Clara had known that Hannah was expecting another child, but the baby had been lost and no more was said about it.

"Must you invite Frank?" JJ asked.

"I can't very well invite Hannah without him."

"I s'pose not, but…"

JJ didn't finish. Clara knew that on the rare occasions they met, he didn't see eye-to cye with his brother-in-law and Frank had a tendency to demean JJ because of his disability, but she could see no way to leave him out if she wanted her sister to come.

"Then there's Grandma Herbert. We could invite Uncle Jack and his family."

"Whatever for? They've never bothered with us in all the times we've needed them." JJ gave a snort of derision.

Clara's shoulders slumped. She knew JJ was right, but it was Christmas, a time of goodwill. "If Jesus's birthday means anything to us it should be about extending the hand of friendship. Even to those who never extend it to us."

"I know." JJ sighed. "But do you 'ave to extend it quite that far?"

Clara gave a wry smile. JJ was right, she knew he was. She wondered for a moment exactly what had passed between her father and Grandma Herbert when they'd argued about JJ all those years ago. Was it enough to cause the chill that had settled in place between them?

"It don't seem fair, that Uncle Jack and Aunt Maggie are both alive and yet our mam and dad have gone." JJ looked out of the window.

Clara could see him biting his lip and wondered if she should go to him, but at sixteen he wouldn't want his sister fussing over him. "No, it doesn't. Perhaps you're right and I'll invite only Martha and Hannah's families."

Inviting Martha was the easy part; Clara would see her at chapel on Sunday. Despite all Martha's moaning about attending chapel when she was younger, she and Stan were now in regular attendance, which meant that Clara saw them often and could delight in seeing the twins grow week by week. Inviting Hannah was an altogether more difficult matter. Neither Hannah nor Frank read well enough to comprehend the contents of the letter if Clara were to write one. She would have to walk to Blaby, in the hope of finding them at home. It was a four mile walk, which took a little over an hour each way at the best of times. If Clara were to go on Saturday afternoon, she supposed, that would afford the best opportunity.

The weather was not in Clara's favour when she set off to see Hannah. Although the ice had cleared by the afternoon, freezing conditions had given way to blustery wind, driving rain toward her as she walked along the lane. At least the wind would be behind her on her return, unless its direction changed.

She couldn't wade through the ford in this weather and would have to take the longer route along the main lane where a bridge would take her over the river.

Eventually Clara arrived at Frank and Hannah's cottage and knocked at the door. By rights, family would knock and go straight in, but she no longer felt she knew her sister well enough to take that liberty. She waited patiently, shivering in the cold.

When no one came, she knocked again, harder this time and then stood back to look up at the cottage for signs of life. Clara frowned. There was no smoke curling from the chimney pot. That meant they were neither at home now, nor had been in recent hours. She couldn't leave a note for them, so how could she let them know that it was she who had called? Her hand went to her chest. She had their mother's brooch, but that was something she didn't want to leave here, or anywhere. She'd worn it every day since Martha had said she wanted Clara to keep it.

In desperation, Clara knocked at the neighbouring door and was glad when it was opened by an elderly man, bent down by years of work; by the look of him as a labourer rather than as a framework knitter. His eyes were bright, and his stoop suggested he hadn't spent his working life seated.

"Excuse me, sir," Clara said.

The man cupped his ear and Clara spoke louder.

"I was looking for my sister Mrs Hannah Carter. Do you know where I might find her?"

The man shook his head sadly. "They left early that's all I can tell you."

Clara wondered if they'd gone to Frank's family, but she couldn't go on a wild goose chase looking for them.

"Please," she said, without feeling a great deal of hope, "could you give her a message for me? I've walked several miles to see her, and I'd be very grateful."

"My memory ain't what it used to be," he said, shaking his head sadly. Then, as if to underline the fact, he added, "Who did you say you are, miss?"

Clara sighed deeply, but tried not to show how hopeless she felt this was. Instead, she chose her words as she would if she wanted the younger children at school to remember something important to tell their parents. She knew then that she was lucky if half of them both remembered to pass on the message and relayed it correctly.

There wouldn't be time for her to call again to see Hannah. All she could do was hope that the invitation to Christmas dinner reached her sister. She thanked the man and took her leave. Dusk would fall soon, and the road would be a hard one in this heavy rain. If she hurried, she could perhaps reach home before complete darkness fell. Walking briskly in heavy rain-soaked clothing wasn't easy and even holding her skirts away from the ground, her progress was slower than she'd have liked. If nothing else, the walk served to make her feel it was more reasonable that Hannah so rarely came to Wigston nowadays. By the time Clara reached home she was exhausted and glad to remove her wet clothes and sink into the chair by the fireside.

In her preparations, Clara had no choice but to assume everyone would come as invited. She knew that Martha and family would be there, but Hannah had not replied. As she thought about gifts for each of them, for a moment she wished she could use a knitting frame and make fine stockings for the whole family. It was a garment they wouldn't normally have, at least not of the quality they so often worked on in the past.

"Oh, JJ," she said over dinner one evening. "Why didn't I think about this sooner? I could have hand knitted something for everyone if I'd given it thought. Now I have time to knit for only some of them."

She didn't expect JJ to have any solution to her problem and was surprised when he said, "Why don't we give 'em gifts between us?"

"What do you have in mind?" Any help would be appreciated at this stage.

"You'll 'ave to wait to find out." He grinned at her.

They agreed between them who would organise each gift, but despite her asking again, JJ refused to say what he was planning to make.

Clara was not normally of a nervous temperament, but when the appointed day arrived, she arranged and rearranged the parlour and wiped away dust almost before it had chance to settle.

JJ was keeping out of her way which was probably a wise move.

She thought of all the reasons that Hannah and Frank

wouldn't come. Perhaps they hadn't received the message and didn't know of the invite. Maybe they were already planning to visit Frank's family. Or maybe they had visitors themselves and could go nowhere. Her darkest thought was that they would choose not to come and, try as she might not to dwell on that possibility, it was the thought which her mind kept returning to.

"You're here." Clara clapped her hands together in delight as Martha, Stan and the twins came in through the back door to the kitchen. "We're in the parlour," she said proudly, taking them through.

JJ took his crutch and pushed himself up from where he was sitting. He shook hands with Stan as though it were a truly formal occasion and the most natural thing to do.

"Have you 'eard from Hannah?"

"Do you know if…" Clara laughed. The sisters were asking each other the same question. She shook her head. "We won't give out presents until after we've eaten. Hopefully they'll be here by then." Clara left JJ playing with the twins and went to fetch drinks for everyone.

She had poured out the cups of tea and put them carefully on a tray to take through. She was walking across the kitchen when the back door opened and revealed a beaming Hannah standing there. Clara's hands shook so violently that she quickly put the tray down on the table before she did any more damage than spill the drinks. "It looks like I need to start again," she said shyly to her older sister, not sure how to greet her after such a long time since she'd come to the house.

"It's just me and Robert. I 'ope that's all right? Frank, he…" but Hannah didn't finish the sentence.

Clara felt a stab of pain for her sister, but relief on her

own part.

Hannah stepped inside to reveal a lanky boy, standing as though illustrating the word gawky, with his awkward angles and his hands deep in his pockets.

"Come in, come in." Clara had longed for this moment, but she had never believed it might happen.

"I'm sorry we weren't in when you came over to us," Hannah said, a little diffidently. Although she was entering the place she had once called home she did so as though she were a total stranger to it and not at all at ease.

"We're in the parlour," Clara said, suddenly feeling herself blush. "What used to be the workshop. Go through, I'll make more tea. The others are already in there."

Hannah shifted uneasily from foot to foot. "Martha? And… John?"

Hannah had never used his nickname with the same ease that Clara did, but hearing his full name still sounded strange to Clara's ears. "Yes, and Stan and the children."

Clara wasn't sure who was looking the more uncomfortable, Hannah or Robert. Where was all the confidence her older sister had? Clara went across to her, and as though it were the most natural thing in the world, she slipped her hand into Hannah's. "Come with me."

Clara led the way along the narrow hallway to the front of the house and into the parlour. As she opened the door, Martha turned and on seeing Hannah she rushed toward her and embraced her.

"I'm so glad you came." She looked around seeming to take in the fact that there were two rather than three of them. Then she smiled at Robert. "I won't hug you. I'm guessing you wouldn't appreciate it."

Clara slipped back out of the room to the kitchen, breathing a sigh of relief and leaving Martha to make the new arrivals at home. She felt a sudden protective surge for JJ and thought she should go back to make sure he was included in everything, but reminded herself once more that she needed to let him speak up for himself. He was all but an adult now.

The kettle was returning to the boil when Clara jumped at the sound of a knock at the back door. She presumed that Hannah's Frank had changed his mind and had come to join them after all. She brushed down her apron, took a deep breath and steeled herself to open the door.

"Samuel." Clara stood staring at the new arrival having no idea what to do.

CHAPTER 19

1861

"Samuel. Whatever's wrong?" Clara's first thought was that something had happened to Mrs Langham.

"Wrong? Why? No indeed." He was rubbing his gloved hands as he spoke. "A very merry Christmas to you, dearest Clara."

"Come into the warm, you look cold out there." She moved back and ushered him into the kitchen. "And a merry Christmas to you, too." On impulse, she reached up and kissed him lightly on the cheek and immediately felt herself blushing.

"I hoped I might speak with you privately," Samuel said removing his gloves. He took a deep breath as though about to launch into a whole speech.

Clara's heart was racing. She wondered if she should invite him to join her family in the parlour, but feared, if she explained she had family there, he would politely excuse himself for fear of intruding.

Samuel took her hands in his. "Dearest Clara…"

He had said no more when Martha burst into the kitchen laughing. "I've bin sent to see where you've got to wi'… Oh, I'm sorry." She raised an eyebrow at her sister and awkwardly pointed along the hall, before turning about and heading back to the parlour.

Samuel dropped Clara's hands. "I'm so sorry. I had no

idea you had company. I should have been more thoughtful of that. I should leave you."

Clara made a decision and smiled shyly as she asked, "Would you like to join us? You could meet the rest of my family."

Samuel laughed nervously. "Part of what I intended to ask was whether you and your brother would dine with my aunt and me today. I only remembered to suggest it to my aunt when I came home. I should have written and asked before now, but time ran away from me. I shall go, and will speak with you another time."

"I had hoped to visit your aunt tomorrow. Shall I see you then?"

Samuel sighed heavily. "I have to leave early in the morning. I've promised help to a family who are being evicted from their home. I cannot leave it longer to be their advocate, it wouldn't be fair."

Clara's heart swelled at the goodness of this lovely man. "Then stay a while now, or perhaps I could call on you when all my family have left. Yes, I'll do that, if you don't mind it being later when I come."

Samuel's face brightened. "Then, dearest Clara, I shall see you anon."

He gave a stage bow, put on his gloves and disappeared back out of the kitchen leaving Clara smiling.

Clara's heart was beating fast as she wandered down to the parlour.

"Sis, where's the tea?" JJ asked

Clara shook her head trying to pull herself back from what felt now to have been a dream. "Tea? What tea? Oh, yes, of course. I'm sorry."

She scurried back to the kitchen feeling as though someone had whisked her brain to a smooth paste. She opened the back door and drew in a few deep breaths of the dank December air. One step at a time. Step one - make tea.

She emptied out the pot and began again. Oh, how she wished that Samuel had joined them. She was sure he wouldn't have called only to invite them for dinner. From how he was before they were interrupted it was clear he had something important to say.

She could hear happy chatter from the parlour which helped calm her a little, but not so much that her hands would do as bidden - to carry the tray without the accompaniment of clattering from the cups rattling on their saucers. She returned for the teapot separately, lest it should fall from the shaking tray.

"Did I 'ear someone at the door?" Hannah asked, looking anxious.

"It was nothing. I was getting some fresh air." She shot a look to Martha so she wouldn't say anything. It wasn't completely a lie, at least not the second part but she sent up a silent prayer asking for God's forgiveness for the dishonesty.

Hannah visibly relaxed again. "For an awful moment I thought it were Frank. He were blind drunk when we left. If 'e comes to his senses this side of sundown I'd be surprised, but it still worried me."

"We'll be fine, Mam," Robert said. "He won't walk all this way."

"No." Hannah looked sad. "He'll just wait for us to go 'ome."

"We'll be fine, Mam," Robert repeated.

It had not occurred to Clara that Hannah's first thought on hearing the door would be one of fear. She wondered how often the boy had to come out with the phrase that they'd be fine.

The rest of their day together passed without incident, but Clara was distracted from her delight in sharing her home with her family by anticipation of what Samuel wanted to speak to her about. She couldn't wait to head to Mrs Langham's house once everyone had left and wondered about excusing herself.

Hannah and Robert set off first, in the hope that Frank had not especially missed their presence. Martha and family stayed on and as time progressed, Clara decided she must say something so that she could still see Samuel. They seemed so completely at ease that she almost wondered if they would notice if she went out for a while. JJ had delighted in playing with the twins when they were awake and crawling or tottering around. In turn they seemed to adore him, and both fell asleep nestled up to where he was sitting with them on the floor, which is where they were at present.

"Martha, can you help me in the kitchen, please?" Clara said quietly to her sister, so as not to disturb those who were dozing.

When Martha followed her, she was grinning. "Now are you gonna tell me what were 'appening in 'ere earlier? I've been dying to ask."

"I don't actually know. Oh, Martha, there's no time to explain now. I've waited all day to see Samuel to find out what he wanted to say. Would you mind if I were to leave you with JJ and go now? I know it's rude, but..."

Martha put her finger over Clara's lips. "Stop there. We've 'ad a wonderful day. We'll 'ead 'ome when the twins wake up. Now get your coat and go. JJ'll understand. And Clara..."

"What?"

"Good luck." Martha smiled. "Whatever 'e wanted to say, good luck."

In her haste, Clara fumbled with the buttons on her coat.

"Let me," Martha came down the hall to where her sister was standing and did the buttons up carefully. Then she kissed her sister's cheek. "I 'ope 'e's worth it."

Clara was out of the door before her sister's words registered. She sighed, thinking of Mrs Langham words and wondering. Perhaps he wanted to tell her in person that he'd found someone in Cambridge, but if that were the case he wouldn't come to tell her on Christmas Day. Or would he? He was, after all, leaving again the following day.

As she turned the corner at the end of Moat Street, a blast of chilly air hit her. She laughed. Yes, she needed to be pulled back to reality. No amount of speculation would provide her with answers. Samuel's purpose in speaking to her might be altogether different. She braced herself against the wind and walked the rest of the way to Mrs Langham's trying to think about anything other than what Samuel might want.

When Clara rang the bell, she was relieved to have the door opened by Mrs Langham's housekeeper; it gave her a little more time to think.

Clara cleared her throat. "Is Mr Hurst at home? Mr Samuel Hurst," she added rather needlessly.

"Come in, miss. He said I should show you into the library when you arrived, and he'll be right with you."

Clara went and sat down, perched on the edge of one of the chairs, while she waited for Samuel to join her. She wondered where Mrs Langham was and hoped she would see her too.

Samuel came in looking as awkward as a schoolboy and with a face as pink as a marshmallow.

"Is Aunty not around?" he asked, looking about him. "No? I suppose she'll appear at some point. We've had such a quiet day, the two of us. It would have been nice to be among a larger number. How was your day? Did…"

Clara, realising his nervousness, went across to him. If their time was limited, she rather hoped he might get to the point. "Samuel, I've had a lovely day too, but what is it you wish to speak to me about?"

"Ah, that." He ran his hand through his hair. "The thing is." He looked around the room as though searching for the words he needed. "I've been offered another teaching position."

"Congratulations. I'm very happy for you."

"No, no, don't interrupt yet, that's only part of it." He took a deep breath. "The position comes with a schoolmaster's house, and I rather hoped…" He took another sweeping look around the library. "Whilst I've barely seen you these last two years, you must know that I've always loved you and I wondered whether you would come with me, Clara and be my wife?" He sank heavily onto the edge of the chaise longue as though the act of getting the words out had left him exhausted.

He'd spoken so fast that Clara almost wanted to ask him to repeat what he'd said, to make sure she hadn't misunderstood. Her heart was somersaulting, wanting her to say 'yes'. She stood dumbstruck, searching for words herself.

"I thought…" Clara felt tears prick her eyes and looked away. She took a few deep breaths to compose herself. "Samuel, my heart is yours, but what of my brother, JJ? I can't turn him out. He is apprenticed here in Wigston and will be for some years. I made a promise that I have always intended to keep. What type of wife would I be if I broke vows I'd already made in order to make others? Besides that, your school governors will never accept you marrying someone with a background such as mine. You work in a public school where they have certain expectations. Imagine how you would be shunned if they knew. As for my own teaching, judging by your aunt's example, that may be easier to resolve, but it is still a concern to me. It is my own means of supporting my brother. I do believe I love you, Samuel, but I cannot say yes, for your sake as well as for mine."

The look of sadness on Samuel's face said more than a thousand words could have conveyed to Clara.

Samuel spoke quietly and without looking at Clara. "I had thought that JJ might live with us. There is room in the house, but I had not thought of his apprenticeship, nor of any objection by the school or the parents. That should never be a problem. You are as good as any woman there is."

Clara sat next to Samuel and took his hand in hers. "I know that is how you think and your aunt too, but that is not how everyone views the world. From what I have seen, those with the most privileges in life can be the first to look down on those who are not of their class."

Samuel sighed heavily. "Then I shall find another position, one that is in a church school, and I shall ask you again." He turned and looked at her directly. "I will find a way." He took her hands in his and raised them to his lips. "Until then, darling Clara, will you wait for me?"

Clara felt the lump in her throat and nodded. This was the right thing to do, wasn't it? It would not be well for Samuel to marry her at present. She couldn't take JJ away from his apprenticeship here and Samuel had so much to lose. She stood up.

"I think I should like some time to think, but yes, I will wait. Please give my greetings to your aunt. Maybe one day things can be different." She took a deep breath. "I hope to see you soon." Then before Samuel could offer to walk her home, Clara made her way to the door. Already she was having difficulty seeing her way through the haze of tears, but she held her head high as she walked along the hall and let herself out.

That night, Clara tossed and turned. She should have said 'yes'. She had no doubt that she loved Samuel, and they could have worked everything out together, even how it would affect JJ. By morning she had made up her mind. She would go to Samuel and tell him her change of heart. Knowing that he was to leave that morning, she rose early. Hopefully she had enough time. It was a little past six o' clock when she set off for Mrs Langham's house resolved to accept his offer, although they may have to wait a while before the marriage could take place.

Once again it was Stubbs, Mrs Langham's housekeeper who opened the door when she knocked.

"I'm sorry, miss but he left about half an hour ago. A carriage took him and his trunk to the station."

Clara let out a howl of anguish that even surprised herself.

"Are you all right, miss?"

"Who is it, Stubbs?" Mrs Langham called from further down the hall.

"Do you want to come in, miss? I'm sure Mrs Langham would be pleased to see you."

"Maybe I can still catch him. I'll come back later." Clara turned quickly and in rushing down the steps caught her shoe in the hem of her dress and fell headlong into the road below.

"Miss. Oh, miss." Stubbs had come down to her and was ready to help her up.

"Bring her inside, Stubbs, at once," Mrs Langham called from the doorway.

Feeling a little dazed, Clara gratefully accepted the help.

As Stubbs assisted her to stand, Clara winced at the pain from her left ankle.

"At least you need something to bind that leg. Once you're settled, I'll ask Stubbs to find something suitable."

Clara was in no state to protest. Stubbs had to bear much of Clara's weight as they made their way through to the library, where Mrs Langham directed her to the chaise longue in the window. Clara sank into the soft velvet of the cushioning. Her first thought was horror at the mud she must be getting on the fabric. "I shall ruin your beautiful chair."

"Sit yourself down and be looked after for once."

Clara had never seen Mrs Langham as formidable as she was now. She realised what a wonderful advocate for Samuel the woman must have been over the years since his parents died and envied him having such an adult to step in when he needed it.

"Thank you, Stubbs. Could you bring me some warm water please?"

Mrs Langham brought a chair across to where Clara was sitting. "Now, my dear, there's the two of us. Can I help you to take those stockings off so we can bathe your leg? And whilst we're doing that, why don't you tell me exactly what has happened?"

Clara realised it would be pointless for her to argue.

She explained the whole of the previous day to Mrs Langham, starting with Samuel's proposal, but including the strangeness of having her family together and all her worries for Hannah.

"And that was when my nephew arrived on your doorstep? Which is why you then called here later." She looked thoughtful.

"You knew why he came?"

Mrs Langham nodded. "As far as I understand, he was rather hoping that you might agree to be his wife. He had asked for my opinion on the subject before coming to you and I could think of no one I would rather have him bring into our family."

At the kindness of Mrs Langham's words and actions, Clara felt the tears rolling down her cheeks. "But there is so much to consider. I don't suppose for a moment the school would be happy with his choice. That was why I said no, together with my promise to care for my brother."

Mrs Langham was gently bathing the large graze on Clara's leg as she spoke. "If I know Samuel, he would be expecting your brother to go with you."

"But JJ's life is here. I made a promise to him when he was born, and I must keep it. Cambridge is so far away. I shouldn't like to make him leave all he knows."

Mrs Langham shook her head. "Cambridge? You wouldn't be near Cambridge. Didn't Samuel tell you? The position is in London. At least it can be reached directly by train. What you say of your differences in birth may alas be true and much as I have brought Samuel up to give such things no consideration, others, regrettably, do not see it in the same light. Poor Samuel will not have considered that issue. As for your brother's apprenticeship, you should speak with him, rather than assuming you know what he would choose." Mrs Langham looked at her intently.

Clara sighed. Of course, Mrs Langham was right.

Mrs Langham broke into her thoughts. "Do you love him?"

"My brother?"

"No, my dear." Mrs Langham sighed. "I know you love your brother. I meant Samuel. I'm presuming you do; otherwise, why would you be here today?"

Clara dropped her gaze. Until yesterday she'd never allowed herself to think in terms of love. "I do believe I do. I enjoy his company and am always happy to see him. I think about him when he isn't here and wish that he were. I feel a fluttering here," she pointed to her chest, "when I know I shall see him again and a sadness when he's gone. Is that love?"

"Oh, my dear girl. I think it would be best for you to talk to him again. Perhaps together you could find some way to work things out."

"That is what I sought to do today. I was almost ready to say I'd go no matter what, but I would be afraid that his employers might not be happy. Will he be back again soon?"

Mrs Langham shook her head. "Not for a while I don't suppose. He's taken his things ready to set up home. Although I rather think he'll rattle around in the schoolmaster's house on his own." She sighed.

"These are not things which should be written. I should go to London to see him. I could take the train." Clara sat up, stretching her leg as she did so and winced with the pain.

"You won't be going anywhere for a few days, young lady. Besides, he has not gone to London directly. He had a matter to attend to in Cambridge and his other belongings to collect. It will be a week before he is in London, which should give your ankle time to recover. That will give you plenty of time to speak with your brother first."

Mrs Langham stroked a strand of hair away from Clara's face, with the loving touch of a mother and Clara felt herself relax a little.

Clara nodded. "I shall go as soon as he is there."

CHAPTER 20

1861

Mrs Langham lent Clara one of her walking sticks to help her with the journey home. Even with her ankle bound, it was painful putting weight on the leg. That would teach her to be in such a rush. It reminded her of her mother's words when she collected her Sunday school prize, and she smiled. If she hadn't learned now, then she didn't suppose she ever would. "Sorry, Mam," she said, quietly into the wind and sighed to herself, feeling chastened by her own stupidity.

As soon as she was home, Clara took out paper and pen and sat at her small writing desk in the back room to compose a letter to Samuel. She would let him know of her intention to visit him in London. The following Saturday would be the second of January and, as long as the trains were running over new year, she would go then. She felt a thrill at the thought that she would finally travel by train, but had little idea of what she would need to do to make that possible. She should have thought to ask Mrs Langham, but until her ankle healed she would not be walking back to see her friend.

She stared at the paper for so long that the ink dried on the nib before she was as far as writing the first stroke of the D in Dear Samuel. She dipped the pen once again and began the note with her address and the date. Should it be

'Dear Samuel' or 'Dearest Samuel', or some other indication of endearment? She stared at the paper once more. Whatever would she say to him?

She blotted the letter, although she'd written nothing for so long the ink had dried again. Standing, Clara winced. She was so lost in thought that she'd entirely forgotten her ankle. She hobbled to the kitchen and made some tea, perhaps that would help her to think. In the end, she wrote the shortest note, telling little more than her intention to visit him and that she would send further word when she knew the arrangements. Then she wrote the address in London which Mrs Langham had given to her. He was due to arrive there by Monday, which would give him plenty of time to receive the letter ahead of her visit. She would ask JJ to post it for her when he came in.

Clara moved to a more comfortable chair in front of the fire and sat with her foot up on a stool. It was still morning, but she found herself dozing after her previous sleepless night. She woke with a start hearing a banging on the back door. The banging did not abate as she hobbled through to the kitchen.

"I'm coming. Who's there?" Clara had an uneasy feeling as she opened the door, which increased at the sight of Frank, Hannah's husband.

He pushed past Clara into the kitchen without invitation. "Where is she?" His speech was slurred.

Clara drew back, alarmed that no one else was in the house with her. "She's not here. I've not seen her or Robert since they left here yesterday afternoon."

As if she hadn't spoken, Frank lurched from the kitchen through the hall looking in the other rooms as he went and then stumbled upstairs.

Clara was shaking and had no idea what she could do.

She didn't want to leave him in her house, but neither did she want to be confronted by him again when he came downstairs. She sat on one of the kitchen chairs to take the weight off her ankle.

It wasn't long before Frank came downstairs and back into the kitchen. He took hold of Clara's shoulders and hauled her to her feet. Clara gasped.

"If I find you're lying to me."

He put his face close to hers and she couldn't avoid his vile beery breath.

"I'll find 'er and when I do…" He threw Clara back into the chair and went out of the kitchen slamming the back door behind him.

Clara sat rigid in the chair. Poor Hannah, that this was her life. She had no idea where her sister was. Fleetingly, she thought she should try to warn her but then realised that it was unlikely any warning was necessary from how Hannah had reacted the previous day, when she thought someone was at the door. Besides, with her ankle as it was, Clara wouldn't be walking anywhere for a couple of days.

She made tea and took it through to the parlour to drink. She was glad to hear the distinctive footfall of JJ approaching the house and felt herself start to relax properly for the first time since Frank had called. But what of Hannah? They should at least make sure she was all right.

"JJ," she called, as soon as she heard him come in.

He came to the parlour door and looked in. "Whatever's the matter?"

"I'll explain later, but more importantly, is there any chance you've seen Hannah?"

"Hannah? Why would I 'ave seen her? Won't she be at home in Blaby? I was at the Baileys' house. What's going on?"

Clara explained about Frank's visit and briefly about her own earlier accident. "I think we should try to find her and make sure she and Robert are safe. They may be at Martha's or Frank's sister's. I think she's still friends with Mary, despite how the family treats her."

By the time JJ returned from looking for Hannah it was late afternoon, and Clara was frustrated with simply sitting with her leg up. "Did you find her?"

JJ shook his head. "Martha's not seen her and no one's at Mary's house. I didn't try Frank's parents. If she's there, there ain't much I could do." He put his crutches down and dropped into a chair. "So, what do we do?"

"Nothing I suppose. What can we do? Frank will hopefully have sobered up and calmed down."

JJ snorted. "Until 'e starts drinking again."

The following day was Sunday, but Clara's ankle was more swollen and much as she wanted to be in the chapel praying for her sister, she stayed home and let JJ go alone. Maybe he would see the Carters and find out what was happening, or Martha might know more.

JJ had no news on his return, but Martha said Stan would walk to Blaby straight from church and let them know what he found out.

It was an anxious day waiting for news and not until near six o' clock in the evening before Stan knocked at the door.

"She's 'ome," he said, somewhat out of breath. "Everything's fine, I think."

Clara let out a long sigh of relief. "Thank you. Was Frank there?"

Stan hesitated. "'E was on his way out but waited 'til I

left before leaving."

Clara nodded. So, Hannah would not have been able to say a great deal, but at least she seemed to be all right. "Thanks, Stan."

When Stan had gone, she looked at the letter lying on the side, waiting to be posted to Samuel. "JJ," she called. "Please can you post this on your way to work tomorrow? And could you buy a copy of the Mercury on your way home, please? I need the train timetable for London."

She didn't think she'd ever heard JJ move so fast as he came back along the hall to where she was sitting.

"What did ya say?"

"I need the train timetable to London. I want to visit Samuel." Clara could feel herself grinning as she said it.

"You can't go on your own." JJ looked horrified.

"I shall have to. There's no one to go with me and besides, I can only afford one ticket."

"What does Samuel think about that?" JJ sat down on the chair which faced hers.

Clara dropped her gaze. "He doesn't know yet. That's what the letter is."

"Don't you think you'd better wait for 'is reply?"

Clara had never known her brother so openly concerned about her before. It made her realise how grown up he had become. "Thank you, but I'm going and that's all there is to it."

JJ raised an eyebrow as he stood up to leave the room. "Be careful, sis. And make sure Samuel at least meets you off the train."

It was a good point which Clara had not thought of. When she wrote to Samuel with her arrangements she would ask if that were possible.

She should have spoken to JJ then about what she had

in mind but somehow couldn't find the words. It wouldn't be an easy conversation.

By Wednesday Clara's ankle was much better and she walked to the station to book her train. Her heart was fluttering with excitement as she asked for a return ticket to London. It was the most extravagant thing she had ever done, probably that she would ever do. Costing almost two weeks' wages which had taken her a very long time to save, it felt incredibly reckless. Much as she worried about using all her savings, she knew in her heart this was what she must do.

"You'll need to change at Kibworth, miss, or else go into Leicester to catch the train. That one doesn't stop at Wigston."

"Will I know when I'm at Kibworth?" Clara could see this could be difficult.

The ticket office clerk smiled at her. "Don't worry. It will be announced by the station master on the platform and if you do miss it, then the train terminates at Market Harborough, and you can still change there; that would give you less time to catch the London train."

Clara nodded. She was already wondering if her insistence that she travel alone might have been a little premature, despite the cost.

As soon as she arrived home Clara wrote down all the man at the station had said. Her heart skipped a beat as she sat and thought about it. She had never previously travelled more than four miles from home. Could she do this? She wrote the letter to Samuel to tell him of her travel details, before any doubts set in.

'I shall arrive into King's Cross Station at ten minutes to eleven on Saturday morning and would be very grateful if you were able to meet me at the platform.'

Clara hoped she would receive confirmation from Samuel before she travelled, but as so far she had received no acknowledgement, she worried in case he had been delayed in Cambridge. She decided the safest option would be to call on Mrs Langham to see if his aunt had more recent news of his whereabouts.

The post arrived before she had the opportunity to leave the house and with it a letter from Samuel.

'My dearest Clara,

It will be a delight to welcome you to London. I will not be so insensitive as to ask if you are sure about travelling but will be waiting on the platform to greet you, if you can advise the time of the train.

Yours in anticipation

Samuel'

Clara smiled. His note made part of what she had asked in her letter needless. Now all she needed to do was think about exactly what she would say to him when they met.

The next couple of days felt endless. By Friday, Clara was so nervous that she could barely think about what she was doing. If she had moved the items on the sideboard around once, she must have done so five times as she occupied herself. She knew now what she wanted to say to Samuel and had written it out so she wouldn't forget anything when the time came.

Late in the afternoon, she heard JJ calling her with an urgency in his voice.

"Clara, Clara."

He was still outside the house, so she rushed to find what was happening.

Leaning against him for support was Hannah, leaving JJ unable to move.

"I found her 'ere as I were coming 'ome," he said,

moving his crutch as Clara took her sister's weight.

"Hannah, what's happened?" Clara put her arm firmly around her sister's waist to support her.

Hannah winced.

"Let's get you inside." Clara inched forward, while trying to help her sister. They made slow progress into the house and found a seat for Hannah. Clara lifted the lamp closer so she could see her sister properly and gasped. "Oh, Hannah, whatever happened? JJ stay here with her while I fetch a cloth and water to bathe those wounds."

Clara went and put the kettle on the stove and while it boiled looked for the salve and ointment which might help to soothe her sister's physical pain.

As she went back into the parlour, JJ mouthed the words, "It were Frank," to his sister. Clara nodded. She'd guessed as much.

"Are there injuries we can't see?" she asked Hannah, but as Hannah said nothing she said to JJ, "I think we should get her upstairs. I won't be able to do this on my own. Can you go for Martha while I make a start on what I can do here?"

Once Clara and Martha had undressed their sister, Clara was able to see the extent of bruising. Hannah's body was also covered in scars from previous lacerations, which looked to have been created with a belt, but no new ones requiring dressing. They made Hannah as comfortable as possible and put her into Clara's bed. Despite her obvious discomfort, Hannah fell asleep almost immediately.

"What do we do?" Martha asked.

"I don't know. I'll sit with her for a while, but someone needs to find out if Robert is all right. We may need to make sure Frank knows where she is before he comes looking."

"I could send Stan, but I think he might lay Hannah's Frank out cold for what 'e's done." Martha shuddered. "Should we tell the constable?"

Clara sighed heavily. "I don't suppose that would get us far. Hannah's Frank's wife. There's precious little they can do. The magistrate would simply order him to keep the peace. I'll go to Blaby once I know she's settled, and JJ can stay here with her."

"At this time of night?" Martha looked horrified.

"It's shortly after seven o' clock. I'll take a lantern and watch my step. If I bind my ankle, it will not be too bad. What choice is there? Robert might be hurt too. Quite apart from him worrying about his mother?"

"Then I'll stay with 'er now so that you can get on your way."

Clara kissed Martha's cheek and left her with Hannah while she dressed for her walk to Blaby.

"I wish I could offer to come," JJ said, sounding forlorn.

"It's fine. One of us needs to stay here in case Frank turns up."

JJ nodded. "Yes, I can do that."

Clara sighed, picked up her lantern and set off for her long walk. There might not be anyone home, but she'd leave word somewhere for her nephew whatever happened. How had life come to this for Hannah? As she walked, she thought about her sister and how precious few were the options available to a woman who'd made a bad marriage. She could leave her husband, but he'd come looking for her if she did. The law gave her little redress. Clara trudged along the lane, taking care to avoid the many uneven areas of the road. She'd walked this way a few times when visiting Hannah, but it was never a route she enjoyed.

She knocked at the back door of Hannah's house, hoping that Frank wasn't at home. There was no response, which she took as a good sign, at least as far as Frank was concerned. From all Hannah had said, Frank was either out of the house or passed out inside. She knocked again and then opened the door and called inside. "Robert, it's Aunt Clara, are you here?" After a pause she called a little louder, "Robert, it's Aunt Clara. Your mam is fine."

This time she heard movement upstairs and Robert, looking white in the face, came to the door.

"Your mam's at my house. Are you all right?"

Robert nodded biting his lip.

Clara could see that his cheeks were tear stained and his eyes red rimmed. "Did he hit you?"

Robert shook his head. "Mam hadn't cooked 'is dinner. I should 'ave protected 'er."

"Your mam will be all right. She's safe at my house tonight. You were unlikely to be able to do anything. Here, let me come in and get you a warm drink. I need one before I walk back anyway. You can tell me what happened."

Haltingly, over the space of the next hour, Robert told Clara of the times that his father had hit Hannah and how, in recent months it seemed to be getting worse.

"'E's never laid a finger on me. Not since I were a nipper. 'E'd take 'is belt to me then, same as any kid. Now I think 'e knows I'd 'it back. I should 'ave stopped 'im 'itting Mam, but I weren't 'ere when it started and by the time I came in 'e were calming down and I'd 'ave made it worse."

Clara was dumbstruck to think of the amount of violence that Hannah had dealt with. If her sister didn't do something, the chances were that her husband would kill her sooner or later.

"You should go. You don't want to be 'ere when Dad gets 'ome. 'E'll be drunk enough to pass out and won't notice Mam's not 'ere until 'e comes round tomorrow. I'll stay 'ere and make up some story that she's gone out early to see ya. I'm used to doing that."

Robert said it all in such a matter-of-fact manner that Clara was the more shocked for how normal it was to him. She patted her nephew's arm. "You're a good lad, Robert. Hannah is lucky to have a son like you."

Robert shrugged awkwardly, which made Clara smile.

It was nearing ten o' clock by the time Clara walked back from Blaby. At least her mind was easy that her nephew was safe and well. As for Hannah, that was more difficult to fix.

By the time she returned to Wigston she was exhausted and was glad to find that Martha had already gone home, and Hannah was sleeping quietly. JJ was sitting in the corner of the room, reading, on-hand in case his eldest sister awoke.

"You have my bed," JJ said. "You need to catch a train in the morning."

"Where will you sleep?"

"I'll be fine 'ere for tonight, but I'm working tomorrow, so I may not be 'ere when Hannah wakes."

"Oh, JJ, she can't be on her own. Did you ask Martha to come back?"

"She says she will, but it won't be until lunchtime."

Clara's mind was racing. The state Hannah was in, she would be best not to be on her own for any time. Besides, what if Frank came to the house? She would send a letter to Samuel first thing the following morning saying she couldn't go that day. She wouldn't be able to stop him going to the station to meet her, but if she explained the circumstances she knew he would understand. She could travel the following Saturday as term would not yet have started and she believed her ticket could be used without an extra fee being paid.

"JJ, I've decided I'll wait a week to go to London. If you can post a letter on the way to work for me, then I can stay with Hannah. You have your bed. You need a good sleep before work, and I'll doze here with Hannah."

JJ nodded. "I thought you might decide not to go. Samuel's a good man. He will understand."

Clara smiled, grateful for the reassurance and then went to write the letter before settling down in the chair beside Hannah.

The following day, Clara was awake and watching over Hannah. When Hannah awoke, she did so with a start.

"You're safe," were Clara's first words to her sister.

Hannah sat up and put her hand to her face and winced. "I didn't know where else to go. It's never been as bad as this. I'm sure 'e didn't mean to 'urt me, it's the drink."

Hannah's eyes were downcast as she spoke, and Clara realised her sister was struggling to believe the words she was saying.

Hannah moved the bed covers away. "I should get back before 'e knows I've gone."

"Let me get you something to eat and drink first. I've already seen Robert, he will look after things until you're ready to go back."

It was with a heavy heart that Clara said farewell to her sister later that morning. She wondered how Hannah would fair but could do no more than tell her she always had a place for her to stay here if Hannah needed it. Then she sat down to write a fuller account and apology to

Samuel and to say she would travel the following Saturday.

CHAPTER 21

1861-1862

Clara heard nothing from Hannah during the following week and hoped she was at least safe. She wished her sister lived close by so that it would be easy to visit her. She did receive a brief letter from Samuel saying that he understood and would be waiting on the platform once again the following Saturday. Clara wondered how long he'd waited the previous week and felt sad to have put him through such heartache. This week, nothing would stop her travelling. Martha was on standby in case Hannah needed help and all Clara had to do was concentrate on catching her train.

As the week progressed, Clara's nervousness about the journey increased, but it was accompanied by a great deal of excitement. When Saturday arrived, she was awake long before she needed to be. As she waited on the platform for the train, she was glad she'd wrapped up warmly to cope with the January cold and at intervals walked up and down.

"There you are, my dear."

Clara gave a start and turned around to see Mrs Langham standing beside her, resting her hand on a fine walking cane.

"Whatever are you doing here?" Clara was too shocked to think whether her response might sound a little rude.

"After you told me you had to postpone your trip to London it gave me the opportunity to arrange to come with you. I would have come last week had I not been otherwise engaged. I thought you might like some company for the journey." Mrs Langham waved her free hand. "Oh, don't worry, I don't intend to get in the way of you young people when we get to London. I thought I might go to the South Kensington Museum and then meet you for the journey home. I shall at least see my nephew, if not for long."

Clara couldn't stop herself from smiling. All her anxiety about knowing when to change trains, and what she should do, was gone and, left only with her nervous anticipation of seeing Samuel, she relaxed.

As the steam train pulled into the station, Clara's heart missed a beat. Standing close to the engine, it seemed so much bigger and more powerful than when watching from the lane, and hearing it let off steam made her jump.

"Come along," Mrs Langham said, guiding her toward the first class carriage.

"Oh, but my ticket is not for this section. The gentleman at the ticket office explained that…"

"Follow me," Mrs Langham said in an insistent tone. "I took the liberty of asking if I might upgrade your ticket once we are on the train, so that you can sit with me. I hardly want to sit on my own for the journey."

Clara had no idea what to say. She should be cross that her friend had interfered without asking. Of course, she would never have said yes to the plan, but in reality, she was very grateful. "Thank you." She decided to accept with good grace and make the most of the wonderful opportunity. Her eyes widened as she saw the comfortable seating and she allowed Mrs Langham to guide her to the right part of the carriage. She wondered what the carriage might be like that she was supposed to travel in and doubted it was anywhere near as pleasant as this one.

"You sit by the window. I've taken this journey before, and I know you will enjoy seeing the places we pass." Mrs Langham used her cane to indicate to Clara where to go.

A window blind obscured the view, but Mrs Langham reached across and raised it.

"I don't suppose you'll see much until long after we change at Kibworth, but it would be a shame for you to miss anything."

Clara smiled. It was still dark outside, but there were lamps at the station, and she presumed that would be the case at their stop at Great Glen as well.

Clara could see little outside in the darkness, but the rhythmic clickety-clack of the train running across the rails captured her attention when they started off. She was transported back to the long-ago sound of the knitting frames being worked by her parents when she was a child. Whatever would they think of being able to travel in such grand style?

The train barely seemed to be underway before Mrs Langham tapped her cane on the floor and said, "This stop will be Kibworth. We have plenty of time to change trains. Follow me."

Once the train came to a complete stop at the platform, a porter helped them both down from the carriage. Clara walked a little behind Mrs Langham as she moved purposefully along the platform. Their next train had not yet arrived at the station but came in shortly afterwards and from the bustle around them it was clear it would be on its way as soon as was possible. Clara was still preparing to sit down when the train moved and she was almost caught off balance, before righting herself and taking her seat.

It would take another three hours to reach London. In that time, they stopped at of places which Clara had never before heard of. She enjoyed watching to see the chimneys of each settlement, with their gently curling smoke as they approached and then the people waiting on the platforms to board the train when others alighted.

"The next stop will be London," Mrs Langham said as they pulled out of the station at Hitchin. "But we have a while until then. I shall take a short nap so that I'm ready for our exertions."

Clara sat watching the fields go by in the wintery light, rehearsing in her head what she hoped to say to Samuel as soon as she had the opportunity.

"We're approaching King's Cross," Mrs Langham said, sitting a little straighter in her seat.

Clara watched in awe as the large station came into view. She had never seen anything like it and was glad she wouldn't be alone. Samuel had said he'd be on the platform and that thought gave her a jolt of excitement. She wondered if he knew she would be alighting from a first class carriage and not further down the train as she had indicated in her letter. She had little time to wait for the answer. She saw him standing a little aside from the crowd as the train came to a complete stop. Mrs Langham gave a nod of satisfaction when she saw him and, gathering her things, stood up to leave the carriage.

As they reached the door, Samuel stepped forward to assist first his aunt and then Clara.

"You came," he said, as though he had prepared for another disappointment.

"Oh, Samuel, did you wait very long last week? I'm so

sorry. I wouldn't have left you standing here for any reason other than an emergency."

He smiled. "I know that. I'm glad to see you made it this week and my aunt accompanied you. Shall we find somewhere for coffee?"

"I've never tried coffee," Clara said, her eyes widening as she took in everything around them.

Mrs Langham waved her hand. "I'll leave you two young things for a while. I'm going directly to the museum. I should be able to get a Hansom cab to take me. Perhaps we could meet at the station tea room before our return train. Three o' clock?"

Samuel nodded. "We'll walk over there with you."

They headed toward the exit where a sign indicated cabs could be obtained.

"Shall we?" Samuel said, holding his arm out for Clara to take.

She felt herself blush at the closeness and her mouth went dry making it hard to speak. Clara waved to Mrs Langham's departing carriage before Samuel guided her in the other direction.

"I thought I might show you some of the sights, if you'd like. We could…" Samuel was talking quickly and sounded nervous.

"Samuel," Clara said, gently. "I came because I need to talk to you about what you said. Can we do that first, please?"

Samuel gave an awkward laugh. "Coffee it is then."

Stepping out of the station, Clara looked around in amazement. She could never have imagined a place so busy, with buildings, traffic and people everywhere. "I thought Great Wigston to be a bustling place until now. You must find it strange, but exciting living here?"

"I'm not used to it yet. It can be tiring having to be quite so alert whenever you go out in the streets. Should we take a cab to where I'd like to take you? It would be a rather long walk, and the streets are so very dirty."

"I have no money left after my ticket. I'll be happy to walk."

"You will, I hope, not mind if I pay for the cab, to save you the discomfort of the walk?" He didn't wait for her reply but guided her back the way they'd come to the line of horse drawn cabs which waited patiently to the side of the station.

Clara felt lost for words. She was used to walking wherever she went but today she wanted to take in the many new things. She gratefully accepted the help to step up into the carriage. As the horse moved off at a trot to the address Samuel had given the driver, Clara felt like royalty. This was so far removed from her normal life that none of what was happening felt real to her.

They drew up outside a small coffee shop and Samuel paid the driver.

Once they were seated inside and their drinks had been served Clara knew that much as she simply wanted to enjoy the surroundings and the fact this was the first time she had visited any sort of coffee shop or restaurant, she must start with what she came to London to say to Samuel. He was looking at her with anticipation as she took a deep breath.

"Samuel, I have been thinking a great deal about you asking me to marry you. Indeed, I have thought of little else, save for the trouble that Hannah is facing. Let me say all I need to say before you speak, for I have a number of things that I don't wish to forget." She paused to compose herself. Speaking in this way to anyone was as alien to her as her surroundings. In some ways the place itself helped as she could almost feel she was another person and not plain ordinary Clara Phipps who felt so unworthy of this wonderful man. She looked up shyly through her lashes as she said, "I do believe I love you, Samuel. I have never felt like this before. If it were only my heart I had to give account to, then my answer would be yes." He made to speak, and Clara shook her head slightly so he would realise she hadn't finished. She took another deep breath and steeled herself to go on. "As you know I have my brother to think of. I love him dearly, but in a different way. I took on the responsibility to provide him with a home and as long as he is apprenticed to Mr Bailey, that home needs to be in Wigston, and I need to continue as a teacher in order to pay for it."

Samuel nodded, but didn't try to interrupt.

"He has eighteen months of his apprenticeship still to serve. After that, well I don't know what he will do, but he might work as a carpenter in Wigston or elsewhere as he chooses. I would want to know he was settled in life before I could say yes to your offer of marriage. I know I cannot expect you to wait all that time for me, but if you ask me again when all that is done then I will say yes, and I will move anywhere to be with you." She let out a long sigh. "There, I've said all I wanted to say." She laughed. "It's all right for you to talk again now, there is nothing more for me to forget."

Samuel reached across the table and took her hands in his. "My darling Clara, I would go to the ends of the earth for you and of course shall wait, if that is what you want. I had already thought that we would include your brother in our home, but I must admit I had not given regard to his apprenticeship. Would you really be prepared to leave your own teaching in order for us to marry?"

Clara nodded. "I think your aunt has shown me that there are many ways I could still use the skills it has given me. I don't need to give up my passion for education because I can no longer have a formal position within a school."

"I shall visit you as often as I can and will write to you every week. May I tell my aunt what you have said? I know, even having to wait, it will make her happy."

Clara smiled. "I will explain to her this afternoon."

With her explanation out of the way, Clara was at last able to relax a little and allow Samuel to take her to see some of the incredible sights which London had to offer. Much as Clara was in awe of Marble Arch, Buckingham Palace and Trafalgar Square, it was Hyde Park and Regent's Park which stole her heart. By the time their tour was finished, and they were ready to meet Mrs Langham back at King's Cross, Clara was exhausted and suspected that on the way home her friend wouldn't be the only one falling asleep. At least their return train was direct to Wigston, although if they slept through their stop they would arrive in Leicester.

With the days lengthening into summer, Clara didn't notice that JJ was coming home a little later than he had in the past. It was when he said, "I've ate already, thank you," that she stopped to think.

"Where?"

"I stayed to eat with Eliza and her family."

"Eliza?"

"Mr Bailey's daughter."

"Oh." Clara nodded. Eliza and JJ had been friends for years through his time in Mr Bailey's workshop. She must have invited him to eat with them.

By late summer of that year, JJ had fallen into a pattern of eating with the Baileys once a week, and Clara was grateful that she enjoyed her own company as well as she did. Borrowing books from Mrs Langham helped and she'd sit up reading until she knew JJ was home safely.

"I'd like to invite Eliza 'ere on Sunday if I may?" JJ said as Clara put her book down on the side table by her chair.

"Why of course." It was the least they could do after all the meals JJ had taken with the Bailey family. "I'll cook us something special as a treat." Clara had enough money to buy extra once in a while and she could bake a fruit pie for their dessert. They had stored apples away carefully which she could use.

When Sunday came, Clara enjoyed preparing the meal. It was a pleasant change to cook for more than the two of them and she wished she did it more often. She set the table carefully, taking pride in the cloth and each of the three place settings. She was doing it as much for herself as to impress Eliza.

When JJ brought Eliza into the house, they both seemed shy.

"Clara, this is Eliza Bailey. Eliza this is my sister Clara."

Clara wiped pastry crumbs onto her apron before holding out her hand. "And I'm very pleased to meet you again outside of a school setting."

Eliza shook her hand and smiled. "John's told me so much about you."

Hearing her brother called John came strangely to Clara's ears. She felt she should return the comment, but the truth was that JJ had said little about either Mr Bailey or Eliza, so she knew hardly anything of the girl, except recollections of teaching her some years before.

Clara had lunch on the table in no time and sat down with them to bowls of soup. It felt a real extravagance to have three courses for their meal. She couldn't remember any time before that they'd done that, and she might not have thought of it, but for the menu where she and Samuel had eaten in London.

"There's something we want to tell you," JJ said as he sat watching her as Clara dipped her spoon in her bowl.

Clara looked up and frowned. She looked from JJ to Eliza and back. "Go on," she said, taking a piece of bread from the plate.

"I've asked Eliza to marry me, and she's said yes."

Clara's spoon clattered from her hand into her bowl. She didn't trust herself to speak but sat open mouthed staring at first her brother and then Eliza. Coming to her senses and remembering her manners she said, "Congratulations. But…"

"Don't worry. It won't be until I complete my apprenticeship, in another year. Then Mr Bailey says he'll help me to set up my own workshop and share work with me to get me started."

"John asked my parents' permission before asking me," Eliza said, putting her hand on JJ's arm.

Clara simply nodded. However had she so misjudged the situation?

"We don't know where we'll live when we marry, but Eliza and I have talked about it and we wouldn't want you to be on your own, so would like it if you were to live with us."

"That's very kind of you," Clara said, while privately uncertain whether she wished to laugh or cry at the absurdity of the reversal of the situation she'd imagined when he was a baby. "This is something to celebrate. I'm happy for you both. It's lovely news." Then with a moment of clarity, she thought of Samuel and smiled. "I think it's high time I told you something too."

CHAPTER 22

1862

Once Eliza had gone, Clara sat at the kitchen table shaking her head and smiling. How could she not have seen what was happening? It had never occurred to her that there would come a time when JJ was truly independent. He wasn't a child anymore. She felt stupid for still calling him by his childhood nickname. It was over five years since their father died and JJ was the only John in the house, so why not use his name?

She wouldn't write to Samuel with the news but tell him in person. He was next due to visit Great Wigston in two weeks' time. She would wait until then. Then it dawned on her, this change in circumstance would mean she would be moving to London. The possibility had not seemed real before. She would be leaving her family behind and seeing them when she and Samuel could visit. Given her family had lived in the area for generations, it felt like a bold step to make. She smiled with the excitement of all the places she could visit and the things she could do. Clara would take great delight in supporting Samuel in his work and could perhaps take on her own pupils at home too.

Much as she wanted to visit Mrs Langham immediately and tell her the news, it was right that she should speak to Samuel about her changed situation first. So, as she had some time free the following Saturday afternoon and the evenings were still long, Clara decided to walk to Blaby to see Hannah and with John's permission, tell her their brother's news.

As she walked along the lane with the sunshine on her face, Clara thought about how different life would be living in a city. At least London seemed to have large parks where one could escape from the noise and bustle. She hadn't seen where Samuel lived, but his description suggested it would feel a little more like where she was used to, rather than how the area around King's Cross had appeared.

She breathed in the fresh country air as she walked and wondered how easy it was in London to get away from the smell of the streets.

"Hannah," Clara called as she knocked on the back door which was already open. "Are you home?"

Robert came into the kitchen. "Hello, Aunt Clara. Mam's upstairs in bed."

"Oh no. Is she ill?"

Robert hesitated. "Not exactly ill." He looked awkward. "I'll ask if she minds you goin' up. It should be all right, Dad's out and I don't suppose he'll be back 'til late."

When Clara saw her sister, she gasped. Once again, the bruises were highly visible, and Hannah's eye was swollen shut.

Hannah reached for her sister's hand and gave a slight smile from her swollen lips. It was obvious to Clara that it would be painful for her sister to speak.

"My darling, Hannah, this can't continue. We have to do something." Clara turned to Robert who was still in the room. "What happened?"

"I weren't 'ere and Mam ain't bin able to say much. I don't really know. 'E came 'ome early yesterday I think - drunk. Mam 'ad gone for a walk so weren't 'ere. He were furious that she'd gone out. It 'appened when she came back. By the time I got 'ere, Dad were passed out and Mam were sitting in the kitchen sobbing. If she don't leave 'im, 'e's going to end up killing 'er. I don't know what to do."

Clara nodded. If Hannah left him, she would need to go somewhere that Frank wouldn't find her. Even so, everyone who knew where she was, would be at risk. The law offered so little protection to married women where their husbands were concerned.

Clara stayed with Hannah for over an hour, holding her hand and telling her John's news as well as some of what it might mean for herself. Hannah said barely a word in all the time she was there, and when Clara had to leave, parting was more difficult than ever before.

"I think she should leave 'im," Robert said when Clara went downstairs. "If I stayed 'ere, maybe 'e'd be all right about it."

"Oh, Robert, surely your father wouldn't accept Hannah leaving him on any basis? None of you would be safe."

Robert shrugged. "I dunno what else to do."

"There's nothing you can do."

"But she's me mam."

The forlorn look on her nephew's face was almost as painful as seeing her sister. She took him in her arms and held him, rubbing his back as she felt his heaving sobs. She didn't say that everything would be all right. It would be wrong to say something which seemed so unlikely to be true.

After a while, he pulled back and wiped his eyes on his sleeve and sniffed. "Thanks, Aunt Clara."

She gave a deep sigh and set off to walk back to Wigston. She wished she has enough time to visit Mrs Langham after all. She could do with her friend's wise counsel. However, in the time she had, her priority should be to tell Martha the state their sister was in. Maybe Martha would have the opportunity to visit her in the coming week.

The following weekend Clara could at last visit both Mrs Langham and Samuel. Her heart was racing as she pulled the bell cord.

When Samuel came to the door, Clara couldn't stop herself from breaking into a broad grin. She would never tire of the sight of this wonderful man.

He took her hand and kissed it. "I've missed you," he said quietly.

"And I you. I have so much to tell you. I hope you will think at least some of it is good news."

Samuel directed her to the library and then followed behind. "Tea is ready and waiting."

Clara went in and greeted Mrs Langham and then proceeded to tell the events of the preceding couple of weeks, beginning with John and Eliza's news.

Samuel's face lit up on hearing that a position for John would be set up when he finished his apprenticeship. He jumped up from where he was sitting and knelt in front of Clara. "And may I ask you now to be my wife?"

Clara laughed with delight. "Not yet, but soon. There is still almost a year to go. Let us see them settled. Until then I need to continue teaching."

Samuel nodded and made a mock pout as he stood up.

"And this is why he wanted a career on the stage." Mrs Langham raised her arms in an act of pretend despair at her nephew.

Then Clara went on to explain about her visit to Hannah. "Somehow I need to help her, but I have no idea how."

Samuel sat quietly for a while. Then he said, "You know that Hannah would be welcome to come to us in London if she needs to. She would be safe from her husband there I think."

"Thank you." Clara smiled. "It might come to that. I know no other way to help. Until she says she is ready to leave him, there is little I can do."

"She would be welcome here too, although that doesn't take her away from this area." Mrs Langham sighed heavily.

"Thank you." Clara was touched and didn't know what else to say. She was saved from saying anything further by Samuel getting up and starting to pace the room.

"I've been thinking more and more about the possibility of going into politics and leaving teaching. There are so many injustices which need to be addressed."

Mrs Langham nodded, and it was clear to Clara that they had already discussed the idea.

"Would you still want to marry me if I were to do that?" He stopped pacing and looked at her seriously.

Clara laughed. "It is you I want to be with, not your teaching. I would be proud to be by your side," she said, feeling some of his excitement rubbing off on her, at the thought of making real changes. "Very proud."

"And you could help me, dearest Clara. There are so many things that you know more about than I do. The things which are important."

Clara sat up straighter and frowned. She had always thought Samuel was the one whose studies were the broadest. "How so?"

Samuel waved his hand around the room. "What do I know about the needs of most of the population, when I have had such privilege? You have taught me what matters more than any school lesson ever has. Your determination to overcome difficulties inspires me."

Clara felt herself blushing.

"There is more to education than all that is written in books," Mrs Langham said, pouring fresh cups of tea for them all.

Clara suddenly remembered them building a snowman and smiled. How true that was.

Thankfully, it wasn't long before Frank was sent by his father to manage building work in Leicester, and to make his life easier, his father paid for him to stay in a boarding house rather than walk to and from Blaby each day. Clara breathed a sigh of relief and hoped that, at least for a period of time, her sister would be safe. Although Robert was apprenticed to Frank, an arrangement was made for him to stay on with a builder in Blaby, so he was still at home with his mother in the evenings. Perhaps a short period apart would help them all to sort out their problems.

Over the following weeks, Mrs Langham began to treat Clara as though she were a daughter, rather than a prospective niece and they became closer than they had ever been.

"I think it's time you stopped calling me Mrs Langham, my dear. You can start calling me Aunt Frances, if that is acceptable to you."

Clara read to her regularly and together they enjoyed the works of Dickens, Chaucer, Shakespeare, Austen and the Bronte sisters as well as Eliot and the poetry of Tennyson, Wordsworth and Barrett Browning. But they also discussed some of the political issues that were of concern to Samuel.

Clara still thrived on her teaching. She was never happier than when she saw a child, who had been struggling to learn to read or write, suddenly begin to grasp those skills and develop a love of books as a result. She would often recount those tales to Mrs Langham whose gentle smile told Clara that she understood how good those feelings were. She had finished telling Mrs Langham about a boy from the village, whose fees were being paid by the chapel and was about to pick up *Nicholas Nickleby* in order to continue reading, when Mrs Langham rested a hand on her arm.

"I've asked Samuel to visit next Sunday. There are matters I'd like to discuss with him."

"Oh." Clara didn't know what to say. "Then I will wait to call until the following week."

Mrs Langham shook her head and smiled. "No, my dear. I'm telling you as I thought you'd like to see him."

"Indeed, I would, but I would not wish to intrude." Clara felt a smile fill her face.

"There is nothing now that I cannot discuss with my nephew with you present. I shall look forward to your company."

When Clara walked home from chapel the following Sunday morning all she could think about was visiting Mrs Langham that afternoon. She chided herself. Normally, she would use the walk home to reflect on the

271

words of the preacher from that morning's sermon, but today if you'd asked her what the preacher spoke about, she didn't think she could have answered.

"You seem happy," John said as he walked along beside her.

"I am," she replied, but said no more.

She went ahead of John to the back door. As she went through the gate she stopped suddenly, causing John to hit her with his crutch.

"Hannah. What are you doing here?"

Her sister was sitting on the step with her arms wrapped around her body rocking back and forth. When she looked up, her face was both bruised and tear stained. Clara rushed to her.

"Oh, Hannah, when will it end?" Clara reached for her sister's hands and helped her up. "Come inside and let me make some tea." She led Hannah to the kitchen table and pulled out a chair for her to sit on.

John indicated she should sit with Hannah, while he went over to the stove and put the kettle on to boil.

"I've left 'im. I know that ain't the real, Frank. The one I married. It were only ever after he'd been drinking. He weren't really like that. Sometimes, when Robert were little it were because I couldn't keep 'im quiet..."

After years of saying so little of the circumstances around her abuse, it was as though the flood gates had finally opened. Clara sat listening, holding her sister's hand and feeling the emotional pain that had plagued Hannah her entire married life.

At one point, Hannah looked up at her. "You know I were expecting another child, when Robert were still small. I wanted to come and tell you all, but it started such a fight. In the end 'e pushed me, and I fell down some steps." She looked down at her free hand as she absentmindedly picked at a hole in her dress. "I lost the baby. There ain't bin no more since then. I think a part of me died wi' that baby."

Clara bit her lip to stop herself asking how badly Frank had hurt her that time. It wouldn't help now, whatever the answer was.

"I couldn't leave while Robert were young and not able to stand up for 'imself. His Dad would 'ave come after both of us. Besides, I couldn't 'ave supported 'im and who else would take us in?"

As Hannah continued to pour out all her years of emotional and physical pain, Clara simply listened. Clara heard the clock strike the hour and her stomach rumbled as though wanting to add its own comment to the lateness for eating. She certainly couldn't interrupt to say she was supposed to be going out. She wanted Hannah to say all that was needed.

Hannah didn't stop talking for a long time, prompted by questions from Clara.

"Where's Robert now?"

"He's stayed wir' 'is dad. 'I wanted 'im to come too, but it'd have made it more difficult."

"There's a home for you here as long as you need it." Clara wrapped her sister in a gentle hug. Despite her bold words, Clara had visions of Frank arriving on the doorstep. Neither she nor John would be in any position to deny him entry if he did. There would be little they could do to stop Frank taking Hannah home.

"I've brought note except the clothes I'm wearing. I'm 'oping Frank'll give up on me. I'm note to 'im. 'E's not 'ome most of the time and when 'e is 'e ain't never sober. Besides, that mother of 'is wanted him rid of me since the day we met. Maybe she'll be 'appy if she's finally gor' 'er own way."

Clara doubted that matters would be that simple. Pride never allowed for such a gentle ending.

By the evening, Hannah had talked herself to exhaustion.

"Come, I'll find you some night things." Clara led Hannah up to her own room. "You have my bed for tonight. I'll sort things properly tomorrow."

It was still early evening, but Hannah was asleep almost immediately. Clara went downstairs to find John preparing supper.

"I thought as we'd missed lunch, you'd be 'ungry."

Clara looked at the clock. It was a little after seven thirty. "I need to run an errand before I eat. You go ahead and I'll be back in a while."

There must have been something in her face, as John said, "Is everythin' all right? Was there something you should 'ave done?"

Clara smiled weakly. "Sometimes God works in strange ways, and we are wise to see his will for us and not pursue our own wishes." Then she picked up her coat and a lantern and headed out to see if she was too late to see Samuel.

"He's been gone some time, Miss," Stubbs said when Clara enquired if Mr Hurst was still at home. "It's been a tiring day for her and Mrs Langham's sleeping, so I won't show you in."

Clara could do little more than nod, as the events of the day caught up with her and she felt the hot tears coursing down her cheeks. She hadn't the strength to bring her thoughts back to control. She didn't turn for home as she walked down the steps but headed for the chapel. She slipped in through the door and took a place in the pews. The only light was the one Clara carried as she sat alone in the chapel. "I have to be strong enough to help my sister, but I'm frightened Frank will come," she whispered into the darkness. "Father God, guide me in how to help her best and keep her safe." And Clara let the tears flow until she felt like a rag rung out on washday. Then she took a deep breath and as she rose, she turned her thoughts back to how life would change with Hannah back at home.

CHAPTER 23

1862

The following morning, Hannah was still sleeping when Clara got up for work. Seeing her looking so angelic in sleep, and yet with so many bruises, made Clara more angry with Frank. How could the law allow a woman to be treated so badly, because she was married to the man who'd inflicted the harm? She wished she could speak with Samuel right then about all the laws that were unfair. Why should she have to give up her teaching when they married? Why could only those men who owned land vote? The more she thought about those things, the more she understood the need for change.

She left food ready on the kitchen table for when Hannah eventually awoke and set off for the school. She still loved teaching. The British School had grown, and it was a delight to see more children receiving education. She felt proud of all that the school was achieving and glad to be part of their work.

Clara never tired of seeing children begin to understand how to read and write and for books to start to have meaning for them. Many of the pupils had difficult lives at home and in Clara's mind, there was little better than to be able to lose yourself from the life around you, by retreating into a world of fiction. She remembered how precious it was to her when she first discovered the wonders which books held, and she did all she could to convey that to her own pupils.

She was in the middle of teaching fractions to some of the older girls when she was called from the classroom by Mrs Farmer. It immediately brought to mind the day they'd found her father and Clara's heart raced. Mr Ward nodded to her to leave the children to him. Clara knew that he would monitor the pupil teacher who now worked with Clara as well as his own.

Mrs Farmer said nothing as she walked along the corridor, which increased Clara's sense of dread. When they reached the office Mrs Farmer showed Clara in and retreated. It was John who was standing waiting for her rather than Mr Cooper.

"Whatever's happened? Is it Hannah? Oh no, please tell me Frank didn't come for her."

"Sit down, Clara. You're gonna need to."

If it were possible, Clara's heart beat yet faster on hearing John's words. She did as bidden but sat on the edge of the seat closest to his.

John took an obvious deep breath before saying, "Frank is dead."

Clara felt relief flood over her and must have visibly relaxed a little because John shook his head looking serious.

"Was it the drink?" she asked.

"Clara, it's bad," John spoke slowly. "'E were coming after Hannah. Robert's been arrested for killing his dad. I need you to come home to be with Hannah. Mr Bailey's gonna take me and Stan in the cart to the police station in Leicester to find out what's 'appening. I'm sorry, I told Mrs Farmer. I didn't want 'er to 'ear it from gossip. She says you're to come 'ome." He paused. "She also said they can't

277

'ave scandal surrounding the school, so you should wait to 'ear when to return."

Clara couldn't speak. She'd heard Robert say how much he regretted not being able to stand up for his mother, but killing his father, surely at not quite fourteen years of age, he wasn't capable of that? Then the rest of what John had said registered with her. "Not come to work? But I've done nothing. Whatever will we do?"

"For now, you're coming 'ome to be wi' Hannah. Martha'll tell you what's 'appened. Let me 'n Stan see what we can find out before we start to worry about ote else."

As they walked away from the school Clara cleared her head. She had so many questions she wanted to ask. "Who came to tell you?"

"Stan went to make sure everything wa all right. Martha'll explain."

Clara nodded. Her mind continued galloping away. She had no idea what they should be doing and wished Samuel were there to help.

Hannah was standing looking out of the window as they approached the house. She looked utterly dazed and showed no recognition of their arrival.

Clara went straight through the kitchen where Martha was making tea and the twins were playing, and into the parlour where she wrapped Hannah in a hug. She felt her sister flinch. Clara thanked God that Frank was dead, but prayed her nephew wouldn't hang for it. He was still a child.

"Do you want to tell me what's happening, or should I talk to Martha?" Clara asked Hannah.

Hannah continued looking straight ahead and said nothing.

Clara decided her sister would be no worse for a few

minutes on her own, while she went through to Martha in the kitchen.

Martha shook her head. "I'm sorry, there's no one else can look after these two today. I 'ad to bring 'em, but they're the last thing Hannah needs right now."

Jane and Ellen were usually quiet girls. Clara smiled. "They might be exactly what she needs to take her mind off waiting. What happened?"

Martha indicated they should sit at the kitchen table.

"Stan wa' worried about what'd happen when Frank went home from the pub. He didn't want Frank coming 'ere looking for Hannah, not given the state she wa' already in. He set off about nine last night to go over to Blaby, thinking he'd get there in time for Frank still being in the pub, but 'e didn't. Frank 'ad gone home earlier. We know all this 'cause one of the neighbours said 'e saw what 'appened. Frank wa' raving. Blind drunk and calling for Hannah. When 'e found she weren't there 'e lost it completely and threw Robert out the house. If it 'ad ended there it would o' been a blessing, but Robert wa' getting up off the ground when his dad came toward him with his fists flying in all directions. Robert reached for the nearest thing available, which wa' a pitchfork and hit his dad over the head wir' it. It wa' one blow, the neighbour said, but he's a strong lad for his age and it wa' a good un. Frank went straight down dead, just like that."

Clara gasped and covered her mouth with her hand. After a moment to recover from the shock she said, "So he did it in self-defence?"

Martha nodded. "The neighbour certainly thinks that and says it's a good thing too. The local constable had to be called, but 'e didn't want to listen to what'd 'appened last night. Said all that would be for the magistrates to decide, and statements'd need to be given later. He arrested Robert and took 'im away, saying as far as he wa' concerned 'itting an unarmed man wir' a pitchfork in his own back yard wa' most likely murder as far as 'e could see."

Clara jumped to her feet. "But he's a child and if the neighbour witnessed what happened..." Though she wondered how much the neighbour would have seen in the dark.

Martha shrugged. "They 'ave to take his statement first. There's some explaining to do. You don't hit someone over the head wir' a pitchfork by accident."

"Robert wouldn't murder his dad. I don't think he's like that. Oh, I wish Samuel were here to help sort it out." She wondered about sending word to Samuel and then a thought struck her. If the school here didn't want any scandal attached to one of its teachers, the same was likely to be true for Samuel. The school he taught at might not be connected to the church, but their rules seemed as strict. Rather than sending to Samuel, she would seek advice from Mrs Langham. Her dear friend might know what they should do.

"I'll sit with Hannah for a while," Clara said, getting up from the table. "Even with Mr Bailey's horse and cart to take them, it will be a while before John and Stan come back from Leicester."

Martha nodded. "I'll stay 'ere too, if you don't think the children are in the way."

Clara shook her head. "I always love them being here. Maybe don't bring them into the parlour until we know a little more of how Hannah is."

Sitting with Hannah made for a quiet day and Clara wished the children were in the room with them. Hannah sat staring into space. All Clara could think to do was keep her warm, hold her hand and talk to her gently.

She jumped when she heard a cart outside, but Hannah remained impassive. Leaving Hannah in the parlour, Clara went through to the kitchen to hear what had happened.

Stan and John were talking as they came in.

"How can the likes of us know what we're s'posed to do? It ain't as though we can pay anyone to 'elp us." Stan sounded bitter.

"Look, lad, let's talk to Clara. Those friends of 'ers might have some idea." Mr Bailey's words carried through to where Clara was waiting.

"We were saying," John said, as they came into the kitchen, "That it might 'elp if you talked to Samuel. We ain't got nowhere." He turned and looked at the others.

"They wouldn't let us see 'im," Stan said. "Nor tell us whether they'd taken a statement from the neighbour."

"Sorry, love," Mr Bailey said, "we all tried. I don't suppose you know someone who knows the local constable do you? He might be able to find sommat out."

Clara nodded. "We could ask people at chapel. Mr Cooper might know. Martha, if you stay with Hannah, I'll visit Mrs Langham now to see what she suggests."

It was a relief to be able to tell the whole story of what had happened in the last couple of days to someone outside the family. Mrs Langham listened without comment until Clara had finished and had brought her up to date.

"Well, my dear, whatever the risks to his employment, Samuel would want to know and will want to help in any way he can."

Clara made to protest, but Mrs Langham raised a hand

ROSEMARY J. KIND

to stop her.

"It is his decision to make as to how he handles it, but I think I know my nephew pretty well and he loves you and that is more important to him than anything. He will want to help."

Clara could feel herself blushing.

"I will write this minute so there is no delay in him receiving the news. Then we will discuss what else is to be done."

Clara sat quietly while Mrs Langham wrote a few lines, presumably summing up the situation, and then called Stubbs to have it despatched without delay.

"Now," Mrs Langham turned her attention back to Clara, "it sounds to me as though your nephew needs a solicitor."

Once again Clara went to respond, but Mrs Langham shook her head.

"I know you can't afford one, but I can. One day you will marry my nephew and all that I have will pass to him on my demise. I will not take no for an answer. This is not charity on my part, it is simply an investment in my nephew's future happiness."

Clara was about to remonstrate, but they needed help, and Mrs Langham provided the only way they were likely to get it. "Thank you. I don't know what to say."

"Then don't say anything. I need to write another note to summon Mr Owston. He's a young, up and coming chap and I think he'll be just the ticket." Mrs Langham turned back to her desk and began writing. This time her missive was a little longer. She looked up part way through. "Shall I instruct him to attend on us here, or would it be better if he came direct to your house?" Without waiting for a reply, Mrs Langham answered her own question. "I think perhaps here to begin with. If you need to return, I can always ask Stubbs to direct him to your home after I've seen him."

Once the second letter had been despatched, Mrs Langham turned her attention back to Clara.

"There is nothing further we can do at this stage. I did wonder why you were unable to join us yesterday. I had hoped to include you when I spoke to Samuel of my financial plans. I see no reason for you not to be included. At some point you will marry and if I can make that easier in some way then I would be delighted to do so. However, I don't think now is the time for that conversation. One thing I will do is to speak with Mr Farmer about you returning to work while your nephew's situation is being addressed."

Clara looked up surprised. "But why should he listen to you? I'm sure they have rules."

Mrs Langham laughed. "They might have rules young lady, but they also have benefactors. And, whilst I do not generally meddle in the way things operate, I don't like to see an injustice being done." She raised a hand. "And before you ask, no I did not secure the appointment there for you. You did that entirely on your own merit. As you know, I did pay for your brother's education, as one of a number of children."

Clara nodded, and her voice caught as she simply said, "Thank you."

Clara had much to think about as she walked back to Moat Street that afternoon. She had never thought of her friend as having so much influence. To her she was just Mrs Langham, or Aunt Frances as Clara was now supposed to call her. How could someone who clearly had so much, treat her as an equal? She stopped suddenly. If she were to marry Samuel as they planned, would people think she had done so for the money? It was a dreadful thought. She hoped that those who knew her would see beyond that, for she loved him dearly.

When she arrived home, Mr Bailey with John and Stan had left, and only her sisters and the children were waiting. Hannah was asleep, which was probably the best thing and Martha was playing with the twins.

She had no idea how long it would be before Mr Owston came, so the best solution was to carry on as normal. Although if that were the case, she would now be at the school teaching lessons. She sighed heavily. She would have left had she married Samuel, but her choosing to do something and having it forced upon her, were quite different things. Quite apart from that, John's wage wouldn't be enough to pay the bills. She joined Martha playing with the children. It was a good distraction, but made Clara think how nice it would be to have a family of her own.

John had returned to work to complete an order that needed to go out. They were grateful for the time Mr Bailey had taken out of the day to help them, but John thought it fair to do all he could in return. Once Martha and the children left, Clara tidied the rooms and then sat staring at the clock, watching the hands tick around minute by minute.

It was almost six when Clara heard a sharp rap on the front door knocker. She jumped. She had assumed they would not now hear from anyone until the following day. She hurried to answer the door, to find a young man, perhaps a few years older than herself, wearing a smart three-piece suit and carrying a leather briefcase.

"Good day, madam. Mr Hiram Owston at your service."

Clara gave a small smile. She had never heard a name quite like his and thought it rather suited the chap. "Please, come in."

She showed him into the parlour, where thankfully all was neat and tidy, following the earlier time with the children. Hannah was still asleep upstairs.

She explained all she knew to Mr Owston, who nodded and made notes in a professional manner.

"Well, it sounds to me as though he acted in self-defence. We do need to ensure that the police speak to the neighbour. They will at least allow me in to see Master Carter. I shall go first thing tomorrow morning."

"Thank you, sir." Clara felt a great deal of confidence in the man who sat before her but was saddened by the thought of her nephew spending another night in a police cell.

He gave a slight shake of his head. "It could still be for the courts to decide, unless the police can be persuaded to drop the charges against him altogether. It's a serious offence."

Clara felt her initial optimism slip away. "If he were sentenced, what would be the punishment?" Silly as it was, she still crossed her fingers as she waited for him to answer.

Mr Owston pursed his lips and looked thoughtful. "If he's charged and they accept a defence of provocation then if we're lucky it will be penal servitude for a relatively short span. Obviously, we will be trying to have him released without that outcome, but you must be prepared. It's not unheard of for a boy his age to be hanged, but I don't think it will come to that."

Clara felt a lump in her throat as she nodded. All they could do was wait.

After Clara had shown Mr Owston out, she turned to find Hannah sitting on the stairs.

"How much of that did you hear?" Clara asked.

Hannah tipped her tear-stained face upward to look at her sister. "Enough to know we must be prepared."

"Oh Hannah, I'm sure it won't come to that."

"I've lost me 'usband, I can't lose me son an'all." Hannah broke down in sobs and Clara sat on the stairs, holding her sister tight until her crying stopped.

CHAPTER 24

1862

Clara slept badly. Hannah was tossing and turning beside her, but without that, Clara doubted that she would have slept. Her mind went from her poor nephew somewhere in a police cell in Leicester, to wondering what Samuel would say in response to his aunt's letter. At least she'd had confidence that the solicitor would do his best, but now she had to wait for news.

Realising she was unlikely to fall back to sleep, she got up and went to sit downstairs. It felt strange not preparing for work. It would be another long day.

She was surprised to find a letter already on the mat when she went down. Her heart jumped when she realised it was in Samuel's handwriting. She'd make up the fire and put the kettle on to boil before she read what he'd written.

When she finally sat down, her hands were trembling as she slit open the envelope.

'My darling Clara,

I was so sorry to read my aunt's letter yesterday. I will travel to Wigston as soon as I can get a train after school finishes on Saturday. Until then, I can do nothing. There is no one here to cover my work and my request for a leave of absence was refused.

Stay strong my darling.

I remain forever yours

Samuel.'

Clara stared down at the letter. Samuel had asked for a leave of absence. Had he not thought of the possible consequences, or was he disregarding them? She sighed deeply and held the letter to her. He would be home, if only for a day, and that was something which would sustain her.

Having no idea what would happen next, Clara sat in the seat nearest the window and thought reading would help her pass the time while she waited. Halfway down the second page of the book, she realised she had taken in nothing of what she had read and started again. She'd barely passed the first paragraph when she sighed and put the book down. Instead, she went to find a duster to clean the parlour. She wiped the sideboard underneath each item and found herself standing holding a candlestick and simply staring into space. This was useless. She almost wanted to wake Hannah to give herself a distraction, but the longer Hannah could sleep, the better it would be for her.

Although she had seen John briefly before he went to work, by ten o' clock, Clara thought it was the longest morning she had ever known and was glad to hear noises from upstairs. She went to boil water so that Hannah could wash. Hannah still said no more than 'hello' and 'thank you' to Clara as she took up first water and then a hot drink and some porridge. Busying herself taking care of Hannah proved a better way to pass the time, so much so that when the mantle clock struck midday, it came as something of a surprise.

She forbore from asking Hannah what she would do, with no income and presumably no home, as the house was owned by Frank's parents. Maybe they would be charitable to their daughter-in-law, given the way their son had treated her, but Clara doubted that. For the time being, Hannah was safe with her and need go nowhere else.

Hannah was still saying little but was sitting watching out of the window onto Moat Street. Whenever a carriage went by, she would stand to see more clearly and then sink down again onto the chair as it passed the house.

Finally, in the early afternoon, a carriage slowed to a halt outside of Clara's house. Hannah gasped and turned to Clara, wild-eyed as though fearing the worst.

Clara looked out of the window. "Thank the Lord," she said, and without waiting for Hannah, rushed to open the front door.

Whilst Mr Owston looked as smart as he had done on the previous day, he was all but supporting Robert who looked vacant and dishevelled. Clara wanted to take her nephew in her arms and comfort him, but Hannah was by her side and must take priority.

Mother and son looked at each other with such a depth of sorrow that Clara's heart broke for them. Whilst what had happened to Frank might ultimately be for the best, these two poor souls needed to live with the consequences, as well as their grief. Clara led Hannah and Robert through to the back room to give them some privacy and took Mr Owston into the parlour so she could ask what had happened.

"There are to be no charges," Mr Owston said, as soon as he was settled.

Clara closed her eyes and let out a long slow breath. "Thank the good Lord for that."

Mr Owston nodded. "I was able to take the neighbour to the station to make a full statement and thankfully he saw and heard all the events unfold."

Clara, knowing the man's state of deafness, wondered how he had managed to hear it all, but would never question that he had.

"The constable who arrested Robert was friends with the deceased. He was keen to find someone to blame for the death of his friend, especially as Robert didn't have a mark on him from any attack by his father. The neighbour, Mr Daniels, was able to recount not only the immediate facts of what happened that night, but enough details of Mr Frank Carter's behaviour as to leave no one in any doubt, both of the injuries caused to your sister and the risk to your nephew, had he not defended himself. Young Mr Carter has had a difficult couple of days, but there will be no charges against him."

Mr Owston picked up his notes and scanned them. Clara presumed he was looking to see if he had missed anything. She doubted that he would have done.

He gave a nod of satisfaction. "I hope, Miss Phipps, that may be the last of my services you need on this sorry matter." He put his notes in his briefcase and stood up.

"Thank you, sir. I am very grateful to you."

"Think nothing of it. All in a day's work." At the front door he put on his hat and, as he left, turned and raised it to her before continuing out to the waiting carriage.

Clara was unsure if Mr Owston would report what had happened back to Mrs Langham. She decided that once she had prepared food for Robert and provided him with hot water and anything else he might need, she would walk over to Mrs Langham to tell her the news. What Robert needed most was a change of clothes, but John would have no trousers suitable for his nephew. Perhaps there were some old clothes of Samuel's that Mrs Langham might spare. Failing that she would walk over to the house in Blaby to fetch some of his own things.

When Clara went into the back room, there was no one there. She frowned. Then she went to check upstairs. Hannah was sitting on the edge of the bed gently stroking Robert's hair as he slept. She raised a finger to her lips and Clara smiled. With having her son home safe, Hannah looked much brighter than she had, although the reality of their situation may yet need to dawn on the pair of them.

Clara mimed eating and pointed downstairs. Hannah nodded in some sort of recognition and Clara went down to leave food ready, which they could eat once Robert awoke. Hannah was capable of boiling any water they might require and would find things easily enough in their small kitchen. Clara smiled realising that most things were still kept in the exact same places as they were when she and Hannah were children, and it was their mam who determined where things should go. Everything changed and yet it stayed the same.

By Saturday, Clara could wait no longer in her anticipation of Samuel's arrival. She checked the times at which trains were due to arrive from London and, presuming he would come direct to Wigston, was on the platform waiting at his earliest arrival time. When he didn't arrive on that train, she walked back toward home. It had been a lovely idea, but now not knowing whether he was on a later train or had alighted in Leicester rather than Wigston she thought it best not to remain at the station. She instead decided to walk to Mrs Langham's and wait for Samuel together with his aunt.

Stubbs opened the door to her but looked a little embarrassed as she did so. "I'm sorry, miss, Mrs Langham has someone with her at present."

It didn't need Stubbs' words, for Clara could hear raised voices, which was most unusual.

"And may I remind you of the words 'are you your brother's keeper?' This is Miss Phipps' nephew about whom we are talking. She cannot possibly be held responsible for his actions. I might also remind you that Master Carter was not charged with an offence. He was acting in self-defence and whatever his father's parents have told you is of no relevance. If you choose to continue this ridiculous stance, I shall have no alternative but to withdraw my funding of the school."

Clara felt her face redden. She quickly nodded to Stubbs and went back down the steps before the speakers came out and found her there. Whatever the outcome of the discussion, she would be best to wait to hear later.

Despite her nephew's innocence of any crime, as Clara walked home, she pondered on what others would be thinking. If she were to marry Samuel, this would all reflect on him and might prevent him from either teaching or standing for Parliament.

When Clara arrived back at her own home, she found Samuel waiting on the doorstep.

"I thought it best to come straight here. I've just arrived and saw you walking toward me, so I haven't knocked."

Clara looked into Samuel's face, his concern for her etched in every detail.

"And I was out looking for you," she said. "Come inside."

Hannah and Robert had clearly eaten, as the loaf was cut and the butter knife still on the table, but they were not there now. Clara set about clearing away the crumbs as she made tea for herself and Samuel.

"It is thanks to your aunt that my nephew was released without charge. I will always be grateful to her."

"But he was innocent of crime. Of course he should not be charged." Samuel was frowning.

Clara sighed. "Not everyone sees it that way. The fact remains that he killed his father with a pitchfork."

"But he did so in self-defence. You do believe that don't you?"

Clara looked up startled and nodded. She didn't think her nephew could ever have killed deliberately, but she rather doubted the testimony of the deaf neighbour. She bit her lip and thought about what to say.

"If you were to marry me now, Robert's actions might reflect on you, and you may never be able to achieve the great things you are surely destined for. I will understand if you wish to find a more suitable wife rather than this poor wretch, whose love you will always have."

Clara jumped when Samuel thumped the table with his fist, causing the cups and saucers to move alarmingly.

"Clara, do you not believe that my love for you is more important than anything and certainly won't be changed by what a few people might say. We talk of all our principles, of believing in justice, equality and fairness, but principles are really rather pointless if you only apply them to other people. As long as you will have me, then one day I shall marry you and until that day I will wait for you, for there is no other girl for me."

Clara nodded, taking Samuel's hands in her own. "I do believe you, but I'm scared I will bring you only grief."

"Dearest Clara," he said, his voice now soft. Shaking his head he ran his hand gently down her cheek. "If only you saw in yourself what I see in you."

When Samuel had gone, Clara sat in the parlour in the gathering gloom, plagued by her own thoughts. Why did she keep pushing Samuel away? She didn't doubt that she loved him or that he loved her and yet she remained convinced that what others might think or say would make a difference to them. Why was she always looking for reasons to stop her own happiness?

Clara could find no acceptable answers. She felt responsible for the care of her brother, sister and nephew, but surely they could take care of themselves? Hannah and Robert had nowhere else to live and, for the time being, had no work either. She had yet to return to her own teaching, but she had a little in savings to tide them over so of course they could stay. She and Hannah were sharing the front bedroom and John had reluctantly agreed to share with Robert.

Why oh why couldn't she put herself first?

She was still sitting there without candle or lantern when John and Eliza came into the house, laughing and calling her name.

Clara rose from her chair, feeling a little dazed and met them in the hallway.

"We're getting married," John announced, the lantern jiggling about as Eliza couldn't stand still.

Clara frowned. "Yes," she said, "haven't you already told me that?"

"No," said John, sounding patient as to a child. "I mean, we're getting married now. We aren't gonna wait."

Clara simply stared at them in the gloom of the hall. "I think we had better sit down so you can explain. I'll make some tea."

Eliza and John fell over each other laughing as they headed for the kitchen and their excitement lifted Clara's mood.

The young couple sat at the kitchen table, while Clara put the kettle on to boil. Then she turned to face them while she waited. "Now, begin at the beginning."

It was hard to get sense out of John and Eliza as each talked over the other in their excitement.

"John doesn't want to share a room with Robert."

"Eliza's dad said it showed that you should take control of your life."

"We're going to live with my parents."

"It will be nearer for work."

Gradually, Clara ascertained that Mr and Mrs Bailey had agreed to help support the young couple until they were in a position to find a home of their own and that the marriage could go ahead as soon as they arranged everything.

"I'm very happy for you both." And she was. Clara wasn't worried for John and Eliza; she was quite certain they would be happy. She thought of her own position with Hannah and Robert and all that she'd said to Samuel. She was aware that John was still talking and had said something about Robert. "Pardon. I'm sorry I was thinking about something else for a moment."

"Mr Bailey said he could offer an apprenticeship to Robert if he'd be interested. I know he was apprenticed to his father, but he may find it hard to obtain another position with a bricklayer."

For the first time in the conversation, Clara felt a genuine sense of relief. She had thought of factory work for Robert, and she knew he would find the change to that sort of work more difficult. This sounded like the perfect solution.

"That is kind of him. He's a good man."

To Clara's immense relief, she received a note the following morning saying that she should return to school the next day. At least now she could see a way to support Hannah until she was ready to become independent. For now, her sister was healing both physically and emotionally and until that had taken place, she was in no state to look after herself.

Returning to the British School the following morning, Clara felt as though she had been away for longer than a few days. She wondered what the other teachers might say and whether she would be called to Mr Farmer's office, but she took up her place in the classroom and, with no more than a nod of welcome from Mr Ward, continued with her class as though nothing had happened.

She was sincerely glad for the semblance of normality and as she read to the children, listened to them reading and worked with them on arithmetic, the events that had occurred seemed to lose some of their significance and become simply part of the backdrop of her life. The more she thought that, the more the things she had said to Samuel seemed ridiculous and far less an issue than she had perceived them to be.

Over the next few days, she thought long and hard about her own situation and wondered why she felt the need to take responsibility for her sister. Would Hannah have done the same for her were it the other way about?

Difficult as it was to make time, she felt she needed to see Mrs Langham. She of all people seemed to understand Clara and might be able to offer guidance.

Once she was seated in the library of Mrs Langham's

house that Sunday afternoon, Clara didn't know where to start. "I think, I probably owe Samuel another apology." She looked down at her hands as she spoke. "I have become so used to making decisions for the people around me and I don't think I've allowed myself to trust that Samuel is perfectly capable to make his own." Hastily she added, "Though I know of course that he is. He is rather more capable than am I." She thought for a moment before continuing and Mrs Langham didn't interrupt. "It has taken Hannah's arrival to make me see my life more clearly. I have spent a lot of the time putting others first and not doing what's best for me. I suppose my parents never had that luxury. They lived a life of duty and that was their example to me. They had to work every hour they could find to feed us and even then, we had days without a meal. I shall never take for granted the opportunity that having some education has given me. Somehow, I need to learn that I am not my parents and that I should allow myself a little happiness."

Having left a brief silence Mrs Langham said, "That is possibly the hardest lesson of all to learn." She said nothing about Samuel and gave no advice as to what Clara should do, but as had happened so often over the years, Mrs Langham gave Clara space to think of the answers for herself.

After that, they spoke of other things and didn't return to the subject of what action Clara should take. Instead, when she left, Clara made the long walk to the cemetery before returning home.

When Clara arrived back at Moat Street, she was clear in her own mind that she would give Hannah a little more time but then talk to her about needing to find work. She would also write an apology to Samuel, something she seemed to be in the habit of doing. That thought gave her a rueful smile. She could only hope that as a good Christian he would go on forgiving her.

It was a further two weeks before Clara was confident that Hannah would be ready to discuss her next steps. They were sitting in the back room on Saturday afternoon when Clara had returned from school. "What will you do to support yourself?" Clara asked, trying to allow Hannah to find her own answers.

"Support myself? But I've never done that. How could I?"

The panic in Hannah's voice was plain and in the past Clara would have found herself backing off, but she had thought about this carefully and knew she needed to press the point.

"Yes, Hannah, support yourself. Frank has left you with nothing. You will need to find a job."

"I don't think I'm in a state to do much at the moment." Hannah touched her face. "My bruises…"

"Have gone now." Clara spoke as gently as she could. "You are perfectly presentable."

"But you are working, and I could keep house for you." Hannah had adopted a defiant look.

Clara sighed and shook her head. "No, Hannah, you will need to find work. You could ask at the factory where Stan works. I believe they have places."

"A factory?" Hannah said it as though such a thought had never occurred to her. "But with you earning enough to cover our costs, that surely doesn't make sense."

Clara stood up and took a deep breath. "I love Samuel and hope to marry him. I may move away from Wigston. You will need to find work." She felt lighter for having stated it so plainly and smiled.

Hannah simply stared at her.

Clara left the room to go outside. She needed some air. She was finally ready to leave Wigston behind.

CHAPTER 25

1862

Teaching that week was hard work. It was the end of the autumn term and Clara's class were in high spirits. Clara was looking forward to the Christmas break as much as her pupils. Although John and Eliza were planning their wedding, they had decided to wait until spring and in the meantime, John would still be at home. With John, as well as herself, Hannah and Robert, the house was busier than it had been for a long time. The holidays would be a good time for them to move some of the furniture around to make it more comfortable.

At last, it was Friday and with no class the following morning, she could begin to relax.

"Excuse me, Miss?"

She looked up to see Sarah Turner, a girl of about eight years of age who worked hard at school but still found it hard to read the words she was given or put her letters in the right order. Clara smiled at Sarah and did her best to help her with her latest confusion.

Then her eyes alighted on another child, Maud Ashton. In her, Clara recognised the same thirst for knowledge that she had had as a child. Maud was rarely at school. The demands of farm work kept her away for much of the year. How Clara wanted to help them all.

When the day was finally over, she packed her things

into her satchel and headed for home. Hannah had, reluctantly, found work at the factory. Robert was with John at the workshop and so Clara set about preparing to eat alone. Despite sharing the house with her siblings and nephew, Clara felt lonely for the first time she could remember. When she'd had no prospect of someone to call her own, she'd had no expectation of company. Now, all she could think of was Samuel.

She was tired but it was still early, and it seemed a shame to go to bed at such an hour on a crisp winter's evening.

Going for a walk seemed a better way to help her shape her thoughts, so she wrapped up warm and set off into the moonless evening. She turned right from their house and walked up Moat Street and past All Saints church and then on in the direction of the station. She heard a train stopping and letting off steam. The sound made her smile and think again of Samuel. She wondered what he planned to do that holiday and when he would visit Wigston, for he hadn't said anything of it when last he wrote. She was still thinking that when she passed the station itself and from the passengers leaving the platform carrying little luggage, realised the train had come from the opposite direction to London. For a fleeting moment she had hoped... but it was a fanciful thought. She decided it was time to turn around and walk home.

Clara was deep in thought when she went in through the back door. She jumped when a figure rose from being seated at the table, and as her eyes adjusted to the lamp light of the kitchen, she gasped. "Samuel." Surely her imagination could not conjure up such an apparition. She wanted to touch him, to make sure he was real.

"I'm sorry to startle you. I doubted that you would be

out for a long time at night, so asked John if I might wait to see you. He's gone upstairs. I arrived by train this afternoon. Are you tired, or could we go for a short walk together? I know that night has fallen, but I simply cannot wait a moment longer."

Clara felt dazed and nodded in reply. It was once they were back out in the street and walking toward the centre of Wigston that she found her voice. "I must have just missed your train. I walked to the station, but it was the train from Leicester which came in."

"Had you gone to meet me?" Samuel sounded eager as he asked.

Clara shook her head. "I would have done so, had I known you were coming. I was about to write you a note."

He stopped walking and Clara turned back to him.

"And what would the note have said?"

"That I would like to see you and if you were not coming home then I should come to London. That I'm ready to leave my family and follow you wherever you need to be."

Samuel grinned broadly and took a bow. "And here I am, at your service. But come, I must show you something before we talk further."

Samuel's pace quickened and, in the darkness, Clara was out of breath trying to keep up, until he stopped outside the National School on Long Street. The school, like the one in which she taught, was now closed both for the day and for the holidays and Clara frowned.

Samuel turned toward her and took her hands in his. "Dearest Clara, I don't want to spend my life teaching privileged children who take for granted their place in society. Of course, I could continue and try to instil in them a sense of the value of every person they might meet, but as many see me as of a lower status, because I have chosen to be a teacher and not a lawyer or doctor, I see it as unlikely that I will make a significant difference there."

Samuel paused for breath and Clara waited patiently to see where his speech was leading.

"What I'm trying to say is that I think I can make more difference following your example and providing education to those who need it most and by starting to work to improve the lives of ordinary working folk who need a voice and an advocate."

At that point in his speech, Samuel sank down onto one knee on the pavement. He held the lantern so she could see his face. "Clara Phipps, what I'm trying to say, but badly, is that from the start of next term I shall be teaching here at the National School in Wigston. I shall live back at home with my aunt, at least to begin with." He took a deep breath before continuing. "Whether you say yes to my question or not, I couldn't bear to be parted from you a moment longer. I cannot ask your father's permission as he is sadly no longer with us and besides, I rather think that you are your own person and that yours is the only word I should seek. Would you do me the very great honour of becoming my wife? If you say yes, then marry me immediately, Clara. Today if it were possible. Nought else matters to me. Let's not wait. We can wed in the chapel if that is what you'd like, but please marry me."

Despite the fact that when Samuel had got down on one knee, she felt certain she knew what was coming next, Clara's mouth went dry, and she was unable to get out any words at all. A few hours ago, she had resolved to tell him how she felt and now here he was, laying his own heart bare and she was struggling to reply.

She laughed for sheer joy and nodded vigorously,

hoping Samuel could see her. She pulled his hands to raise him to his feet. Eventually, she found her voice. "Yes, yes, oh yes. That was what I wanted to see you to say. I wanted to tell you all that had happened these past days and say I'll wed you anywhere and go with you to anyplace you feel called. There is nothing I want more in the whole world than that very thing. But can you truly be here in Wigston?"

Samuel nodded. "I have to return to London for the next week in order to pack my belongings and bring them home, but after that we need never be parted."

"We must tell your aunt." Clara pulled at his hand and began along the road. "It is not quite too late to do so now."

Laughing and with Samuel telling her about having applied to the National School some time previously, they made their way to Mrs Langham's house.

"Tomorrow we will go to the vicar. Or your minister, of course. But we will go without delay." Samuel strode up the steps to the front door of his aunt's house. "Aunt Frances, Aunt Frances," he called almost before he was through the door. "Clara said yes."

Mrs Langham came out of the library with a broad smile on her face. "That is wonderful news." She embraced first Clara and then Samuel. "Come my dears," and she led them into the library. "We must make plans. Or perhaps it is too late for tonight."

Samuel said, "Tomorrow, before I return to London, we will book the ceremony. Let us wed as soon as the banns have been read. As long as you are happy, my darling, we will not wait a moment longer."

Clara sighed. "And I must speak to Mr Farmer about leaving my post. That is the part of this which makes me sad."

Mrs Langham nodded. "There will be other avenues for your talents, my girl. None of your studies need be wasted. Now, I know it's late, but there is one thing I would like to give you before Samuel walks you home." Having said that, Mrs Langham left the room and Clara sat wondering what her friend had gone in search of.

"Here you are." Mrs Langham handed over to Clara a large parcel, wrapped in brown paper.

Clara looked from Mrs Langham to Samuel and back again. "Should I open it?"

Mrs Langham shook her head. "Not while Samuel is here. I hope you won't think me impertinent, but I saw this material in London and bought it in the hope you might use it for your dress."

Clara gasped. It was too soon for her to have given any thought to what she would wear, but as she had little available money and now would have no job of her own, she was grateful. "Thank you." She gave Mrs Langham a warm embrace.

Samuel carried the parcel home for Clara and placed it carefully on the small side table in the parlour.

"Goodnight, my darling Clara," he said, taking her in his arms and kissing her on the lips for the first time.

Clara felt breathless from the excitement and longed for the time that they would not be parted.

Once Samuel had gone, she sat quietly in the parlour, her heart still racing. She wouldn't find sleep yet if she went to bed, so although it was late, she cleaned the table in the parlour and carefully opened the parcel of cloth. Once unwrapped, she could understand why it was so heavy. It contained lengths of the most beautiful brocade, shot silk and satin. Clara stared at it in wonder.

Whilst Clara's own dressmaking skills were good, she

had never worked with fabrics as fine as these. "However am I to turn this into a dress in time for my wedding?"

"You should ask Mam," Robert said, looking over his aunt's shoulder.

Clara frowned. "Hannah," she called her sister from the kitchen. "Is Robert right? Have you worked with fabric like this?"

Hannah blushed and nodded. "Mary, Frank's sister's a seamstress. When we lived in Wigston, I used to go to 'er 'ouse and 'elp 'er sometimes when Robert wa' small."

"I had no idea. Why don't you work as a seamstress now?"

"I hadn't thought that I could. Perhaps if we make your dress then I could start to do work for others too. I'm always tired when I come 'ome from the factory, but I'm sure we could do it between us." Hannah picked up the pen and paper from the desk and having dipped the nib into the ink she drew a few lines to sketch out a dress.

Clara gasped. It looked perfect. How had she never known her sister could draw? There seemed to be a lot of things about Hannah she was only now discovering.

Although Samuel had to return to London on the Saturday, they were able to begin their wedding arrangements before he left. Whilst Clara would have preferred to wed in the chapel, Samuel would be employed by the church and their attendance there would be expected. Much as she'd have felt more comfortable in the place she knew, she did feel a thrill of excitement to be marrying somewhere that seemed so grand. The banns would be read in All Saints that Sunday and Mrs Langham accompanied Clara to the service so they might be present to hear them.

It was the first time Clara had set foot inside All Saints church, even though it was so close to where she lived. When she entered the building, she felt awestruck by its architecture when compared to the chapel she was used to. She was even more glad of the company when she realised how clueless she felt on the format of the service. She wished Samuel could be there with them, but she followed Aunt Frances's lead on what responses to give and when to kneel. When they reached the part where the banns themselves were read, Clara gave a little start. However much that was what she was here to listen to, it was still a shock hearing her own name being read out.

After that she lost herself in thoughts of what the wedding itself would entail and the work which she and Hannah would start that afternoon on her dress. She was imagining what it would be like to walk down the aisle in her dress, escorted as she would be by John, when she heard the congregation around her saying their final amen and silence descended upon the church for a few moments before people stood, ready to leave.

By the time Clara had attended the following two weeks' of services, she was starting to feel more comfortable with the pattern of worship and, with Samuel by her side, thought that if they chose to worship here after their marriage, she might yet be happy with the choice. Before that, they had the wedding itself to look forward to.

When the day arrived, Eliza helped Clara prepare her hair and when all was finished Hannah helped her to dress. Clara's wedding gown didn't finish in a train, nor did the hem quite reach the floor. Hannah had considered the needs of John in walking Clara down the aisle. It was a hard enough process, needing an arm free for Clara to take, without something to catch his crutch on as they walked.

"You look amazing," John said, as he saw his sister's gown for the first time. "Mam and Dad would've been proud of you."

"I think they'd hardly have believed this was happening. I find it hard to believe myself." Clara took John's hands in hers. "Thank you."

He blinked at her. "Whatever are you thanking me for? You're the one who's always been in my corner, my whole life."

Clara smiled. "But you taught me what it meant to persevere and never give up on a dream. Without that I would still be framework knitting and we'd be in poverty."

John shook his head. "You weren't born to be like the rest of us. When we were young you were different from the other children I knew - in a good way. It was you who taught me that all things were possible if I wanted them badly enough." He kissed her lightly on the cheek. "Shall we go?"

It was a short walk to All Saints, but Samuel had arranged a carriage to collect his bride and take her to the church.

"He's worried you'll change your mind," John joked as he helped her up to her seat.

Clara smiled and shook her head. She had no remaining doubts. She hardly had time to think how nervous she felt, despite her certainty, when the carriage was brought to a halt. Clara took a deep breath, before accepting the offered help to alight.

"All right, sis?" John asked.

She nodded.

"Shall we?" he offered his free arm.

Their touch was gentle as they walked into the church. Clara didn't want to put weight on John which might overbalance him. She was so proud of him and could think of no one, other than their own dear father, who more deserved to be there to give her away.

As well as their immediate families, there were many well-wishers in the church, including parents of some of the children Clara had taught. But Clara's gaze found Samuel. He looked so earnest standing at the front of the church with his best man by his side. Having no family of his own, and his friends being a great distance away, it was Martha's husband, Stan, who he'd turned to. Dressed in a smart suit, Clara thought she'd never seen her brother-in-law looking more uncomfortable. She smiled.

The music stopped and Clara looked from the vicar to Samuel and gave a slight nod that she was ready. She wanted to remember every moment of this day that she had thought would never come, and yet already seemed to be galloping away from her with a life of its own. It felt like barely a moment or two until the vicar was declaring them man and wife and soon after they were walking back up the aisle together.

The guests were invited to celebrate back at Mrs Langham's house. As they filled the dining room, Clara took in all that was happening. Mrs Langham looked as though she had never been happier as she watched Martha's children toddling between and around the guests.

Eliza was standing next to Clara and was also watching the twins. "Clara," she said diffidently, "do you think John and my children will be like their father?"

"All children are like their fathers to some extent. It makes me laugh when I see some of the children at school together with their parents. The boys especially..." Clara broke off, suddenly realising what it was Eliza meant. "I don't know. I suppose it is possible, but if that happens, they will have the best father in the world to know how it is for them and the best mother in the world to love them as they are."

"They won't have the best sister in the world to work with them every day, so they don't give up." Eliza rested a hand on Clara's arm. "John may not tell you, but he has never stopped telling me how much you have done to help him have a normal life."

Clara felt herself blushing.

"You are like a saint in his eyes." Eliza was earnest as she spoke.

Clara coughed, not knowing how to deal with the compliment. "And if your children should be born like John, then their aunt will help them just as she helped their father."

One or two of Clara's family, especially Robert and Stan, looked uncomfortable rubbing shoulders with some of Mrs Langham's acquaintances. But it was Hannah who Clara was most interested to watch. She had been approached by two or three ladies who were clearly asking if she could make gowns for them. Hannah's talents were wasted in the factory and maybe other opportunities would open up for her.

Clara was so far away thinking about Hannah that she jumped when Samuel came across the room and took her hands in his. He lifted her left hand gently to his mouth and kissed it. "My wife." He shook his head and laughed. "Those are words I never dared dream I would be able to say. He dropped her hands and caught her around the waist and swung her around. "My wife," he shouted in a voice of sheer joy, making those around them move back and laugh.

"Put me down." But despite her embarrassed protestations Clara couldn't help laughing herself.

"Aunt Frances, aren't I the luckiest man alive?" Samuel said, once Clara's feet were firmly on the ground.

"You may well be," Mrs Langham said, smiling. "But I'd like to borrow your wife for a few minutes if I may? Come my dear there is something I would like to show you. Your guests won't miss you for a short while."

Clara followed Aunt Frances out of the room and up the stairs. Although she had gone up there the previous week when Aunt Frances asked her approval on the rooms that she and Samuel were to have, Clara still hadn't been further than the first floor. This time it was to the floor above that she was led. Mrs Langham guided her to a large room at the back of the house, overlooking the garden. It was set out with half a dozen desks and chairs and looked for all the world like a regular schoolroom.

"This is my wedding present to you, my dear girl. Fill it as you choose." Mrs Langham smiled. "Be that with your own children, children you wish to teach or adults who need your help. They will all be welcome."

Clara gulped, she didn't know what to say. She felt a knot in her throat and her eyes became moist. She kissed Aunt Frances's cheek. "How can I ever thank you?" She walked inside and went to the front of the schoolroom. She turned as though to face her pupils and realised Mrs Langham had quietly left her on her own. Clara looked at the room and sighed. It was perfect. Hopefully, she and Samuel would be lucky enough to have children of their own, but her life would be full, whatever happened.

The framework knitting industry might be significantly reduced, but factories for knitwear and boot making had taken their place. She knew plenty of children who still needed to help earn money for the family, or who were kept home to help with the chores. They would miss out on any but a Sunday school education unless someone stepped in to help.

Then Clara's thoughts turned to her sister Hannah. There were so many people like Hannah, who reached adulthood but were still unable to so much as read or write their name.

Clara's mind was a whirl with ideas. She would teach as many women and girls as her time allowed. The education she had been fortunate enough to receive, would not be wasted. In her own small way, she too could change lives for the better.

THE END

GLOSSARY OF LANGUAGE

I have tried to use the colloquial language to give a flavour of how they would speak. Most is self-explanatory (I hope). I've included some explanations below to help. Bear in mind that this is spoken not written normally, so spellings may be inconsistent with other work where this has been done. The use of colloquial speech would have been far more extensive in their speech, but I have sought to balance reader understanding with authenticity. An example of this is the regular us of 'on' instead of 'of', so, 'both of us' would become 'both on us', and 'ger' instead of 'get'. I have not done this as it makes for more difficult reading.

At the start of a word, the dropping of the first letter (usually h) is denoted by '. Also 'me' is often used instead of 'my'.

ain't - is not
an'all - as well
bin - been
dunno - don't know
dun't - does not
d'you - do you (more likely d'ya)
fret - worry
frit - frightened
gerron - get on
gerronwirrit - get on with it
gonna - going to
gorra - got a
jitty - narrow footpath
note - nothing
ote (said like oat) - anything

shurrup - shut up
summat - something
wa' - was
wanna - want to
warra - was a
warrit - was it
wharra - what are
wi' - with
wir'im - with him
wir'us - with us
wirrout - without
ya - you or your

PLEASE LEAVE A REVIEW

Reviews are one of the best ways for new readers to find my writing. It's the modern day 'word of mouth' recommendation. If you have enjoyed reading my work and think that others may do too, then please take a moment or two to leave a review. Just a sentence or two of what you think is all it takes.

Thank you.

BOOK GROUPS

Dear book group readers,

Rather than include questions within the book for you to consider, I have included special pages within my website. This has the advantage of being easier to update and for you to suggest additions and thoughts which arise out of your discussions.

I am always delighted to have the opportunity to discuss the book with a group and for those groups which are not local to me this can sometimes be arranged as a Skype call or through another internet service. Contact details can be found on the website.

Please visit https://rjkind.com/

ALSO BY ROSEMARY J. KIND

Violet's War
While Billy's fighting for King and Country, Violet's fighting for the right to play football.

Vi for Victory
It wasn't the Great War that stopped Vi reaching her goal, it was the men who protected their turf.

The Blight and the Blarney (Prequel to Tales of Flynn and Reilly)
Whatever it takes to stop your family from starving.

New York Orphan (Tales of Flynn and Reilly)
How strong are bonds of loyalty when everything is at stake?

Unequal By Birth (Tales of Flynn and Reilly)
How far will Daniel and Molly go to fight injustice and is it a price worth paying?

Justice Be Damned (Tales of Flynn and Reilly)
How do you fight for justice against those whose interests it does not serve? William Dixon is about to find out.

The Appearance of Truth
Her birth certificate belonged to a baby who died, so who is Lisa Forster?

The Lifetracer
Connor is out of time to stop the murders. Now his young son's life is in danger – Who is The Lifetracer?

ABOUT THE AUTHOR

Rosemary J Kind writes because she has to. You could take almost anything away from her except her pen and paper. Failing to stop after the book that everyone has in them, she has gone on to publish books in both non-fiction and fiction, the latter including novels, humour, short stories and poetry. She also regularly produces magazine articles in a number of areas and writes regularly for the dog press. As a child she was desolate when at the age of ten her then teacher would not believe that her poem based on 'Stig of the Dump' was her own work and she stopped writing poetry for several years as a result. She was persuaded to continue by the invitation to earn a little extra pocket money by 'assisting' others to produce the required poems for English homework!

Always one to spot an opportunity, she started school newspapers and went on to begin providing paid copy to her local newspaper at the age of sixteen.

For twenty years she followed a traditional business career, before seeing the error of her ways and leaving it all behind to pursue her writing full-time.

She spends her life discussing her plots with the characters in her head and with her faithful dogs, who always put the opposing arguments when there are choices to be made.

Always willing to take on challenges that sensible people regard as impossible, she set up the short story download site Alfie Dog Fiction which she ran for six years. During that time it grew to become one of the largest short story download sites in the world, representing over 300 authors and carrying over 1600 short stories. Her hobby is developing the Entlebucher Mountain Dog breed in the UK and when she brought her beloved Alfie back from Belgium he was only the tenth in the country.

She started writing *Alfie's Diary* as an internet blog the day Alfie arrived to live with her, intending to continue for a year or two. Two decades later it goes from strength to strength and has been repeatedly named as one of the top ten pet blogs in the UK.

For more details about the author please visit her website at https://rjkind.com For more details about her dogs then you're better visiting https://alfiedog.me.uk

ACKNOWLEDGMENTS

The Greater Wigston Historical Society and in particular Mike Forryan.

The Wigston Framework Knitters Museum.

My sister, Mags Kind, for your advice on the language.

My writing buddies, Patsy Collins and Sheila Crosby, without whom I would never have finished this book.

www.ingramcontent.com/pod-product-compliance
Ingram Content Group UK Ltd.
Pitfield, Milton Keynes, MK11 3LW, UK
UKHW020228210425
457661UK00007B/312